E.R. PUN

DEATH OF A BE

Ernest Robertson Punshon was born in London in 1872.

At the age of fourteen he started life in an office. His
employers soon informed him that he would never make a
really satisfactory clerk, and he, agreeing, spent the next
few years wandering about Canada and the United States,
endeavouring without great success to earn a living in any
occupation that offered. Returning home by way of
working a passage on a cattle boat, he began to write. He
contributed to many magazines and periodicals, wrote
plays, and published nearly fifty novels, among which his
detective stories proved the most popular and enduring.

He died in 1956.

Also by E.R. Punshon

E.R. PUNSHON

DEATH OF A BEAUTY QUEEN

With an introduction
by Curtis Evans

DEAN STREET PRESS

INTRODUCTION

"I don't like religion in murder cases—complicates things so."

Superintendent Mitchell

In 1902 Ernest Robertson Punshon, a twenty-eight-year-old life assurance agent residing at 17 Makin Street, Walton-on-the-Hill, Liverpool with a retired schoolteacher aunt, had recently published his first novel, *Earth's Great Lord*, a romance of the Australian outback; yet the nascent author was not above participating in weekly writing competitions held by *The Academy*, a London literary review. In July of that year Punshon succeeding in winning *The Academy*'s one Guinea prize, for the "best description of a dream," beating out thirty-five other competitors. Punshon's dream, as he detailed it, was a child's nightmare about sin and divine retribution:

I dreamed that I stood on a low sandy shore. Before me stretched a great sea, murmurous with tiny waves. Beyond the horizon, hidden from my sight but not from my knowledge, sat an angel. At his feet were a number of envelopes bearing the names of men. These he was opening one by one at regular intervals and from each in succession flashed out a huge light spreading over half the sky and proclaiming eternal judgment, the salvation or damnation of the person whose name had been written.

Presently I became aware that the next to be opened would declare my own fate. I ran blindly to and fro, watching dreadfully, till at last the great light flashed out, the sky flamed with the sentence, and as I strained to read it, I awoke.

I suppose that at the time of this dream I would have been about ten years old. I distinctly remember my frantic efforts to be very good indeed for several days thereafter.

The conflict between imperatives of wrath and mercy forms the theme of E.R. Punshon's fifth Bobby Owen mystery, *Death of a Beauty Queen* (1935), a novel in which the author depicts psychologically credible murder in a realistic environment. The dead lovely of the title is scheming Caroline Mears, knifed in her dressing room on the night of her triumph in the beauty competition at Brush Hill Central Cinema. Caroline Mears had been determined at all costs to make it to Hollywood and see her name—altered, she imagined, to "Caroline La Merre"—"flared in electric splendor in every busy street throughout the world"; but now someone has forever short-circuited her shining dream of global fame and fortune.

It becomes the job of what to E. R. Punshon's growing audience of devoted readers was the now pleasingly familiar team of Superintendent Mitchell and Sergeant Bobby Owen (along with a cast of supporting policeman) to discover who murdered Caroline Mears. Numerous suspects are on hand in the case, starting with Lilian Ellis, a hot-tempered rival beauty who aimed—rather less ambitiously than Caroline, but certainly no less anxiously—to use a strong finish in the contest as a stepping stone to securing a coveted mannequin position at the Brush Hill Bon Marche; but also including a company of males who for varying reasons had become interested in Caroline's fate: Mr Sargent, "owner—under his bankers of course—of the cinema"; photographer Roy Beattie, rather a partisan on behalf of Lilian Ellis; an unnamed "tough looking bloke" who stormed past the doorman the night of the contest, looking for a "Carrie Quin";

Claude Maddox and Leslie Irwin, young gentlemen trailing in Caroline's wondrous wake; and the puritanical Paul Irwin, Leslie's righteous father, who as a member of the borough council had fiercely fought to force Sunday closures of Brush Hill cinemas. The elder Irwin fervently believed that Caroline Mears was a designing wanton who, left to her own devious devices, was sure to wreck his son's promising young life.

From his own family history E. R. Punshon was well aware that men could founder on the shoals of sensual allurements. His mother's older brother, Richard Webb Halket, once Deputy Commissioner and Chief Assistant of the Chinese Imperial Maritime Customs in Shanghai, had embezzled heavily from his office, served a two-year prison term, frequented brothels and finally been successfully sued for divorce after deserting his wife, Rose Bloom Halket, and three children and cohabiting with a barmaid, Dora M'Guff, in Woolloomooloo, Australia. Surely one need not necessarily have been possessed of a puritanical mindset to have looked askance at these disreputable episodes from a life.

In *Death of a Beauty Queen*, however, it is religious zealotry that comes in for criticism from several of the characters, including Bobby Owen himself. Mr Sargent—a biased party, to be sure—denounces Paul Irwin as "an awful old fanatic….Sticks at nothing to get his own way, because he's so sure he's right and doing the work of the Lord, and everyone else is in outer darkness." At another point in the novel, Superintendent Mitchell observes: "Religious people of the Paul Irwin kind are so jolly sure all the rest of us are vile sinners they're always ready to believe the worst—of other people." For his part, Bobby not only references the famous free-thinker Voltaire but also invokes the wisdom of the feminist and pacifist Christian minister Maude Royden, a Liverpool contemporary of Punshon's: "I remember once hearing Maude Royden say, in a sermon, that when a member of her congregation came to her and said: 'God is telling me to do something,' her first thought was always: 'Now what crime or folly are you going to commit?'"

"It's so easy to take your own wishes for divine," concurs Superintendent Mitchell, "and so convenient, because then you know you're right, you and God against the world." Yet rather than wrathfully cast stones at moral transgressors, we can always, of course, choose mildly to turn the other cheek. In *Death of a Beauty Queen*, there is, in addition to an interesting murder puzzle (with one particularly clever clue), a complex and compelling human drama, enriched with memorable portrayals of major and minor characters alike. Dorothy L. Sayers astutely emphasized this latter point when she warmly reviewed the novel in the *Sunday Times*. "Some readers prefer their detective stories to be of the conventional kind," allowed Sayers, "they like to enjoy the surface excitement without the inward disturbance that comes of being forced to take things seriously." Yet Sayers believed the future of crime fiction lay with serious-minded authors like E.R. Punshon, who had the desire, as well as the capacity, "to persuade us that violence really hurts." *Death of a Beauty Queen* was, she concluded, "a fine and interesting novel, where the emotional discords are resolved in a strain of genuine pathos…."

I hope that modern readers will agree, as I do, with Dorothy L. Sayers that in *Death of a Beauty Queen* we have a Golden Age detective novel that, if not alone in its time, was, along with select others from its day, ahead of it. In the novel the knife blow that slays the beauty queen does not simply remove a piece from a chessboard in some antiseptic murder game; it sparks a deadly fuse in a succession of poignant human tragedies. *Death of a Beauty Queen* merited Sayers' commendation eight decades ago, just as it amply merits revival today.

Curtis Evans

CHAPTER I

BEAUTY'S STAB

SHE came out quickly, self-confidently, royally, with none of that hesitation or apparent self-mistrust that had marked the entry of some of the other competitors on the stage of the Brush Hill Central Cinema. Turning, she faced the crowded audience, and stood, superb and lovely, her tall figure outlined against the neutral-tinted curtain that formed certainly an equal background for all, but that also showed off very effectively her gown of gold brocade, cut in the new sweeping 'stream-line' fashion.

For just the fraction of a second there was complete silence, and for just that moment her self-confidence wavered, so that a passing fear flickered an instant in her light, rather hard, blue eyes – her worst feature, perhaps, but one not very noticeable at first or at a distance. Then it passed as she understood that her confidence had not been misplaced, that it was her beauty itself that had imposed upon this crowded audience the silence she had mistaken during one brief instant for indifference, but that in reality was appreciation far deeper than the facile rounds of clapping some of the other competitors had earned.

But now the applause began, low at first, then swelling into organ notes that filled all the building, that bathed the soul of the girl standing there in an almost physical delight.

It flowed about her; it enveloped her; she made little movements with her hands as if to draw it closer to her; she seemed to herself no longer human but half divine; she seemed to float above the world – above all the rest of humanity – borne up to the very heavens on the wings of this tumultuous cheering. Instinctively she closed her eyes. A profound instinct, a strange sub-conscious knowledge in her inner self, told her they had in them some quality that at times was apt to check the enthusiasm of her admirers, and let her curled, exquisite eyelashes droop upon her rounded cheek. It was a gesture she had practised. It had a modest and demure air; it gave, she was well aware – for she knew these things as a child knows how to breathe or smile or cry – an added attraction of contrast to her somewhat flamboyant beauty, to her masses of golden hair, her large, strongly marked features of almost perfect shape and harmony, her imposing height, so that she seemed a veritable goddess of old Grecian dream, even though to some eyes it might have seemed also that there showed a hint of a possible coming grossness.

Still the applause continued. It beat into her soul like fine music on one who understands; she glowed in it like metal white hot in the furnace; she felt it wafting her away to all those delights of fame and wealth and power wherefor panted her soul. To herself she seemed to soar high above the life of common, everyday humanity, to be freed from all those trammelling bonds of necessity and need that hitherto had irked. To her it was as a release from everyday existence, from life itself, and in such a moment how could she remember that a release from existence and from life means merely – death?

Hollywood! That was the magic word of power this cheering seemed to her to spell. How glad she was that now she could start for Hollywood at once, and could scorn the tuppenny-ha'penny little engagement at the Colossal Film Studio, Palmer's Hill, that was the prize to-night, and that this continuous applause seemed to certify already hers. She supposed that the news of this triumph to-night would at once be recorded everywhere, for all her favourite film papers agreed in telling her how continually the wide world was 'scoured' for possible 'stars' by the magnates of the films. So, knowing all about her, they would welcome her eagerly; they would 'groom' her a little, and then her career of triumph would begin.

From under her half-closed lids, with those long curling

lashes that veiled so well the hard appraising look her eyes sometimes showed, she bestowed an approving smile upon the spectators. They were applauding still – as, indeed, was only right and proper. How proud they would all be to remember this night, in times to come when her name was famous everywhere, and 'Caroline Mears' flared in electric splendour in every busy street throughout the world. Well, she did not grudge them their satisfaction, even though she felt they ought to pay a little extra each for the privilege – a little extra in cash that should be hers for herself alone. Only, was 'Mears' too ordinary a name for the bright magnificence of the lights that she foresaw? She decided on the instant to change it to 'Demeres' – or 'Le Merre' perhaps. Yes, 'Le Merre' it should be – or, no, 'La Merre,' of course, and a slight pucker of anxiety creased for an instant the satin-like smoothness of her brow as her glance picked out, standing alone at one side of the auditorium – those hard, clear, brightly shining eyes of hers possessed wonderful sight – a tall, straight man, apparently of middle age, who stood there, erect and stern and rigid, taking no part in the general applause that now was slackening a little.

What was he doing there, she wondered? Anyhow, she had the money; and what did it matter if his glance beat upon hers with a hint of a force before which that of her beauty was as that of ice before fire ? With an effort, but only with an effort, she averted her gaze.

In the wings, Mr Sargent, owner – under his bankers of course – of the cinema, and organizer of this Beauty Contest, with its prize of a film engagement, that had moved all Brush Hill to its depths, was beckoning to her to come off now the cheering was dying down, and Martin, the time-keeper, whose job it was to note with a stop-watch the duration of the applause each competitor earned, said to him:

'You'll need a crowbar, Mr Sargent, to prise that girl off.'

'She's a winner all right,' Sargent answered. 'They're beginning clapping again.'

'Asked 'em to, she did,' observed Martin; and added

dispassionately: 'Some of the rest of 'em aren't so dusty. Lilian Ellis, for one – that comes on next.' Then he said: 'Someone told me Paul Irwin was in front.'

'Irwin? Councillor Irwin?' Sargent repeated, startled. 'Why, what's he snooping round for, the old killjoy? Wanting to make more mischief?'

'His boy's behind,' Martin explained. 'Young Leslie – sweet on this girl, they say, and likely old man Paul thought he would have a look at her.'

'Half the young fools in the place are sweet on her,' growled the manager. ' If it's only that – she's turned him down anyhow. I'll go and have a word with the old man, though,' he added, looking uneasy again.

For Paul Irwin, a member of the borough council, was no friend to cinemas, or, for that matter, to any other form of public entertainment, and had fought hard to get the Brush Hill cinemas closed on Sundays – indeed it was for that purpose he had been elected to the council to represent a group holding certain strict old-fashioned ideas. For Mr Irwin's powers and influence the cinema owner had considerable respect, and he hoped sincerely the old campaign was not going to be reopened.

Again he beckoned to the girl on the stage to come off, and again she took no notice, but, with a bow and a smile to right and left, appeared rather to invite renewed applause. Yet her glance that stabbed so keenly from under her half-closed eyes was again upon that tall and rigid figure of the man of whom Sargent and Martin had just been speaking.

'Well, I don't care,' she was telling herself. 'He can do what he likes – it's enough to pay my fare to Hollywood, and I can start to-morrow if I like.'

In the wings, Martin said to Sargent:

'Well, you've got to get her off somehow or we shall be here all night – there's Lord knows how many of 'em waiting their turn.'

Sargent nodded, and walked out on the stage. He bowed to the audience, who stopped applauding, a little puzzled by his unexpected appearance. He bowed to Caroline, who understood it very well, and who turned on him angry eyes that did not harmonize too well with her smiling lips, and then he took her hand.

'Got to give the others a chance, you know, my dear,' he said to her, in an undertone, as he conducted her off the stage to a fresh round of applause.

If Miss Caroline Mears had ever heard of that celebrated retort: '*Je ne vois pas la nécessité*,' she would probably have quoted it now – at any rate it very accurately represented her sentiments. As it was she said nothing, and consoled herself with the reflection that she had managed to stop on the stage longer than any of her rivals and so would probably be best remembered when it came to the voting.

'Lilian Ellis next,' said Martin, in a loud voice. He was slightly bored with the whole business, and, besides, he knew Mrs Martin was keeping hot for him a nice plate of fried fish and chips. 'Now where's she got to?' he demanded wearily.

'I'm here,' a small voice answered, as there came forward – though looking more than half-inclined to run for it – a girl who had been standing and shivering and panicking in a corner close by, waiting for the summons that had seemed so long in coming, while the courage she had with pain and grief screwed up to sticking point oozed slowly, surely away, till now very little indeed of it was left her.

She was tall, too; nearly as tall as the magnificent Caroline herself, though built on much less generous lines – 'scraggy' was in fact the description Caroline had done her best to broadcast of her – and she was as dark as Caroline was fair, with very large dark brown eyes and dark rippling hair. Her features were a little on the small side, though finely moulded and in perfect proportion, and, if it was the beauty of the soft radiance of her eyes that generally attracted attention first, a minor beauty she could equally have boasted was the perfection of her teeth. Their regular and pearly whiteness flashed like a ray of light through her rare

smile, but unfortunately she had never learnt the trick of
showing them to advantage. Her lips were generally pressed
firmly together to express the resolution and distrust a hard,
unlucky life had taught her, though it may be her smile was
all the more captivating when it came because it so seldom
lit up the gravity of her young face. At the moment she was
perhaps hardly looking her best, for her nervousness was pal-
pable, and had induced a slight perspiration, while a chilly
draught, blowing straight into the corner where she had
been waiting, had resulted in a certain unfortunate redness
of the nose. Now, as she moved forward in answer to Martin's summons, she and Caroline came face to face, and,
with real admiration, Lilian whispered:

'You looked lovely. They did clap, didn't they?'

Caroline's glance flashed over the other girl and recognized a dangerous rival. There was, it had to be acknowledged, something attractive, something in an odd con-
tradictory way both appealing and compelling, about her.
Feature by feature, item by item, Caroline was confident of
her own superiority – with the possible exception of those
lustrous teeth silly little Lilian had luckily no idea how to
use to advantage. Not that Caroline was dissatisfied with
her own, polished and shining and large and strong, real
'ivory castles' of the advertisement that could crack a nut
with ease but, if hers were 'ivory castles,' Lilian's were
like two rows of well-matched pearls, and added their share
to that rather inexplicable attractiveness the child certainly
possessed. People were such fools, too – Lilian's smile might
win them to give her an applause to rival that just now
awarded to Caroline. Like summer lightning across the sea
all this flashed through her mind – though intensely felt
rather than clearly thought – and showed her dream of
Hollywood endangered. She said:

'Disqualified – isn't it awful?'

Lilian looked bewildered.

'Disqualified,' Caroline repeated, in a rapid whisper. 'I
stopped too long on the stage – against the rules. You've got

to run away just as soon as the clapping starts, or they disqualify you. Mind you're careful.'

'Oh, I will – oh, I am sorry,' Lilian exclaimed, in consternation at such a catastrophe. 'Oh, they won't really – –'

'Now then, Miss Ellis, ·stage waiting,' Martin bawled. 'Come along there – got to finish some time to-night,' he protested, thinking longingly of fish and chips – so much more to a practical, middle-aged man than all the lovely ladies that are or ever were.

Lilian found herself on the stage. This surprised her, for she had no idea how she had got there. The one clear thought in her mind was that she must be careful not to get disqualified. If that happened she would lose her chance of getting the job as permanent mannequin at the Brush Hill Bon Marché she had applied for, and had been as good as promised if she met with any success to-night. Mr Ginn, the staff manager, was in front to-night, she knew, though of course it was quite impossible to distinguish him in that sea of white faces, all intimidatingly staring. She could only hope he thought she was satisfactory, for a job at the Brush Hill Bon Marché meant a lot to a girl with a fretful, invalid mother to support as well as two small brothers of inconceivable appetites and an absolutely bewildering habit of growing out of their clothes almost as soon as they put them on. At any rate, the one thing she had to be careful of was not to risk poor Carrie's fate and get herself disqualified.

No one was clapping as yet as they had clapped the unlucky Caroline. In point of fact, as she had only just stepped into their view, the spectators had as yet hardly had time, but to her it seemed that she had been standing there a hundred years or so. But, if they were not clapping, they were all, as she perceived to her extreme astonishment, staring their very hardest. It was rather awful. It needed courage to stand there and endure that. And she had never had much courage, only temper – as her mother had found out once or twice when she had pushed complaining a little bit too far, or those two boys of whom a shameful legend of her youth proclaimed that she had chased them with a dinner-knife all down the street merely because they had been having some fun with a lame kitten. Indeed in the school she had been attending at the time the shocking story was still repeated of how, when a horrified mistress asked her what she had been intending to do with the dinner-knife, she responded firmly:

'I was going to chop them up.'

But, in an emergency like this, temper and fierce display of dinner-knives were no use, only firm courage was required, and, above all, care to run no risk of sharing Caroline's unhappy fate of disqualification.

The clapping started, a little hesitatingly, for no one was quite so sure about this thin and nervous-looking girl as they had been about the flamboyant, self-confident Caroline. But the clapping continued – it even grew in volume. Bewildered, Lilian listened. It seemed to her to have gone on for long, and vividly she remembered Caroline's warning. If she were not careful she would share the same unhappy fate. To avoid it, one had to run, it seemed, when the clapping started. And now it had started.

She ran.

The clapping stopped. Someone laughed. Laughter's infectious, and this audience was in a happy mood. It spread; it ran like the wind from one to another. A gust of uproarious merriment followed Lilian as she fled, till one might have thought it blew her from the stage. The judging committee in the big stage box shared in the general hilarity to such an extent that most of its members forgot even to mark her card. Mr Sargent said:

'The little fool's ruined her chance all right.' He added reflectively: 'I thought at first she was going to be the high spot of the evening.'

Martin called:

'Next, please; next number.' He said to Lilian as, bewildered and breathless, she paused near by, 'What in blazes made you play the giddy goat like that?'

CHAPTER II

FATHER AND SON

Now, on the stage, there followed each other a somewhat monotonous procession of pretty girls, for so variable is the mind of man that, strange as it mûst seem, even pretty girls may come in time to bore. But this profound truth is not one that as yet has come to be recognized by the producers of musical comedies who still believe that true joy lies in endless repetition.

To each competitor in succession, however, good-natured spectators gave a round of applause that had generally a spear-head of enthusiasm in the one special spot in the auditorium where had assembled the friends and admirers of the girl at the moment apparent. But near where stood the silent, grim, watchful personage the keen eyes of Caroline Mears had picked out, whose presence, too, had been mentioned by Martin to Mr Sargent, such clapping and applause seemed always soon to die away. It was as though his mere presence – upright, immovable, and stern – spread a kind of unease around, acting as a check and a restraint.

'Blooming block of ice,' Sargent muttered ; and if ' blooming ' is not the most appropriate adjective to apply to a lump of ice, neither is it the one that the proprietor – under the bankers – of the cinema actually employed.

He had come round to the front of the house, and, having paused only to rebuke an attendant he found flirting in the corridors when she ought to have been selling ices in the auditorium, he was now, from behind a curtain hanging over a door at the back, regarding Councillor Paul Irwin with marked disfavour.

'Even chances he's going to start another agitation – bring it up at the next council meeting, perhaps, and tell them a

beauty contest's a public scandal,' he thought ruefully.
'Well, I can tell him his precious boy has got the chuck from
Caroline if that'll smooth him down, but I wish the old
blighter would keep his nose out of the place.' He went
through the door to where the councillor was standing.
'Well, Mr. Irwin, sir,' he said warmly, 'it's an unexpected
honour to see you here to-night – a real pleasure.'

Paul Irwin turned his eyes slowly upon the other. They
were strange eyes – deep-sunk and vivid – burning, if the
expression may be allowed, with a kind of cold fire, as it is
said that in extreme frost uncovered steel and glowing embers
will each burn the incautious hand that touches them. His
actual age was sixty, but he could easily have passed for a
vigorous forty, so apparent were the strength and energy
still showing in every gesture he made, every word he spoke.
In his hair and trim beard – he was probably the only
bearded man in the audience – not a single grey hair showed
as yet, and, from each side of his great hooked nose, his deep-
set eyes glowed with a kind of restrained and fierce energy
that well held the passing years at bay. They gave him,
indeed, with their far-off look as if they searched for distant,
hidden things, something of the air of a watching, patient
eagle waiting upon heights inaccessible to all but itself. The
lines of the close-shut mouth were straight, as though a ruler
had drawn them, and were pressed together as by a constant effort of the will. As a young man he must have been
unusually handsome ; now, in his maturity rather than his
age, for of age his vigour gave no hint, he had a daunting
and formidable air that came very largely from the impression of concealed tension that he gave, as if the very stillness
of his attitude, the marked impassivity of pose and features
alike, suggested some coiled spring the merest touch might
release into fierce vehemence of action. He was dressed in
well-worn clothes that were even a little shabby, but with a
shabbiness that seemed of indifference rather than of poverty,
and he had on a broad-brimmed hat of black felt – his one
little affectation in dress, for no one, summer or winter, wet

or fine, had ever seen him wearing any other kind. He said now, speaking very quietly, but still with that manner of force in reserve that seemed natural to the man:

'It is neither honour nor pleasure to be here, either for me or for – –' and a slow, condemnatory movement of his hand indicated all the audience.

'Oh, come, Mr Irwin,' protested Sargent uncomfortably.

'I know you and your friends call me a killjoy,' Irwin went on. 'It is not true. For one thing, no one can kill true joy, and, besides, joy is always good. But where's the joy or the good, or the fun either, of watching a lot of empty-headed girls preen themselves one after the other like a lot of peacocks on a terrace in a park?'

'Oh, well, now then, Mr Irwin,' protested Sargent feebly. 'Besides, as far as that goes, aren't peacocks good to look at?'

'Yes, and good for nothing else,' retorted Irwin, in the same level, controlled tones in which nevertheless one could feel his passion beating against the bars of his self-restraint like an angered tiger at the bars of its cage. 'Foolish girls showing themselves off like toasted cheese in a trap for silly mice,' he pronounced.

Mr Sargent turned so as to bestow an unseen wink on the vacancy behind him. He thought:

'I know what's biting the old man, and making him talk like the day of judgment.'

Aloud, he said:

'Oh, that's a bit hard on 'em – on us all. What's the good of being pretty if no one ever sees you? It's a talent and gift like any other, and it oughtn't to be hid.'

'Hid?' repeated Irwin, with a terrific emphasis, as he flashed his eyes at the stage where a girl had just entered in what she fondly believed to be a real mannequin glide; and he was going on to say something more when Sargent interposed quickly:

'I see your boy Leslie is behind to-night.'

The old man always held himself so stiff, so rigid and

upright, he could not well grow more so. But all the same there was an almost visible increase of tension in his voice and attitude as he said slowly:

'I thought you always told us you never allowed anyone behind who was not there on business? Is Leslie there on business?'

Sargent shrugged his shoulders.

'That's all right in the ordinary way,' he declared. 'Speaking generally, we never do. It's the sack for any of the staff who lets in anybody not on business. But a night like this is different. There's dozens of competitors, and they've all brought their fathers and their mothers and their uncles and their aunts, and they're all rushing in and out because they've forgotten their nail-polish or they've just thought of some new gadget for their frocks or their hair or their noses, and then there's telegrams and bouquets and chocolates being fetched along without stopping – why, it's all more like the first day of the winter sales in the West End than a well-managed, self-respecting cinema. How can we sort out the chap who's bringing a competitor the lipstick her life depends on – and she'll throw a fit of hysterics if she doesn't get it good and quick – from the chap who only wants to kiss one of 'em good luck?'

Mr Irwin looked grimmer than ever.

'Promiscuous kissing,' he commented. 'That, at least, I think could be controlled. And you tell me Leslie is taking part in all this?'

In spite of himself his voice softened as he pronounced his son's name – for the moment a kind of radiance showed through the austerity of his tone and attitude and then was gone again. At his side, Sargent was indulging in a little bad language, though only thought, not uttered. 'Promiscuous kissing, indeed!' A nice twist the sour old puritan had given his words. Who could tell what that phrase might not have grown to in a day or two? But he judged it prudent to control his wrath. Irwin had a large and influential following in Brush Hill, and altogether was a personage with whom a quarrel was best avoided. So Sargent permitted himself only the mildest of protests.

'I don't think I said anything about promiscuous kissing,' he remarked; 'and I'll tell you one thing, Mr Irwin. This is the last Beauty Contest that'll ever be held here – never again. Handling that crowd of girls, all of 'em all worked up, all of 'em making eyes at you because then they think you'll give 'em the best chance, and all of 'em dead sure you're favouring the other one – handling a horde of hungry lions is nothing to it; nothing at all,' declared Mr Sargent, pausing to wipe a forehead that had begun to perspire gently at the mere memory of all he had been through that night.

'If Leslie is behind,' Mr Irwin said unexpectedly, 'I suppose there can be no objection to his father joining him?'

Mr Sargent fairly jumped, the suggestion surprised him so. But he accepted it very willingly. The crabbed old Puritan would be able to see for himself that 'behind' was no sink of iniquity, that no mysterious 'orgies' were going on there, but that it was merely a workshop like any other, where the always serious and often tedious business of entertainment was seriously and often tediously practised. Besides, the old man would soon discover there was no 'promiscuous kissing' – the phrase still rankled – going on, and, if any story founded on those two unlucky words got about, Mr Irwin's visit would provide an effective reply. Of course, it was hard luck on young Leslie Irwin – a little like throwing him to the wolves. The boy would have the scare of his young life when he saw his formidable old father in the one place where he must have thought he would be safe from meeting him. But then Mr Sargent had his own reason for not objecting to that happening.

'Why, certainly, Mr Irwin,' he answered. 'Always pleased for any responsible person like yourself to have a look round. We'll go now, shall we?'

They went along the deserted corridor together, and in the abrupt and direct style he practised – for the injunction to be wise as serpents, harmless as doves, was the one scrip-

tural injunction he never felt had any personal application –
Mr Irwin said:

'I suppose you know well enough it's the Caroline Mears
girl has brought Leslie here?'

'Oh, half Brush Hill knows that,' retorted Sargent, with
a note of resentment in his tone that entirely escaped his
companion's attention, absorbed as the old man was with
his own thoughts.

He put out his hand now, and laid it heavily on Sargent's
shoulder.

'It would ruin the boy,' he said. 'He shall never marry
her – never.'

'Ow-w, my shoulder,' gasped Sargent, almost doubled
up under the weight of that fierce grip.

'I am sorry,' Mr Irwin said, releasing him. 'I feel strongly.
I mean it. The boy shall have no wife so light-minded, so
worldly – a girl with nothing in her head but dancing and
running about and all kinds of frivolity.'

Sargent was rubbing his shoulder – whereon, when he
undressed for bed, he found the marks of his companion's
fingers still visible. He said in the same sulky and resentful
tones:

'That's all right. I should feel that way myself. It would
never do. Only, how are you going to stop it? They're both
of age.'

'I will find a way. I will not have Leslie ruined – ruined
body and soul,' the other answered, with a slow concentrated
force that had about it something almost terrifying. 'That's
what it would mean,' he added, more quietly. 'I've seen it
happen. I would give my own soul to make sure it does not
happen to Leslie.'

As always when he spoke of his son, his voice softened to
gentleness, for the moment a sort of radiance surrounding
him, though soon it passed, and soon he was his own stern
self again.

'Oh, well,' Sargent muttered, scared a little by the almost
demoniacal energy that throbbed in the other's tones,

'there's no need to worry. As a matter of fact, I happen to know Miss Mears has given him the chuck – I mean, she's breaking off her friendship with him, completely and entirely.'

'With Leslie,' repeated Mr Irwin, and something that was nearly a smile plucked momentarily at the corner of his mouth. He made a little gesture of incredulity with one hand – such a gesture as a man might make if he heard that another had refused a fortune. 'She'll never do that,' he said slowly. 'She may pretend, for her own purposes, but that's all. I doubt he'll never be safe while she's alive – never. Only death will make him safe from her.'

'It's through here,' Sargent said, opening the door. He turned, and looked up suddenly at Irwin, who was some six or nine inches the taller. 'Maybe you're right,' he said, 'and death's the only cure.'

He had spoken with some energy. A stage-hand, who was passing, heard, and turned to stare. Sargent saw him, and shouted angrily:

'You, there, get on with your job, can't you?'

The man vanished in a scutter, and Sargent said morosely:

'They spend half their time yarning and gossiping instead of working. Come this way, Mr Irwin.'

CHAPTER III

'BEHIND'

PAUL IRWIN had never since his childhood been in any
place of public entertainment – museums excepted, if they
come within the terms of the definition – and never even in
his wildest imaginings had he supposed that one day he
would find himself behind the scenes of a theatre or a cinema.

He had no idea, therefore, that what he was now witness-
ing was not entirely normal, or that in the ordinary way
activity 'behind' is as disciplined, controlled, and regular
as that in any warehouse or office, all present knowing their
jobs and intent only on carrying them out.

That every corridor should be swarming with excited
girls; that rushing about in every direction should be equally
excited relatives and friends; that a bewildered stage-door-
keeper should have given up all efforts to keep out un-
authorised persons without legitimate reasons for claiming
entry, since while he was arguing with one man, who might
prove to be the father of a competitor bringing her some
fal-lal she had to have or die upon the spot, various others
on equally important errands, or on no errands at all, would
be dashing wildly by; that girls in smart evening dresses
that Paul took for undress, and girls in undress he hoped was
smart evening attire, should be darting in and out of over-
crowded dressing-rooms sometimes as many as a dozen had
to share since there was nothing like enough accommodation
for such a tribe of competitors – all this he supposed to be
quite normal. He had no idea, even, that the confusion
and the excitement were growing worse every minute, for,
by now, Wood, the door-keeper, had finally thrown in his
hand, and was complaining bitterly to a crony of the oppro-
brious epithets heaped upon him by a young man he had
endeavoured to eject in the belief that he was a mere in-

truder, but who had turned out to be Roy Beattie, the 'art' photographer, as he liked to call himself, who had been specially invited by the management to take photographs of the most popular competitors, singly and in groups.

'Called me a pumpkin-pated foozledum,' bitterly complained Wood, who measured an insult more by syllable than by significance. 'How was I to know he was here legitimate? – and not like half the rest of 'em, letting on to be fathers or uncles or brothers of girls they've never seen before except to cuddle in a corner. Why, there was one tough-looking bloke said he was pa to a Carrie Quin, or some such name, and, before I could look at the list and make sure there wasn't any Carrie Quin, he did a bunk past.'

'Can't you fetch 'em out again when they try that on?' asked the crony.

'In a general way,' answered Wood, 'that's what I do – so quick they never know what's happening till they're outside again smarter than ninepence. But to-night, if I got busy after one, half a dozen more would be slipping in. Besides, this bloke wasn't a young smartie, so I didn't worry; looked more like it was handbags he was after than hugging and kissing round the corner.'

'Does seem, to-night,' agreed the other sympathetically, 'like a special crazy evening at Bedlam more than anything else.'

'Here's the photographic bloke again,' said Wood, bristling. 'I'm not going to take any more of his pumpkin-pated-foozledum language, even if it costs me my job.'

'Sock him one in the jaw,' urged the crony, traitorously thinking that, if thus Wood did lose his job, then there might be a chance for anyone happening to be on the spot at the moment.

But Roy Beattie's intentions were quite peaceable and friendly. He was a tall, fair-haired, blue-eyed youngster, good-looking and powerfully built, more like, in appearance, the typical athletic 'hearty' than an 'art' photographer whose work tended to be somewhat finicky and precious.

'Just look after that for me, will you?' he said, handing
Wood a small dispatch-case. 'Take care of it – I've just got
some ripping studies of Miss Mears I don't want mixed with
the others.'

Wood took the dispatch-case, and at the same time glanced
at a paper by his side.

'She's the favourite, at evens,' he announced. 'Lilian
Ellis was runner up, but she's done herself in the way she
bunked off the stage.'

Beattie went red. He was, in fact, a somewhat ingenuous
young man, with little in his life but 'studies' and 'expo-
sures' and 'effects,' even though he believed himself most
sophisticated, and, on the strength of a stay in Paris and a
little chatter about new theories of art, in the very forefront
of contemporary thought, with a profound experience of life.
At the moment, or rather during such rare moments as he
could spare from photography, he was, like other ingenuous
and innocent young men of his type, an enthusiastic Fascist,
just as he might have been an enthusiastic Communist had
their fairy-tales been the first he had chanced to hear. But
perhaps in any case the dark ominous threat of the black
shirt would always have appealed more to his sense of drama
than the Communist red he thought rather commonplace
and gaudy – and then you can do so much more in photography with blacks and shadows than you can with reds.
Now, though, he went red himself, as he stretched out a long
arm, terminating in an enormous hand, and took possession
of the paper Wood had referred to.

'Do you mean you've been making a book about the girls'
chances?' he demanded. 'Infernal cheek -- I've a jolly good
mind to show it to Mr Sargent.' He put the paper in his
pocket. 'If anyone wants it,' he said, 'they can come and
ask me, and I'll tell 'em what I think of 'em.''

He walked off indignantly, leaving Wood quite breathless, and a little way down the corridor came on Sargent
himself, still in the company of Paul Irwin. Had Sargent
been alone, Beattie might quite possibly, in the heat of his

indignation, have complained about this betting on the
chances of the different competitors that had struck him as
such a piece of impudence; but Paul's presence had on him
the repressing, almost chilling, effect, it often exercised on
younger people. Then, too, an indignant matron had just
recognised the cinema owner, and now came hurrying up,
eager to unburden herself of a grievance.

'You said there wouldn't be any favouritism,' she protested; 'and there's my girl got to share her room with such
a crowd none of them can't even turn round – and only one
glass between them all – and there's that Caroline Mears got
a room all to herself.'

'She had to go somewhere, hadn't she?' Sargent defended
himself. 'I couldn't push her in where there wasn't any
room already. I know we've had to ask competitors to put
up with crowded conditions, and we couldn't make the
crowding worse by putting more in a room, now could we?'

'That's no reason why Caroline Mears should have a
room all to herself,' insisted the still indignant matron, 'and
my girl not able even to get hold of a glass to see herself in
– and "Private" and "No Admission" stuck on her door,
so her ladyship shan't be interfered with. "No admission,"
indeed,' she snorted. 'Shows who's meant to win.'

'We've nothing to do with the judging, that's for the committee alone' – Sargent explained mildly – 'and that notice
on the door has nothing to do with Miss Mears. What's happened is that Miss Mears's name was left out of the list by
some accident. Her name wasn't down for any dressing-
room, and they had to come and tell me one competitor had
been forgotten – no accommodation provided, and every
dressing-room crowded to capacity. I told them they had got
to put her somewhere, and they said there wasn't any somewhere. They said: "We can't ask her to do her dressing in
the corridor, can we?" So I said: "Well, there's my private
office – stick her in there; only mind you leave the 'No Admission' notice on the door, or someone will go barging in
while she's pulling up her stockings." So that's what was

done. The "No Admission" notice is just one I put on my-self, in the hope of having a corner to myself to-night. No chance of that now, though. The fact is, we've just had to manage the best way we can. This way, Mr Irwin.'

He hurried on, leaving a still profoundly dissatisfied lady behind him. Mr Irwin said:

'Miss Mears's name having been forgotten seems to have turned out rather a good thing for her.'

'She doesn't think so,' retorted Sargent. 'You ought to have heard her shouting about having to dress in a man's office without so much as a looking-glass in the whole place, except the one she had in her handbag.'

They were passing now a side passage that branched off from the one they were following. At the end of this passage, where it turned towards the entrance used for scenery, was a door marked 'Private' and further adorned with a piece of square cardboard, on which had been painted, with a brush dipped in ink, in large, intimidating letters, the words: 'Keep Out – No Admission.' The door was half open, and standing on the threshold was a youngster of twenty-one or two, or thereabouts, his hand upon the door-knob. He was a slightly built youth, handsome, with small, well-formed features, and a skin like a girl's for its smoothness and soft-ness. His eyes were good, too, set well apart, and very clear and bright, and veiled by long, curling lashes. The mouth, small and pouting, and the rather pointed chin, did not sug-gest any great strength of character – indeed the whole ex-pression might have been thought weak and perhaps a little effeminate, though the set of the shoulders and a certain spring and ease in movement suggested a vigorous enough physique, as the ready smile, the bright and smiling eyes, suggested also a joyous gaiety of disposition. The resem-blance to old Paul Irwin was marked – no one could have seen them together without at once understanding they were father and son – yet it was hard to say in what this resem-blance consisted, for there was no strong likeness in feature, and the contrast between the severe and dour expression of the elder and the laughter-loving joyousness of the younger was sufficiently striking. They might, indeed, have stood for opposing types of the 'grim' and the 'gay,' though just now the boy looked anything but gay. For the instant he recognised his father all the fun and laughter fled from his face; he gave a gasp, a little jump, banged the door of the room, and vanished at a run.

Sargent began to laugh, but checked himself as he saw the old man wince with sudden pain.

'I've never seen the boy run from me before,' he said, though more to himself than to his companion.

'Oh, he just felt caught out,' Sargent remarked, a little sorry for the old man, who seemed to feel so keenly an action that in the circumstances appeared quite trivial and natural.

'I never thought to see him run from me,' Paul repeated, in the same low voice. He was evidently deeply hurt. 'Leslie always trusted me before,' he said, and again it was almost a kind of radiance with which he spoke his son's name.

'Oh, you know, when a girl comes along ...' said Sargent vaguely.

'Yes, it's her doing – well, she shall never marry him,' Paul answered, with slow and fierce determination. 'It would be his ruin.'

'Well, she's given him up – I know that,' Sargent insisted. 'You needn't worry.'

'I'm not worrying,' Paul retorted, 'for I am taking steps to make sure – quite sure. If she cared for him, it might be different, but all she wants him for is what she can get from him.' He raised both hands in a gesture that was eloquent of controlled and strong resolve. It was evident that the cinema owner's assurance that Caroline had given Leslie up made no impression on his mind. He could not conceive it as even thinkable that any girl should be willing to give up his Leslie. Turning sharply upon Sargent, he said, in different tones:

'Your "No Admission" notice doesn't seem to be very

effective. Leslie had evidently been in to see Miss Mears. You allow visits to the girls' dressing-rooms, then?'

'Most certainly not,' declared Sargent angrily. 'We can't prevent some youngsters from misbehaving, but it's most irregular – most improper. Though I must say I thought Leslie was just going in, not coming out.'

'Coming out, I think,' insisted Paul coldly.

Before Sargent could reply, someone calling him by name came hurrying up, and Sargent turned, by no means sorry for the interruption.

'Well, I'm here. What is it now?' he asked.

'It's about the Ellis girl,' the new-comer said. 'There's complaints that Miss Mears tricked her into running off the stage the way she did by telling her she would be disqualified if she didn't. Some of them are saying she ought to have a chance to show again.'

'Certainly not,' answered Sargent. 'If she's fool enough to believe all she's told it's her look-out. No one can show twice – out of the question.'

'If you ask me, I think Miss Mears ought to be disqualified herself,' the other grumbled. 'It was a dirty trick to play.'

'Most likely it was only meant for a joke; she never thought it would be taken seriously,' suggested Sargent.

'Well, you had better come and talk to Miss Ellis yourself,' replied the new-comer, who was one of Sargent's associates. 'She went right in off the deep end when she understood. Looked like murder, and went tearing off to Miss Mears's room. I thought there was going to be trouble, but she came back. She said she hadn't dared to go in for fear what she might do. You had better come and try to smooth her down, if you can.'

'Oh, all right,' said Sargent wearily. 'You'll excuse me, Mr Irwin. This is the sort of thing that happens when you try to run a Beauty Competition.'

'It was a dirty trick,' his associate repeated. 'Miss Mears may be a beauty, and she may be the winner, but she ought to be penalised all the same.'

'She will be,' Paul said, in his grimmest tones. 'No one ever escapes just punishment, I will see if I can find Leslie,' he added, to Sargent, and, turning his back, walked slowly, with long strides, down the passage leading to the door marked 'No Admission.'

He had taken off his hat, and his hair he wore a little long stirred in the draught blowing down the passage from an open window by the big door where scenery was taken in when occasion required.

CHAPTER IV

MURDER!

WHETHER telepathy and thought-transference are facts or no, whether the tale is true that in primitive communities news, especially bad news, tragic news, is transmitted at a speed even modern science can neither rival nor explain, it is at least certain that a rumour can pass through a crowd as lightning flashes from sky to earth.

Certainly the great audience assembled in the Brush Hill Central Cinema for the choosing of the Brush Hill Beauty Queen had been growing a little restless, and, collectively, was glad of a fresh distraction. A girl of beauty is no doubt a joy for ever, but a whole procession of them all through a long evening is apt to blunt the edge of appreciation. Cheers and yawns go but ill together, and it had become a trifle wearisome to clap and stamp every time there appeared a fresh pretty girl almost exactly like the last pretty girl. By eleven o'clock, freckles and a snub nose would most likely have won warmer appreciation than the brightest of eyes and the most cleverly designed complexion.

As for the judging committee in the big stage box, one member had already fallen asleep. Luckily a fellow committee-man had awakened him before his snores had been recognized for anything but the grunt of less and greater approval he had previously been emitting. But whereas score-cards had at first been marked in precise detail – so much more for the enchanting tilt of a nose, so much less for a mouth a trifle too large, something extra for a graceful walk, a minus for a stumble or for hands that looked a little large – though, indeed, one committee-man, a fervent admirer of a certain renowned film star, had been giving plus marks for really substantial hands and feet – by this hour of the night a general estimate had become the rule, and .

shortcomings and defects that earlier had been smiled at tolerantly, a weary committee now tended to regard as fatal.

'Wasting time, that's all it is,' grunted the man who had just been awakened, and who was consequently in a very bad temper. 'That last girl had thick ankles – oughtn't to have been let on. We've all given Miss Mears top marks. She's bound to be the winner.'

The joint honorary scorers at the back of the box agreed. It was their task to add up the marks assigned to each competitor, add in agreed proportion the number of seconds the applause of the audience had continued, and then certify and announce the result. One of them said now:

'Yes. C. Mears is well ahead.'

'What's that?' asked the chairman. 'Caroline Mears?'

He was a prominent local politician, and possessed the sort of voice necessary to prominent local politicians, both for emphasising their own arguments and bawling down those of opponents. So the question he had meant only for the hearing of his fellow judges was plainly audible to members of the audience sitting near.

'Caroline Mears?' someone repeated. 'Which one's that? Is she the winner?'

'Can't be,' a neighbour protested. 'The thing's not over yet.'

'Well, what's happened to her, then?' a third asked.

'Something happened to Caroline Mears?' inquired, excitedly, yet another.

People near looked round interestedly. In their weary state, half hypnotised into a condition of torpor by the seemingly endless procession of loveliness passing across the stage, a new interest was very welcome.

'Caroline Mears?' they repeated to each other. 'Something happened? Why? What?'

But no one knew. The name, the question, passed over the assembly like a breeze blowing across a field of ripe corn. 'Caroline Mears?' people said to each other, and one could follow the progress of the name across the auditorium as one could follow the wake of a darting fish through calm water. 'Carrie Mears?' they repeated to each other. 'What about her?' 'She's the winner.' 'She can't be, not yet.' 'She's disqualified.' 'What for?' 'There's been cheating.' 'Who? How?' 'Well, anyhow, something's happened.'

A general restlessness developed. The unlucky girl at the moment on the stage was hardly noticed. She might not have been there, and her frock and her complexion, on which so much anxious care and attention had been bestowed, were quite wasted. Even some of her score-cards never got marked, for the members of the committee, too, were asking each other what all the excitement was about, and the prominent local politician said, in the bellowing undertone that was his idea of a whispered aside:

'What's started them off like this? Has anything happened? Is something wrong?'

'Something wrong,' repeated again one or two who overheard, and the phrase flashed through the auditorium so that scarcely had it been uttered before it reached the uniformed commissionaire at the entrance.

'Something wrong?' he repeated, and beckoned to a passing policeman. 'Seems there's something wrong,' he said. 'Just stand by a moment, will you?'

'What is it?' asked the policeman.

'I don't know,' answered the commissionaire. 'Carrie Mears, they say.'

'Who is she?' asked the policeman.

But the commissionaire didn't know that, either, and, within, the very last competitor flatly and thankfully now refused to appear. She had been pushed into the competition by a proud mamma; she had been dreading the ordeal for weeks; funk had kept her awake the last night or two, she knew she was looking a 'perfect wreck,' and she knew, too, that the frock her mother had chosen for her didn't suit her in the least. Joyfully she was able to point out that it was evidently useless for her to go on.

'No one's looking; no one noticed that last poor thing a scrap,' she said. 'Something's happened to Carrie Mears.'

'What's all this?' demanded Mr Sargent, appearing suddenly. 'Carrie Mears? What about her?'

'Better go on and try to quiet 'em down,' said Martin, the time-keeper. 'There'll be a panic in a moment – Lord knows why.'

'What's the matter?' Sargent repeated. 'What's happened?'

'Nothing – that's why it may be serious,' Martin answered. 'Old Paul Irwin went running off after that boy of his he's dotty on, saying something about Carrie Mears making a public show of herself and the judgment of heaven he thinks he has in his pocket, and I suppose that started people talking. You had better stop it before trouble starts too. Tell 'em Carrie Mears is the winner – she is all right. None of the others had a chance after Lily Ellis did for herself.'

Sargent walked out in front. People were already on their feet, puzzled and anxious. His appearance produced an immediate hush. People turned to look and listen. He began:

'Ladies and gentlemen, you'll be glad to hear that the last bus hasn't gone yet, there are still taxis to be had, and the tube is still running. I've just sent round to inquire, as some of you seem in such a hurry.'

That made some people laugh, faintly puzzled others, and quietened them all. He went on:

'In a few moments the name of the winner will be announced. The judges' committee is now engaged in confirming its decision. As you are all aware, the prize is nomination as Brush Hill Queen of Beauty. [Loud cheering.] The winner will be crowned Queen of Beauty on this stage, next week, by a very distinguished film star and actress – one you all know and admire, and who is a tremendous favourite not only with you here in Brush Hill [more applause], but all over the world. [Renewed applause at this intimation that the world was following the Brush Hill lead.] I won't an-

B

nounce her name to-night. [Signs of disappointment.] I'll keep that for you as a little surprise – and it will be a surprise.'

He paused and beamed. As a matter of fact he kept the name secret because as yet he did not know it. Up to the present the luminaries of the cinema world he had approached had declined, not thinking Brush Hill sufficiently important to be worth the shedding upon it of the light of their countenances. But he was sure to be able to get someone or another, and the smaller her renown the bigger the letters in which he would announce her. He went on:

'And, then in addition to that very great honour, there'll be the very substantial prize of a month's engagement with the Colossal Film Company, whose splendid picture, "The Sheik's Own Darlingest," you all enjoyed so much last week. Almost – I say almost advisedly, for there are exceptions – but almost every favourite film star began her career with the Colossal Film Company, and I think you may be quite confident that what we are really doing to-night is selecting a future star whose fame will soon be on a level with that of – of Greta Garbo herself.'

His voice had taken on a note of real awe and reverence as he pronounced that wondrous name. His hearers gave a little gasp, and looked at each other with new respect. They had not quite realized that that was what they were really doing, and it seemed so dazzling and important to them that they all felt quite dazzled and still more important. It is not every day you have the chance to put out your hand and elevate someone hitherto unknown to a Greta-Garbian fame. Sargent, who was really a clever man and knew his job, saw, with satisfaction, he had produced his results, and that all danger of a panic was over. He went on:

'The final judgment rests with the committee. But I believe their choice has been made. I wonder if you can guess it? If you can, and guess right, why, then, we can all take that as a very important and impressive confirmation of the committee's decision.'

There was a momentary pause. Then someone muttered
'Carrie Mears,' and someone else repeated it, and then a
third called it aloud. It was taken up at once; it became a
general cry; from the whole auditorium one universal name
was uttered:

'Mears! Mears! Mears!'

Mr Sargent beamed on them.

'I'm inclined to believe you're right,' he announced.
'Most gratifying if it turns out, as I think it will, that the
verdict of the committee and the verdict of the audience
coincide. I will ask the genial and popular chairman of the
committee, so well known to all of you, whether he can
confirm that.'

The 'genial and popular' gentleman in question stood
up. He, too, beamed upon the audience. He adored hearing
himself described as 'genial and popular.' He adored,
equally, making speeches. He began:

'Ladies and gentlemen, it is with the utmost pleasure
that I am able to announce, on behalf of myself and my
esteemed colleagues, that Caroline Mears – –'

He paused, for Martin had just come hurrying on to the
stage. He was ghastly pale, and the hand he held out towards Sargent was shaking violently. He said, in a shrill high
whisper:

'Carrie Mears has been murdered ... she's lying there
stabbed ... ask if there's a doctor in the house.'

But Sargent only gasped and stared. He heard, but he did
not believe. He could not. He remained standing there,
mute and staring. Everyone waited. Even the chairman
waited, silent. Martin himself called out, addressing the
audience:

'I'm sorry ... it's one of the competitors taken ill ... is there
a doctor here?'

CHAPTER V

FIRST INQUIRIES

By good fortune there were, as it happened, two or three doctors in the house, and there was also one, a Dr Bryan, who was a member of the judging committee, though this fact both Sargent and Martin had, in their agitation, forgotten for the moment, Now it was Dr Bryan, who, hurrying from the box, and guided behind by an excited attendant, reached first Sargent's office where the victim lay.

The policeman who had been kept on the spot by the lucky foresight of the commissionaire was already on guard at the door. He had, too, sent a phone message to the Brush Hill police station, and inside the room he had allowed no one but two women attendants, of whom one, fortunately, had some knowledge of first aid. Near by, the 'art' photographer, Roy Beattie, was standing, leaning against the wall for support, and looking very pale and excited, and a little as if he might be sick at any minute. His clothing was stained with blood; his face and hands were dabbled with it. He was explaining, confusedly and incoherently, to everyone near that he had entered the room to speak to Miss Mears, and had found her lying on the floor behind Mr Sargent's big roll-top desk with a knife sticking in her throat.

'I pulled it out ... it bled awfully ... a great spurt ... then it stopped,' he said again and again, and the policeman notebook in hand, busily writing, would look up, and remark from time to time:

'Don't you say nothing ... don't you say nothing just yet awhile.'

Then he would resume his writing, and Beattie would always answer:

'No, that's right ... I won't,' and then, almost in the same breath, would begin telling his story all over again to the next new-comer he saw staring at his blood-stained clothing.

' The policeman, who knew Dr Bryan by sight, drew back to allow him to enter. The unfortunate girl was lying supine, the fatal knife on the floor near by where Beattie had thrown it down, the two attendants, bewildered, scared and useless, kneeling by her side. The wound at the base of the throat had bled with a dreadful profusion, and the horror of the scene was heightened by the triple contrast between it, the dying girl's festive attire in the latest and most extreme style, and the drab office surroundings, the letter files, card index, deed boxes, and all the other appurtenances of modern business.

One was aware of a ghastly incongruity – it seemed murder had no place in this decorous, conventional apartment, and violent death no claim on youth that had gone so bravely, richly, gaudily, attired.

Dr Bryan's diagnosis was swift.

'She's still alive,' he said. 'It's not the wound so much – it's shock and loss of blood. The only chance is to rush her to hospital for blood transfusion, and most likely it's too late for that to be any good.'

A colleague, who had just arrived, agreed with him. An urgent call was put through to the nearest hospital. The policeman looked worried, for this was a sad departure from the 'nothing must be touched' principle firmly implanted in his official mind ; and, though the message to the police station had gone through first, it was the ambulance that first arrived.

Shortly afterwards the officers from the local police station appeared, and then, in swift succession, Superintendent Mitchell of Scotland Yard, summoned from home just as he was taking his usual nightcap - a modest whisky and soda – before retiring to bed, Inspector Ferris, who had chanced to be on duty at the Yard when the Brush Hill message came, the usual experts - finger-print, photographic, and so on – and two or three assistants, including a young sergeant named Bobby Owen, who stood very much in Mitchell's good books, but was held by his critics to be really rather dense, even if somehow or another he showed at times an odd capacity for blundering on the truth.

'Oh, you just keep on making one silly-ass blunder after another till at last one of them turns up trumps,' he had once explained, when asked to account for a success that had made him stand well with his superiors. 'Facts always stick together, and mistakes never do, so, when you find things begin to fit in, you know all you've got to do is to peg along.'

As Mr Sargent's office was not a large one, and as Mitchell was anxious that it should be as little disturbed as possible until a complete examination had been made, there was at first some confusion. One zealous subordinate, for instance, was only prevented just in time from clearing away a broad-brimmed black felt hat lying on one of the chairs. Finally Mitchell turned out everyone, except the local C.I.D. inspector, a man named Penfold, and the young sergeant, Bobby Owen. The photographers and the finger-print experts, and the rest of them, he promised should have their turn afterwards, but first he himself wanted to have a good look round.

'The girl was using it as a dressing-room?' he asked. 'Is that it? Funny idea to use the manager's office for a dressing-room. Is she any connection?'

'No, sir,' answered Bobby, who had already made one or two swift inquiries. 'I understand it was the only room left; all the ordinary dressing-rooms were crowded out.'

Mitchell looked as if he thought this was an explanation that itself required an explanation. He was staring all round the room, his slow intent glance passionate in its intensity upon every item in turn. There came a knock at the door. It was to say a message had been received from the hospital reporting that the patient had passed away, almost immediately upon arrival, before there had been time for any attempt to save her by blood transfusion.

'A bad business,' Mitchell said slowly, and one could

almost see his body stiffen with the intensity of his resolve to bring to justice the perpetrator of so abominable a crime. 'The doctor said there wasn't much chance,' he added. He looked at the big, broad-brimmed hat lying on a chair near. 'I wonder who that belongs to,' he said. 'The manager perhaps, as it's his office. I suppose the murderer wouldn't be so kind as to leave it – he must have got covered with blood, that ought to help. Looks like a love quarrel – someone she's turned down, perhaps. Have to check up on that. Owen, ring up the hospital and ask them to be careful of all her personal belongings – her handbag, and so on, it doesn't seem to be here. Tell them I'm sending a man round to get them. See to that, will you? Jones might go.'

'Very good, sir,' said Bobby, and left the room to carry out his instructions.

Mitchell followed, surrendering that room to his assistants, and asking if another could be placed at his disposal.

'A photographer, going in to take her picture, found her, I think?' he asked. 'Was that it?'

The policeman beckoned to Roy Beattie, who was still waiting near, to come forward. Mitchell, after giving a few other directions, asked Beattie to accompany him to the little cubby-hole of a room that the distracted Martin had managed to discover for his accommodation. Bobby followed, to report that the hospital had answered his phone message by declaring that there had been no handbag or any other personal belongings brought with the dead girl – nothing but the actual clothing she had on.

'She must have had a handbag – they all have,' Mitchell said. 'Tell Ferris to have a search made. If it can't be found, someone must have pinched it. Tell him to make all possible inquiry, and then come back here. I want you to make a note of what Mr Beattie has to tell us.'

Bobby was back from his errand, with his notebook open and ready, before Mitchell and Beattie were settled.

'Did you know Miss Mears?' Mitchell began by asking.

'She came to my studio about a year ago,' Beattie answered. 'I made some pictures of her. She was hoping to get an engagement as a film actress, and she wanted photographs to send with her applications. I don't think she succeeded, but she came back once or twice, and we became friendly.'

'Anything more than friendly?' Mitchell asked.

'No, no,' Beattie answered, flushing. 'She was awfully pretty ... you couldn't help feeling ... there was nothing between us, if that's what you mean. Of course, I liked to be with her. I admired her tremendously.'

'I see,' Mitchell said gravely. 'Now tell me about tonight. It was you who made the discovery, wasn't it?'

'Yes,' Beattie answered. 'I went to her room and knocked. I didn't get any answer.'

'One moment,' Mitchell interposed. 'You are here taking photographs, aren't you? Is that for a paper, or for the management?'

'For myself,' Beattie explained. 'I'm in business for myself. I only do special work – not ordinary studio work, I mean. I got exclusive permission to come behind to-night. I was going to make pictures of the winner and the runners-up; there was to be a big group picture on the stage as a wind up.'

'Were you about to take photos of Miss Mears, then?'

'No, I had done that before,' Beattie answered, with a certain hesitation that made Mitchell look at him sharply.

'You have them, I suppose?' he asked.

'I gave them to the stage-door-keeper to look after for me,' Beattie explained. 'I didn't want them mixed up with the others I had taken. Hers were special, you see. Everyone thought she was sure to be the winner.'

'Yes, so they tell me,' Mitchell agreed. 'Winner – and then this instead. You had some reason for wanting to see her again?'

Beattie looked more hesitating and more uncomfortable still. Bobby's pencil paused, hovering over the page. Mitchell waited, very quietly, and yet with a kind of formidable patience that made his very stillness impressive. At last Beattie burst out:

'There was a story going about – someone else is sure to tell you. I don't suppose it's anything to do with it. Some of them were saying she had played a mean trick on one of the other girls.'

'What was that?' Mitchell asked.

'It's a Miss Ellis – Lilian Ellis,' Beattie explained uncomfortably. 'She's very pretty too – not like Carrie Mears, but ... well, everyone thought she had the best chance after Carrie Mears, and some thought she might turn out winner. And it got about Carrie had told her the rules were she would be disqualified if she stopped on the stage too long, and Miss Ellis believed her, and ran off again before the judging committee had time to give her any marks.'

'And you were going to ask Miss Mears about it?'

'Yes.'

Mitchell hesitated, and drummed lightly on the table with his finger-tips, as was his custom when he was worried or perplexed. He said quietly: .

'Well, let's leave that for the moment. Will you tell us exactly what happened after you knocked? Oh, by the way, there's a hat here.' He showed the big, broad-brimmed felt hat he had brought with him from the manager's office. 'Isn't yours, is it?'

'No,' Beattie answered, shaking his head.

'Don't know whose, I suppose?'

'It looks like one Mr Paul Irwin wears sometimes,' Beattie answered. 'I don't know if it is.'

'Have to ask,' observed Mitchell carelessly, putting it down. 'After you knocked, what happened?'

'There wasn't any answer,' Beattie continued, 'so I opened the door and looked in, just to make sure there was on one there. All the lights were out except a reading-lamp on the desk. I thought the room was empty, and I was just going away again, only I thought it funny the reading-lamp on the desk was lighted, and then I got the feeling ...

I can't describe it exactly ... I felt uneasy somehow, as if
something was wrong ... I didn't know what ... and I saw
the room was empty, and, all the same, I thought it wasn't
... I called her name and there wasn't any answer, and then
I thought I heard a faint sort of breathing sound, as if
someone was asleep, only not very comfortable – a sort of
half breathing, half choking. The switch is near the door,
and I turned on the electricity and went further into the
room. I could see her then, lying on the floor behind
Sargent's big desk. It had hidden her before.'

'I noticed that,' Mitchell agreed. 'I saw behind the desk
would be hidden from anyone standing in the doorway.
Go on, please.'

'I thought at first she had fainted or something. I went
across to her. I was hurrying, and my foot slipped in something.' He paused and shuddered, remembering what that
something was. He continued. 'I went down on my knees.
I tried to lift her. She was looking at me, and I think she
knew me, but I'm not sure. She didn't say anything. I saw a
knife just at the bottom of her throat. I caught hold of it
and pulled it out. That made the wound bleed worse than
ever for a moment, and then it stopped suddenly. I tried to
stop it with my handkerchief, but it stopped itself. I didn't
know what to do. I think I hardly believed it. There was
blood all over me. I got up and ran to the door and there
was a man passing, and I shouted out to him that Miss
Mears had been murdered. I think he thought I was mad.
Someone else came, and I told him, and he looked inside
the room and then he ran off, and I think I went faint or
something – I only remember leaning against the wall and
trying to tell a policeman, who had turned up somehow, all
about it, and his keeping on telling me not to say anything.'

He paused and then, after an interval, he added abruptly:

'I had got myself all over blood.'

Mitchell took no notice of this remark. He was again
drumming with his finger-tips on the table before him. He
said:

'Was Miss Mears alone when you were taking the photographs you spoke about? Was there no one with her?'

'No, she was quite alone.'

'Isn't that rather peculiar? Hadn't she any friends with her? I should have thought all these girls would have been running in and out of each other's rooms all the time?'

'Well, you see,' Beattie answered, 'there was this story about the trick she had played on Miss Ellis. Some of them were rather indignant about that. I think Miss Mears knew what they were saying, so she stopped in her own room. It was because she was all alone, and I thought it funny, that I asked what was up, and some of them told me about the trick she had played Miss Ellis.'

'Is that why you went back to see her again?'

'Well, yes, in a way. I thought it was a dirty trick if it was true. I thought I would ask her. I thought if it was true I would scrap her photos and not show any of them – I had exclusive rights.'

'By way of punishment?' Mitchell asked gravely.

'Well, to pay her out, if you like. That's really why I gave those I had taken of her to the door-keeper, so as not to mix them up with the others I was getting developed right away.'

'You are friendly with Miss Ellis?' Mitchell asked.

'Yes, in a way – yes,' Beattie answered, flushing slightly, just as he had done before when asked the same question about Miss Mears, and again Mitchell looked at him slowly and gravely.

'You were angry at the trick you heard had been played upon Miss Ellis?' he asked.

'I wanted to know if it was true what they were saying,' Beattie answered uncomfortably. 'I didn't believe it,' he added.

'Perhaps I had better not ask you any more questions just now,' Mitchell said slowly. 'If there is anything more you wish to say, well and good.'

'My God,' Beattie cried out at that. 'You don't mean you think I did it?'

'We are trying to find out what to think,' Mitchell answered. 'You don't wish to make any further statement?'

'I think I've told you everything I know, and it's the truth,' Beattie muttered.

'If you don't mind,' Mitchell said, 'I'll ask you not to leave here for the present. Owen,' he added, to his assistant, 'tell Mr Penfold that Mr Beattie has kindly promised to wait a little in case he can give us any further information.'

'I suppose that means you are going to arrest me,' Beattie said moodily.

Neither of them answered. Bobby went out into the corridor with him. A tall young man was hurrying down it towards them. He had on the leather jacket and overalls motor-cyclists often wear, and behind him a policeman was following, calling to him to come back. He took no notice, and his thin gaunt face, his blazing eyes, his mouth half open with twitching, nervous lips, all seemed to show that he was in a very excited condition. His clothes were muddy down one side, as if recently he had had a fall, and indeed his whole appearance seemed a little wild. The policeman caught him up and laid a hand upon his shoulder, and he shook it off with a fierce, powerful movement of his whole body.

'I tell you, I've got to know – I must know,' he almost shouted.

'What's all this?' Bobby asked.

'Is it true? Is it true what they're saying outside?' the stranger asked him. 'God, is it true?'

'Is what true?' Bobby asked, and the other answered:

'Is it true Carrie's murdered?'

'I am afraid so,' Bobby answered. 'Did you know her?'

The stranger stood still. He covered his face with his hands, and one could see his body shake with his emotion. He said, not very loudly, but very distinctly:

'It can't be true. It's only this morning she promised to marry me.'

CHAPTER VI

THE MISSING HANDBAG

MITCHELL, whose keen ear had caught the note of emotion and excitement in the voice of the new-comer, came out into the corridor. The motor-cyclist, by an apparent effort, straightened himself, and yet still kept one hand against the wall, as if for support. His lean, cadaverous face, too, was quivering with the agitation he was trying to control; his eyes were wild and dreadful. One had the impression that his self-control might give way at any moment, and that he knew this and was using all his nervous energy to prevent it. He said hoarsely:

'Where is she? I must see her.'

'Miss Mears's *fiancé*,' Bobby explained to Mitchell. 'He says they were engaged this morning. He has just heard – –'

'I can't believe it,' the motor-cyclist interrupted. 'It's not possible. ... Is it true?' he asked, almost as if hoping that even now it might appear there was some mistake or misunderstanding. Then: 'Who did it?' he shouted fiercely.

'We are only beginning our inquiries,' Mitchell answered. 'Possibly you can give us some information. So far we haven't got much to go on. Owen, carry on, and then come back here – oh, and tell Penfold again to concentrate on that handbag. Every woman has a handbag – you must if you've no pockets. It must be somewhere. Tell Penfold to report the moment he has any information.'

The cyclist drew a long breath. He said to Mitchell, quickly and eagerly:

'Her handbag's missing. ... Carrie's handbag? Then it's been stolen ... then the murderer's got it ... find it and you've found him.'

'Yes,' agreed Mitchell thoughtfully. 'Yes ... quite so ... so

far we haven't much information about Miss Mears's identity. I take it you can help us there?'

'Yes, but I must see her. I must see her first,' the other
answered. He looked at Mitchell, and said, quietly and
steadily: 'Is she dead?'

Mitchell made a sign of assent. The other turned and
walked the length of the corridor. He stood at the further
end of it for a moment or two, and then came back. He
seemed quieter now, more composed, as if he had braced
himself to greater self-control.

'I'm sorry,' he said. 'I'm sure you will understand ... I
can hardly realize even now ... it's so awful.' He paused,
shuddering, and continued: 'How did it happen? Have you
no idea who did it?'

'Not much at present,' Mitchell answered. 'It will be our
duty to find out ... we always do in the long run.'

'Always?' the other repeated. 'Always?' he said again,
and mentioned a recent sensational case at Brighton concerning which, up till then, little had been discovered.

Mitchell made no attempt to justify his 'always.'

'I suppose there's nothing you can tell us ... no one you
suspect for any reason?' he asked.

'No, no. I can't believe ... I can't imagine anyone doing
such a thing ... it seems, so ... so unnatural, incredible ...
could it have been an accident ... or – –?'

'Or what?'

'Nothing .... it's only that murder seems so .. so incredible.'

'I think you were going to say something, or make some
suggestion,' Mitchell insisted, and, when the other still shook
his head, Mitchell said: 'You were thinking of the possibility of suicide?'

'No, I wasn't – not thinking; it just came into my mind,
only because it all seems so impossible, and then she said
something once. She didn't mean anything; it was only just
talk.'

'What was it?' Mitchell asked.

'It wasn't serious; it was because she was so keen on be-coming a film star. She burst out once she would kill herself if they wouldn't give her her chance on the pictures. Of course she didn't mean it. I told her not to talk rot. She never said anything like it again – at least not that I ever heard.'

'It may be important,' Mitchell said, and led the way back into the room, where almost immediately they were joined by Bobby.

'Mr Penfold has gone to complete inquiries about Miss Mears's identity,' he reported. 'There don't seem to be any friends or relatives of hers here. I gave Mr Ferris your in-structions about the handbag. He says there is no trace of it so far. He is sending round to the hospital, to make special inquiries there, and, of course, continuing to look here. He wants to know if he should offer a pound or two reward for its recovery.'

'You ought to – more. I'll stand it, if you like – ten pounds – twenty – as much as you want,' the cyclist interrupted ex-citedly. 'It must have been stolen. Find it, and you've found the murderer.'

'Seems an odd thing for a murderer to steal,' observed Mitchell thoughtfully. 'Unless she had jewellery in it. But she seemed to be wearing all her trinkets, and she would hardly be likely to bring much money with her to-night. Do you know of anything valuable there might be in the bag?'

'It would be the bag itself,' the other answered. ' It was a very good one – real crocodile, worth five or six pounds. If it's missing, it must have been stolen. Afterwards. If it had been taken before, or even if it had been mislaid or lost, she would have been sure to say something.'

'That's right,' agreed Mitchell. He added to Owen: 'I don't think we'll do anything about a reward just yet. If the murderer took it for any reason, the offer of a reward will only let him know we are looking for it and he'll destroy it. If any third person has it, it'll be handed over all right with-out any reward offered.'

'Anyhow, it's a clue,' the cyclist said.

Mitchell nodded.

'Even an important one,' he said. 'Though that's not certain yet. Now, sir,' he continued, 'perhaps you'll tell us your name – I don't think we know it yet – and any information you can give us that may be useful in any way whatever.'

'My name is Maddox,' the cyclist answered. 'Claude Maddox. I'm with my uncle's firm – South American Trades, Ltd. My uncle is managing director. I suppose I shall be that myself some day, when he retires. I worked for the firm in South America for some years – from soon after leaving school, I went out almost immediately. I came back home to take up an appointment in our London office. Miss Mears worked in an office near ours. I used to see her in the lunch-hour. I suppose I fell in love with her at first sight, as they call it. She kept me at arm's length a long time. She thought I hadn't been properly introduced. But I didn't care how much she snubbed me. I managed to get her to let me speak to her at last, and we got friendly. I asked her several times to marry me. She kept putting me off, but this morning she promised. I bought the ring in Regent Street after lunch.'

'Have you given it her?'

'Yes. I met her as she was leaving work to hurry home and get ready for this show to-night. You didn't see it? She wasn't wearing it?'

'I don't think so,' Mitchell said.

'She told me she wouldn't – not yet; not to-night. I expect it was in her handbag. I expect that's why it was stolen.'

He gave a description of the ring – diamond, set with small seed pearls – and mentioned the shop in Regent Street where it had been purchased. It had cost £5, he said. Bobby took careful note of the details, and after one or two more questions, and after Maddox had explained that he had been cycling most of the evening, Mitchell remarked:

'Wasn't that a little unusual? If you and Miss Mears had

just got engaged, I should have expected you to be here.'

'I wanted to be,' Maddox answered. 'I was rather sick about it. But Carrie asked me not to. I couldn't very well turn down the very first thing she asked.'

'Had she any special reason for that?'

'Well, you see' – Maddox hesitated – 'the fact is ... you see she was awfully pretty ... and fascinating.' He paused and had some difficulty in continuing. One could see how his deep emotion shook him from head to foot. Mitchell waited quietly, and presently Maddox regained his self-control and was able to continue: 'There were several fellows who wanted her,' he explained. 'There was one chap who takes rather swell photographs – his name is Beattie, I think – that handbag of hers was a present from him. And another fellow called Irwin.'

'Irwin,' repeated Mitchell sharply, and his glance went to the big, broad-brimmed felt hat he had brought with him from the scene of the tragedy.

Maddox followed the direction of his eyes.

'His father always wears a hat like that,' he said. 'I don't know if that's his, but it's like it. He runs the Building Society here, you know – the father, I mean; Paul Irwin. His son is Leslie, and he used to boast that Carrie and he understood each other, and their engagement was practically settled, only they were waiting till they could get round the old man. He's very strict in his views – puritan – didn't like her, or think her the right sort for his precious son. Leslie said he would come round in time – he always did. Carrie told me there was nothing in it. She had just been out with him once or twice, and he chose to think that meant more than it did. I think she was afraid there might be a bit of a row if he knew about us, and she wanted to keep us apart. He and I had already had words over it – over his boasting, I mean. I told him he was a cad to talk that way. I expect he only did it to try to warn me off. Anyhow, we had a row, and I suppose she was afraid we might have another to-night. So she asked me to keep out of the way till she had

had a chance to tell him. I think she thought she could make him reasonable about it and promise to be friends. I suppose it would be rather a shock to him – I know it would to me; it would have made me half mad if I had thought I was going to lose her. Perhaps it made him the same way.'

'Do you mean you think – –?' Mitchell began, but Maddox understood and interrupted instantly.

'That he did it? Oh, no! Oh, that's impossible! ... He's not that sort ... he's no pal of mine, but he's not a murderer ... impossible!'

'I hope so,' Mitchell said slowly, 'but we must consider everything, even the impossible.'

'Leslie Irwin would never do a thing like that,' Maddox repeated.'No one could.'

'All the same, someone did it,' Mitchell said, in the same slow abstracted tones. 'The question is, Who and why? What was it made you think of going out on your motorcycle to-night? Anywhere special you wanted to go?'

'Oh, no. It was just that I was too restless to stop in, knowing all that was going on here and wondering how she was getting on, and all that. I couldn't settle to anything. I could hardly eat any supper, I remember, and afterwards I got out the old bus and went for a spin. I went a good way out – along the Edgware Road, and out into the country somewhere. I didn't much mind where, and I didn't notice particularly. I turned back about half-past nine, I suppose – or perhaps about ten. When I got near London again, I thought that, though Carrie had asked me to keep away, I could ring up the cinema and ask how she had got on. So I stopped at a call box and rang up, and, when I asked for her, I got a reply there had been an accident; and, when I asked what accident, they said, "Stabbed – murdered." Well, I thought it was a joke or a lie or something, and I didn't believe it. But they rang off, and I couldn't get any reply, so I rang up again from another call box, further on, and this time, when I asked, I was told the police were in charge and then they rang off, too. Well, then I fairly got the wind up. I came along just as fast as the old bus would go. I had two falls on the way – luckily I didn't hurt myself.' He glanced at the mud-stains showing on his clothing. 'I might have done. That mud's from Brush Hill Common; somehow I came off all right, but it was a bit of a narrow squeak. When I got here, there was a crowd outside. They were saying – –' He paused. He got to his feet, drawing himself to his full height: 'You've got to find who did it, and why,' he said. 'You've got to find her handbag, too, and then you'll have found her murderer.'

'We'll do our best,' Mitchell assured him quietly.

CHAPTER VII

THE FINGER-PRINT

THERE came a knock at the door. Bobby went to open it.

'Inspector Penfold, sir,' he said to Mitchell.

'Tell him to come in,' Mitchell answered, and turned to Maddox. 'I want to hear what the inspector has to tell us,' he explained. 'You won't mind waiting a little longer, will you? There might be some other points you could help us on.'

'I will stay as long as you like,' Maddox answered heavily, 'if there is any chance of helping you find the – the murderer.'

He pronounced the word with difficulty. It was as though the word brought home to him the fact, and that he dared not face it. His lean, cadaverous face showed plainly, in the worn, haggard look it bore, the tension he endured. His walk, even, was not too steady as he left the room, and Bobby looked after him with sympathy.

'Poor devil. He's feeling it,' he said.

'Yes,' agreed Mitchell. 'Yes. Not far from a breakdown, I think.'

'No wonder,' Bobby observed. 'Pretty awful, the girl you've just got engaged to murdered the same day.'

'Yes,' agreed Mitchell again; and went on, half to himself: 'Which is worse – to be murdered, to be the murderer, or to be the helpless looker-on? Well, Penfold, what have you got to tell us?' he added, to the local man who had just come in.

'Miss Mears lived at – –' Penfold gave the address. 'It's not more than ten minutes from here. It's a converted flat in a fair-sized, semi-detached house. She and the aunt with whom she lived had the four rooms on the first floor. Miss Perry – that's the aunt – is old and not very strong, and very

seldom goes out. Apparently she sits and knits and listens
to the wireless all day long. A woman comes in, three times
a week, to clean. Other relatives, an aunt and a cousin or
two, live in Exeter. Miss Perry is one of those people who
believe in keeping themselves to themselves, and they don't
seem to have many friends. Miss Mears worked as a short-
hand-typist in the City.' He gave the name and address of
the firm who employed her. Their offices were close to those
of Maddox's firm – South American Trades. Penfold continued: 'I don't imagine Miss Perry and Miss Mears got
on very well. But the girl wanted cheap lodgings, and the
aunt found the money she paid useful, so they put up with
each other. As a result, Miss Perry doesn't know much about
Miss Mears's private life – just disapproves of it generally.
But she says she knows she was mad on the pictures – wanted
to be a film star – and liked boys running after her. Applies
to practically every girl in London, I should say,' Penfold
commented, in parentheses, and continued: 'At least, most
of 'em are cracked on the pictures, want to be film stars,
and like as many boys in tow as they can get. Miss Mears
never brought her boys to the flat, and Miss Perry only
knows the names of one or two – the photographer, Beattie,
and Leslie Irwin. Miss Perry let me lock the door of Miss
Mears's room so it can be examined later. She took it
fairly calmly when I told her what had happened. I think
she regards it as a natural judgment on a flighty girl, but is
quite anxious to see judgment done on the murderer, too.
She seems one of those people whose religion chiefly consists in expecting a judgment on others.'

'Does she know this Leslie Irwin?' Mitchell asked.

'No. She approves of his father though. Mr Irwin led the
local opposition to the Sunday opening of cinemas, and Miss
Perry always approves of people who disapprove of what
other people want – if you see what I mean,' he added
doubtfully.

'Do you know anything yourself about Mr Irwin – the
father, I mean, of course.'

'He is a lawyer, but he doesn't practise privately. He is secretary and solicitor to the Brush Hill Building Society. It's a big concern - very flourishing now. There were rumours about it at one time, but it's made big progress ever since the war, thanks to Mr. Irwin. He's made it. Mr Irwin's father was one of the founders back in the last century and the general idea is that Leslie Irwin is to follow his father and grandfather. He's an articled clerk to a City firm at present, but acts as his father's secretary, too - in training for the old man's job.'

'Know anything about him?' Mitchell asked.

'No, except that he's honorary secretary to the Brush Hill Amateur Dramatic Society, and they say had a big row with his father over taking it on. But he managed it rather well. He joined the Brush Hill Literary Institute to study German - which his father did approve of. Then he joined one or two more classes, added the Literary Institute dramatic class, and worked on to the A.D.S. before the old man quite knew what was happening. In the blood apparently - the grandfather was a friend of Irving's and Toole's, and used sometimes to take a share in dramatic productions.'

'Interesting family,' observed Mitchell thoughtfully. 'There was a hat in the room where the girl was murdered,' he went on. 'It seems it may belong to Mr Paul Irwin.'

Penfold looked very surprised and bewildered.

'That's very funny,' he said. He got up and went across to look at the hat towards which Mitchell had pointed. 'Mr Irwin usually wears a hat like that,' he admitted cautiously.

'I suppose he will be on the phone - -' Mitchell began, and then paused. 'No, I think you had better go yourself. Take my car, it'll be waiting. Ask Mr Irwin and the boy to come round here - oh, and, Penfold, the murderer can hardly have avoided getting covered with blood. But the funny thing is there's no sign or trace of any bloodstains outside the room itself, and no one, apparently, has been noticed with anything of the sort on his person or clothing -

except the photographer who discovered the poor girl.
There's the chance that the murderer covered himself up
with a raincoat, or something like that – it's drizzling a
little, so a raincoat would seem natural. But just keep your
eyes open for anything to suggest that either of the Irwins –
father or son – has changed his clothing or washed his face
or hands recently.'

'Very good, sir,' Penfold answered. 'Ferris asked me to
tell you he can't get track of Miss Mears's handbag. They
are quite positive at the hospital it was never there. No one
here seems to know anything about it. One or two say she
had one, and they think it was in crocodile-skin. Mr. Beattie
says he noticed it lying on the table while he was taking
her portrait. He noticed it because it was a present of his –
cost three guineas, he said, it was real crocodile, and he
recognized it again at once. I think there's no doubt it's been
stolen.'

Mitchell looked a good deal disturbed, and began again
his old trick of beating a tattoo on the table with his finger-
ends. To him this case had seemed at first to be beyond all
doubt what is called a love drama – one of those in which
hot primeval passion breaks through the customs and
restraints of ordinary everyday life, and men fall back again
into their first savagery of unchecked desire. Every now and
again such cases occur to prove how thin is the crust of our
sophisticated civilization, to prove how near the surface
still boil the primordial instincts, and how easily man can
relapse into the animal whose only will is to possess or kill –
or both. Odd, how near man is still to the beast, and how
easily the pale, routine-ridden city dweller, with his wireless·
and his cup of tea and penny bun every afternoon, can turn
again to the red savagery of the dawn. Such cases are strange
and difficult for the philosopher and the psychologist, but
not generally difficult for the police officer. Here, for instance, it had seemed at first there would be little difficulty
in discovering what ardent and passionate lover the engagement to Maddox had disappointed, and little likelihood

there would be any necessity to look further for the culprit. But already there were complications. One had arisen from the evidence of Maddox himself. Now there was this question of the missing, and apparently stolen, handbag.

'Never heard before of a murder for a three-guinea hand-bag,' Mitchell remarked. 'It can't be that she came into the room unexpectedly and found an intruder there, and then he just hit out wildly with a knife and ran for it, because the evidence is she was in the room all the time continuously from when Beattie saw her there – and saw the bag, he says. If any stranger came in afterwards, why didn't she shout for help? Or is it that she tried to, and he – stopped her? Or can the bag have been taken by way of a blind? If whoever did it is really some lover who thought she had been fooling him, and who was a bit off his head, as they are occasionally, for girls will still play with fire, and when passions get loose anything may happen, he might have taken it with the idea of suggesting theft as a motive. But that's not likely; crimes of passion aren't calculated.'

He paused again, worried and puzzled by this apparent intrusion of the vulgar motive of theft into what had seemed a tale of passion and despair and love. Bobby said:

'Perhaps there was something valuable in the bag or something the murderer wanted – love-letters, or something like that? It might be letters he had asked her to bring with her.'

'It might be that; worth remembering anyhow,' agreed Mitchell. 'Well, carry on, Penfold.'

'There's just one other thing, sir,' Penfold said, as he rose to obey. 'I don't know what it means, but it may be important. There are a lot of finger-prints in the room here and there, but there are none on the handle of the knife. It has a rough surface.'

'I noticed that,' Mitchell said.

'But there's one on the blade of the knife. It looked like a woman's, and, as there was talk about a quarrel to-night between Miss Mears and a Miss Ellis, a chance was taken to

compare the print on the knife blade with Miss Ellis's finger-
prints. The knife-blade print seems identical with that of
the little finger of Miss Ellis's right hand. They'll have to
get a clearer imprint and compare them more carefully
before being quite sure, but they say there's no real doubt.'

'There was a quarrel between them about stopping on
the stage too long, or not long enough, wasn't there?'
Mitchell asked. 'That's why Miss Mears was sulking all
alone in her own room, I think. First it looked like a love
tragedy – youngsters carried away by their own passion and
killing as a mere relief to feelings they haven't sense enough
to get the better of. Then with this bag business it looked
like turning into a motive of common robbery, and now it
seems as if it may be just jealousy and a fit of temper. I
think we must have a talk with Miss Ellis. Find her, Owen,
will you? I suppose she's still here. Ask her if I can have a
word with her. Don't frighten her, you know. There may be
a dozen explanations of that finger-print.'

But that hardly seemed very probable to Bobby as he
left the room upon his errand, for in fact less than a finger-
print has before now brought a criminal to execution.

The corridors, rooms, stairs, passages, that only a little
before had been thronged by such eager, excited, animated
crowds were indeed crowded still, for few had had any
desire to leave the scene of so sensational and mysterious a
tragedy, but presented now a very different spectacle.
There was no more running to and fro of laughing, chattering girls, eager to compare experience: no more merry
speculation on the outcome of the competition; no more
friendly teasing of each other; no more grave debates as to
whether this flower would not have been better here rather
than there, or that ribbon or lace more effective there
rather than here; no more proud boasting by confident
mothers and aunts; no more swaggering up and down by
fathers and uncles convinced no girl was like their girl, let
the judges say what they liked. Pale and frightened, little
groups gathered together, exchanging whispered specula-

tion, watching with terrified eyes the grave-faced officers of
police going about their business. Incongruous and strange
indeed was the background to the grim business in hand
that was furnished by that company of girlish competitors
in their youth and loveliness and fashionable finery, and, as
Bobby threaded his way among them, all whispering ceased,
all eyes were turned to watch with dread his progress. It
seemed as if they more than half expected to see him make
a sudden pounce, and cry:

'Here's the murderer.'

Cold and draughty as were these corridors and stairs, it
seemed nearly everyone was collected in them. Few apparently had cared to wait in the comparatively sheltered
dressing-rooms. It was as though· they feared that death
that had struck once that night with such suddenness and
effect might soon strike again, and that only in company
were they safe.

Bobby had no difficulty in finding Lily Ellis. She made
one of a small group, including several of her friends and
relatives, and Bobby's invitation to her to come and talk to
Superintendent Mitchell evidently frightened her badly.

'It is merely that you may be able to give some useful
information,' Bobby explained, more reassuringly than his
feelings quite justified. 'Perhaps you would like someone to
come with you?' he added.

An aunt, a Mrs Francis, volunteered at once to be her
companion. The offer plainly cheered her niece, who began
to look a little less like a convicted criminal ordered to
instant execution. Nevertheless all eyes followed her as she
moved away in the company of Bobby and the aunt, nor
was it difficult to see that what was now merely an excitement of interest and curiosity might easily turn into hostility.
The whisperings and the nods and the stares could well be
imagined changing to clamorous condemnation, and Bobby
heard quite plainly murmured references – there was perhaps no very strenuous effort to keep inaudible – to the
quarrel there had been between her and the dead girl; of

how Lily Ellis had a temper of her own; of how she had been heard to cry out passionately that she could kill Carrie for playing her such a mean trick; of how she had then rushed off to tell Carrie exactly what she thought about it.

He stole a look at her as they all three went along the corridors to the little room where Mitchell waited. There was a certain lightness, almost a fragility, about the girl that did not suggest the murderess, and yet the lines of that close-shut mouth, and a certain air of resolution that marked her grave, dark beauty, suggested one who could take strong determined action if need arose. And murder's a thing so soon done; death a finality so easily achieved. A weapon ready to hand, a gust of passion such as it was said this girl's calm demeanour hid, a blow aimed with small intention, and there's tragedy ready made.

So Bobby mused to himself as he opened the door of the room where Mitchell waited, and all three of them went in together.

CHAPTER VIII

LILY ELLIS'S STORY

HOWEVER, before he began to ask them any questions, Mitchell succeeded in putting both Lily and her aunt much more at their ease. It was the elder lady in whom at first he seemed most interested, fussing about a cushion for her back, about her chair being out of a draught, and so on, till Lily began to feel that after all no such importance and significance attached to this summons to her as she had at first feared.

Only when Mrs Francis, a stout little elderly lady, wearing a very badly applied make-up of powder and lipstick and rouge she was not in the least used to, and a hat in the new pancake style that could not possibly have suited her worse, was at last comfortably settled, did Mitchell turn to Lily, as if suddenly remembering her presence.

'Now then, Miss Ellis,' he said cheerfully. 'Now that's all right, I'm sure you won't mind telling us what you know about this affair.'

'But I don't know anything – anything at all,' protested Lily, quickly nervous again.

'That's just what no one can be sure of,' Mitchell assured her. 'It's extraordinary how much people who think they don't know anything can tell us at times. Often small details they hardly even know they know turn out the most important. We'll begin about yourself, shall we?'

A few leading questions soon elicited details of the girl's birth, education, present circumstances, her hope of obtaining the post of leading mannequin at the Brush Hill Bon Marché, the difference such an appointment would make in a home where there was an ailing mother and two small brothers.

'If you had won the competition to-night, it would have

meant a good deal to you then,' Mitchell observed, with a certain reluctance in his voice as though the point were not one he much wished to make.

'Oh, yes,' Lily agreed eagerly. 'Or even being second or third. I didn't expect to be first exactly, but I knew if I came out near the top it would most likely be all right and I should be taken on.'

'If we hadn't been sure she would be the winner – that is, if the judges had eyes in their heads,' Mrs Francis interposed .firmly, 'never would any of us have agreed to her entering. In my young days no self-respecting girl would ever have dreamed of such a thing, but Lily has her mother to think of and the boys, and there's so little we can do to help with business what it is.'

'Everyone must understand that,' Mitchell agreed, checking a flow of explanation that seemed likely to continue for some time.

He was looking grim and uneasy at the same time. There was one point established. Winning the competition had meant more to Lily Ellis than a mere gratification of feminine vanity – more even that vague hopes of future success. It had meant being able to provide better for those dependent on her. His fingers beat their accustomed tattoo that always meant he was deeply worried. He said, a little abruptly now:

'You knew Miss Mears?'

'Only a very little. I met her at a dance once, and once or twice besides. Mr Beattie introduced us.'

In reply to some more questions Lily explained that it was at the same dance she had first met Roy Beattie. A friend had introduced her to him, and then he had introduced her to Carrie Mears. Mr Beattie had asked her to call at his studio and let him take her photograph, but she had never done so yet, though she had promised that perhaps some day she might. Mitchell rather gathered that at this dance the young photographer had shown Lily rather more attention than Carrie had quite approved. She had regarded his scalp as dangling permanently at her waist, and had not relished seeing it transferred elsewhere. That meant then, it seemed, that there had been a note of rivalry, possibly of some ill feeling, between the two girls even before this evening, and Mitchell scowled again as this new fact forced itself upon his recognition. Claude Maddox had also been at the dance, but not Leslie Irwin, for, while dramatic societies were bad enough, dances, in the eyes of old Mr Irwin, were worse – very much worse, in fact. To have attended a dance would have been sheer defiance – it would probably have meant for the young man the risk of an open breach with his father. Besides – perhaps an even more conclusive reason – Leslie was no dancer, having no natural skill in the art, and never having had any lessons, while both Claude Maddox and Roy Beattie were expert performers.

'Did you know Mr Maddox and Miss Mears were engaged?' Mitchell asked, and Lily shook her head, and said she had heard a lot of guesses about the direction Carrie's favour was likely to take, but nothing definite.

'To come to to-night,' Mitchell continued. 'I believe there was some kind of misunderstanding between you and Miss Mears?'

Lily flushed again, and looked piteously at her aunt for assistance. Mrs Francis tried to give her version of the affair, but Mitchell checked her.

'It is Miss Ellis's own account I would like to hear,' he explained. 'That is, if she has no objection.' He added to Lily: 'Of course I am only asking if you feel disposed to help us. If you would prefer not to, you need only say so. But in that case, you will understand, I shall have to depend on other people's versions, and I would rather have yours. Still, if you would prefer to wait till you've had a chance to talk to your solicitor and have his advice – –'

'Oh, no, no,' Lily interposed. 'I do want to help all I can, only it's all so dreadful, and as if it couldn't be – well, real. Only it is. What happened was that Carrie told me she had been disqualified for stopping on the stage too long, and I must be careful or I might be too – disqualified, I mean. So I ran off as quickly as I could after I went on, and they all laughed at me, and they said it was a trick of Carrie's so the judges wouldn't have time to mark my card.'

'Too bad,' said Mitchell. 'That meant you thought you had lost your chance. Were you upset at all?'

'I was most awfully angry – furious,' Lily exclaimed, with sudden energy, as for the moment she forgot everything else but the indignation that had burned in her when she discovered the trick played her. Her eyes blazed, she straightened herself with a tense and formidable energy one felt could easily translate itself into action; the tempest of her anger seemed, indeed, entirely to transform her. Then, as quickly as it had come, it passed : 'Oh, I forgot ... oh, poor Carrie,' she said.

But Mitchell's face was dark and heavy, and he seemed to droop a little as he sat there, silent now, a little as if he dared ask no more questions. For the first time in his life he had a feeling of being old and rather tired, of not wanting to go on. With almost every word the girl spoke she seemed to be drawing the net closer about her. He glanced at his young assistant, Bobby Owen, taking all this down in his notebook. It relieved him a little to see that the young man was not affected in quite the same way. His air was still eager and intent – he was taking down what was said with interest, even with excitement, but hardly seemed to grasp the direction in which it was all tending.

Mitchell braced himself to continue. Truth was his mistress, to be followed at all costs, whithersoever she led, no matter what was revealed when her veil at last was drawn aside. Truth, that is the first, the fundamental, the foundation of all value, without which there can nothing be that is worth man's while – or God's. There was a new note of hardness and sternness in his voice – Bobby noticed it, and wondered; Lily recognized it, and was again afraid – as he went on:

'I take it you mean you realized at once you had lost your

chance of winning the competition through this trick Miss
Mears played you?'

Lily did not answer. She was feeling oddly frightened
now, and the anger that had flamed for a moment in her
eyes had changed into a puzzled and bewildered terror.
Mitchell was looking not at her, but at the polished surface
of the table before him. On it his fingers were now not beating a tattoo, but pressed heavily, as if to hold it down. He
thought to himself:

'Well, they would find my finger-prints there all right.'
He looked up, and asked:

'Did you say anything when you understood?'

She shook her head, and Mitchell turned over some notes
that were lying before him.

'There is no need to answer if you would prefer not to,'
he said, 'but I think you ought to know my information is
that you were heard to say: "I could kill her".'

'Oh, she didn't. You never did, did you, Lily?' Mrs
Francis cried.

But the girl still made no answer, and then at last, when
she had moistened lips that had become suddenly dry, she
almost whispered:

'Yes ... I remember now ... I had forgotten.'

'She didn't mean it,' Mrs Francis almost shouted at Mitchell. 'Why, everyone says things like that. I often say I
could kill the baker, he will come so late; and I'm sure when
people come banging at the door the way they do – –'

'If you please,' Mitchell interposed, holding up one hand.
He went on: 'My information is, Miss Ellis, that, after you
said that, you went hurriedly, running indeed – "at a run,"
is the expression used – towards Miss Mears's room.'

Mrs Francis tried to speak again, but this time it was Lily
who checked her.

'Please, aunt,' she said, and then continued to Mitchell:
'I suppose that's true, I was so – so furious. I didn't seem
able to think anything or feel anything except how angry I
was. Everything seemed to go all funny and red, and I re-

member running down a long, long passage, and thinking I would just tell Carrie how beastly it was of her to do a thing like that.'

'Do you care to say anything more?' Mitchell asked. 'It is entirely for you to decide.'

'Yes. Everything,' Lily answered. 'Carrie had a room all to herself. I knew where it was, because a girl showed it me, and said it showed who was the favourite. The door was shut, and I rattled the handle, but it wouldn't open, and then I seemed to come to myself, and I remember thinking: "What's the good of saying anything? It's all over now."'

'A good thing you didn't go in,' interposed Mrs. Francis, loudly and defiantly. 'It's just as well as it's turned out you went away again without going in.'

The hint was plain, but Lily did not speak. She gave a little gasp, and was still silent. Mitchell, with his eyes not on her, but on his notes on the table, was silent, too. Bobby had understood now, and a kind of horror-stricken wonder was showing in his eyes. He thought:

'Mitchell thinks she did it, does he? Oh, he can't ... a girl like her ... Why not? ... A pretty face proves nothing.'

Mitchell looked up from his notes again. He said, in the dry hard note that had come into his voice:

'I think I ought to tell you, Miss Ellis, that a finger-print that seems to be yours has been found on the blade of the knife used in the attack on Miss Mears.'

After he had said this, there was silence for some moments. Mrs Francis had become very pale ; not even all the powder and lipstick and rouge so unskilfully distributed on her features could hide the stress and rigidity of terror they displayed. Lily was very pale, too ; her eyes half closed ; her clasped hands trembling, even though she held them pressed together so closely ; her breath rapid and uneven. Mitchell got to his feet, and went over and stood by Bobby, as if to look at his notebook, and then came back to his seat at the table.

'Miss Ellis,' he said. 'Murder has been done here to-night,

C

or what seems like murder. It is our duty, and we must do it, to discover the actual truth of what happened. It is quite likely you would prefer to say no more now. You would be wise to take the advice of – –'

But she interrupted with a sudden, startled cry, as if this were a new idea to her and one more terrifying than any other.

'No, no,' she exclaimed. 'I'm quite ready to tell exactly everything – just as it was. I did stop at the door, because the handle stuck, and I couldn't get it open at first, and I thought it was all over and no good saying anything, but then remembering that made me get all angry again, and I thought anyhow I would tell Carrie I knew what she had done, and it was because she was afraid the judges would like me best. I was still pulling at the door, and it came open and I went in.'

'Were all the lights on?'

'Yes, I think so. Yes, they must have been.'

'Was she alone?'

'Oh, yes. She was standing near a big desk. She laughed when she saw me, and said, "Hullo, Lily." I said: "Carrie, you pig." That was all, just that: "You pig." She knew what I meant, and she said: "My dear girl, it was just a joke; no one could ever have thought you would take it seriously. If you're such a fool, it's not my fault." That made me angrier still. I could have slapped her or anything only the table and the desk were between us and I couldn't reach. I put my hand on the table. I don't think I really meant to throw anything at her – oh, I don't, not really.' Her voice rose; then instantly died down again. 'I think what I really wanted was to do something to make her stop laughing at me. It was horrid to see her laughing at what she had done. I felt I was touching something hard and cold, and when I looked I saw it was a knife. Then I went away. That's all.'

'Thank you,' Mitchell said. 'I won't ask you any more questions at present, except one. Did you see anyone else near the room when you left it?'

'No – no one, I don't think so – no one.'

'Thank you,' Mitchell said again. 'What you have told us will be written out, and to-morrow, after you've had time to think it over, you will be asked to read it again, and sign it if you find it accurate. It is not for me to give you any further advice. Your solicitor will be able to do that better than I can.'

'Can I go now?' Lily asked, almost whispering.

'Certainly,' Mitchell answered, rising again to open the door for her.

Mrs Francis put her arm round her niece and helped her to her feet, and then, quite suddenly, kissed her. Mrs Francis's hat was dreadful, and her badly put on make-up she had felt due to the occasion was in ruins, and the last dab of powder she had meant for her nose had landed somewhere under her left eye, and she was fat and stumpy and altogether without dignity, but a splendour was about her as she said, very loudly and clearly:

'Well, Lily didn't do it; and, what's more, I don't care a damn if she did.'

CHAPTER IX

MR SARGENT'S STORY

'AND that,' said Mitchell thoughtfully, when the door had closed behind Mrs Francis and her niece, 'is probably the old lady's very first swear word – quite a good one, too.'

He went back slowly to his seat, and then, catching sight of Bobby's face, smiled a little sadly.

'You don't think a young attractive girl could possibly commit a murder?' he asked. 'Remember the Thompson-Bywaters case? Oh, a pretty, pleasing face can hide thoughts neither the one nor the other.'

' But you don't really think, sir, that Miss Ellis – –?' began Bobby, and then stopped. 'I can't believe' he began again, and then paused once more.

'Our job is to follow where the evidence leads,' Mitchell said, with that grim look of the hunter on his face that Bobby was coming to know so well. 'I think the girl's story is true, as far as it goes,' he continued, 'but does it go far enough? She told her tale frankly, but then we had found her finger-print on the knife, and that had to be accounted for some-how. The thing is, does the story stop where she stopped, or is there a continuation? From her own account she was very excited – "everything went red," you remember – and she admits she had a shock when she felt her hand touching the knife on the table. Well, what happened, then? Is that "all," as she says? Or did she pick the thing up – and throw it at the other girl?'

'I suppose,' Bobby admitted gloomily, 'if it was like that – I mean if the knife was thrown from a distance, either by Miss Ellis or by someone else – then that would account for the apparent absence of bloodstains from clothing and so on?'

Mitchell was beginning again that drumming of his

finger-tips on any convenient surface that always betrayed
a mood of profound unease. He resumed presently :

'She admits an impulse to hit the Mears girl in her
anger at the trick played her. We know' – the story had
already reached Mitchell's ears, recounted, as it had been,
to Inspector Ferris by one of Lily's more intimate friends –
'that there's some evidence of a violence of temper in her,
if it's true she once took a dinner-knife and chased a couple
of boys down the street. It is possible she flung the knife in
a temper, as the first thing she put her hand on, without
meaning murder at all – just as a gesture of disapproval, so
to say, as she might have flung an inkpot or a book. Nine
times out of ten, it would have missed ; nine times out of ten,
if it had hit, it would have done no harm. This time it hap-
paned to hit – to hit with the point forward, and to hit a
fatal spot, just at the base of the throat. It's possible, even,
that, after she had picked up the knife and thrown it, she
just turned round and rushed away and didn't even know
what she had done.'

'If it was that,' Bobby observed, 'then it would be man-
slaughter, I suppose, and not murder at all?'

'That would be for the jury to say,' remarked Mitchell.
'And, besides, was it like that? But the first thing to do is to
find out where the knife came from. How did it happen to
be lying there at that particular moment? A knife like that
isn't usually lying about in business offices. We must see if
Mr Sargent can tell us anything about it. We had better ask
him now, as Penfold seems so long turning up with Mr
Irwin. Find Sargent, will you, and ask him if I can see him
for a few moments? Oh, and ask the door-keeper if he has
any record of phone calls to-night, and if he received one
from Maddox. Better confirm every detail of what everyone
says, as far as we can.'

Bobby left the room on his errand, and was soon back.

'Mr Sargent is coming immediately,' he said. 'I spoke to
the door-keeper. He is supposed to keep a record of phone
calls, but there's been a lot of confusion and excitement all

to-night, from the very first. Since it happened, he says the phone has never stopped ringing. There's no chance of identifying any one call.'

'Pity. 1 always like things confirmed when possible,' Mitchell observed.

'He told me one thing,' Bobby went on. 'He says a rough-looking man was asking, earlier in the evening, for a Miss Quin he said was one of the competitors. There's no such name on the list, but while Wood was looking for it this man pushed by. I told Wood – the door-keeper, I mean, Wood's his name – I thought you would like to hear about that.'

'We'll have him in next,' Mitchell said. 'That is, if Penfold hasn't got back with Mr Irwin by then. Looks as if he had got lost – he's been gone long enough. Ah, come in, Mr Sargent,' he added, as the door opened and the cinema proprietor appeared. 'There are just one or two things I want to ask about.'

'Anything I can do to help, of course,' Sargent said. He looked pale and worried. 'A terrible business,' he said. 'It's going to do us a lot of harm.'

Privately Mitchell was not of that opinion. He was inclined to believe that from the business point of view this night's tragedy would be more likely to mean a great increase of business. But he did not pursue the point. Instead he began by asking a few unimportant questions, while at the same time observing Sargent closely, with that careful intent gaze of his that seemed to absorb, as it were, every possible detail. He saw a short, sturdily built, middle-aged personage, with the sharp, alert little eyes that suggest the keen business man, a loose sensual mouth that seemed to proclaim instead the man of pleasure; large, prominent, well-shaped nose that hinted at the man of action and a good forehead to speak of intellectual capacity. An interesting face, Mitchell decided – one of possibilities; one in which all would depend on which of those four conflicting tendencies prevailed. But then, too, it might well be that they cancelled out and left little behind.

Before long Mitchell came to the question of the knife. Sargent's reply was short and decided. He had already seen the knife. He had no knowledge of it whatever. He had never before seen one like it anywhere in the building. He was quite sure none resembling it had ever been in his office. Nor could he conceive how it had got there.

'Whoever murdered poor Carrie Mears must have brought it,' he declared.

'That would mean premeditation,' Mitchell mused. 'By the way, is that yours?'

'Mine? No!' answered Sargent, looking at the broad-brimmed felt hat Mitchell had brought with him. 'It looks like Mr Irwin's. Where did it côme from?'

'It was in your office – on a chair, close to the body,' Mitchell answered.

Sargent looked very puzzled. He picked the hat up, looked at it, and then put it down again.'

'It's Mr Irwin's all right,' he said, 'but I don't know what it could be doing there.'

'Did Mr Irwin know which was Miss Mears's room?'

'Yes, he did. He came behind with me. He wanted to speak to his son, Leslie Irwin. As it happened, we saw Leslie coming out of the room, and he was rather upset about it.'

'Ah, yes.' Mitchell's voice was flat; it showed no sign that he found this statement of any special interest. 'Why was that?'

'He didn't approve of her – didn't want there to be anything between them,' Sargent explained. 'He felt quite strongly about it – thought she wasn't good enough for his precious boy; thought she was too frivolous and worldly and would ruin him, body and soul together. He is an awful old fanatic, you know. Sticks at nothing to get his own way, because he's so sure he's right and doing the work of the Lord, and everyone else is in outer darkness.'

Sargent spoke with some bitterness, for in the controversy about the Sunday opening of the cinemas in the Brush Hill district he had, from his point of view, considered some of the tactics and statements of the party led by old Mr Irwin distinctly unfair and even dishonest. Indeed there was possibly some foundation for his view that Mr Irwin was always so certain of the profound righteousness of his aims that he was apt to consider equally righteous all and every means for attaining them.

'About what time was this?' Mitchell asked.

Sargent considered. He wasn't very sure. But Carrie had left the stage about ten, and Beattie had discovered her soon after the half hour. On the whole Sargent considered it must have been about a quarter past ten, though he couldn't be certain to a minute or two.

'Where were you and Mr Irwin at the time?' Mitchell asked.

'In the passage – just where it leads down to my office,' Sargent answered, though a little uneasily, as if he did not much like this close questioning. 'We saw Leslie Irwin in the doorway, and when he saw us he cleared off quick. I expect he hoped his father hadn't seen him, and knew there would be a row if he had. Mr Irwin followed him – at least, that's what he said. I don't know how his hat got in the room, unless he went in. I'm sure he had it when he left me.'

'What did you do?'

'Nothing. I was only having a look round. I was looking for Martin – one of the staff – to speak to him, but I couldn't see him at first. After a time I found him. I was just beginning to speak to him when we heard a commotion, and someone told us there had been an accident and Carrie Mears had hurt herself.'

'You didn't see either of the Irwins again?'

'No. I thought most likely Leslie had gone home and the old man had followed him, I told him there was nothing to worry about, Carrie didn't want to have anything to do with Leslie. But I don't think he believed it. He thought everyone was as cracked about his boy as he was himself.'

'Had you any reason for saying Miss Mears didn't want anything to do with Leslie Irwin?'

'Well, she told me so herself.'

'I see. By the way, that reminds me. Isn't it a little unusual for one of the competitors to be assigned your private office for a dressing-room?'

'Well, she had to go somewhere; everywhere else was full,' Sargent explained, but, though he answered readily and easily, Mitchell was aware of an impression that the question had been expected and prepared for. 'You must remember what it's been like, fixing everything up,' Sargent went on. 'I can tell you it's no joke finding places for all that tribe of girls and their mothers and their fathers and their uncles and their aunts – pandemonium, that's what it's been all night, a regular pandemonium.'

'But why your private office for Miss Mears?' Mitchell insisted.

'Well, it's this way,' Sargent answered. 'Pandemonium, it was all right, all evening; and then, to make it worse, we found Miss Mears's name had been left out of the list, and she had been forgotten – no place provided for her. Naturally, she raised Cain, so I told them for the Lord's sake put her anywhere to keep her quiet, and when they said there wasn't anywhere that wasn't full up to the ceiling, I told them to shove her in my room – I had had it in my mind as a possible last resource all the time, of course.'

'I'm told Miss Mears was the favourite; everyone expected her to win and be crowned Brush Hill Beauty Queen,' Mitchell said. 'Rather odd she should be the very one to be overlooked?'

'Well, you see, that's just why,' Sargent explained again. 'We ticked them all off to different rooms in order of entry, but I remember telling Mr Martin, I think it was, that Miss Mears was quite likely to be the winner, and she had better have accommodation near – you see, some of them we had to put right down in the cellar, five minutes' walk from the stage. And so, I suppose, with her name being left out for the time, it got forgotten altogether, and we had to push her in at the last moment.'

'I see,' said Mitchell. 'Apparently the murderer knew just where to find her, too.'

'What struck me,' observed Sargent, 'is that perhaps it wasn't that. Perhaps it was some fellow taking advantage of the fuss and confusion – I told you there was a regular pandemonium behind, all evening – to have a go at the safe in my room. Then, when he found her there, he knifed her and ran for it.'

'That'll have to be considered,' agreed Mitchell, 'but there seems no reason for the knifing. If he hoped the room would be empty, and found her there instead, he need have merely said, "Beg pardon," and gone away again. Was there anything in the safe?'

'Well, no – not to-night,' Sargent confessed. 'The takings are still in the box-office safe – we don't generally transfer them till after the place closes.'

'There's no sign of the safe in your room having been tampered with, and there's nothing missing – except her own handbag. And she was already there in the room, so she can't have disturbed a thief at work and been stabbed while he was making his escape. If there was a thief, there doesn't seem any reason for him to have attacked her. I think you said she told you herself she didn't want to have anything to do with Leslie Irwin. You were on fairly intimate terms with her, then?'

'Oh, no. Only in a business way,' Sargent protested, his voice sullen and hesitating now, as if he did not wish even to admit that much. 'She was very keen on getting a start, acting for the films. She came to see me here once or twice, to know if I could help her.'

'Did you try to in any way?'

'Well, of course, there wasn't much I could do really. I told her – well, we talked it over once or twice, at dinner.' He added defiantly, 'We went up West, now and then, to have dinner together. I tried to choke her off, but in the end I had to promise to introduce her to some of the big people.'

'Did you do that?'

'Well, no. You see' – Sargent stopped, and laughed in an embarrassed way – 'I expect I blew a bit about my influence and the people I knew. Of course, I do know some, but just as an exhibitor. I don't reckon any introduction I could give would be much use. That's really what I wanted to explain – to let her down lightly, if you see what I mean, after she had got to expecting too much. That's why I treated her to a dinner or two, to ease her off.'

'To ease her off,' repeated Mitchell doubtfully, thinking the method was one hardly likely to be successful, and wondering greatly how much this story meant. 'Was it at one of these dinners she told you she didn't want to have anything to do with Leslie Irwin?'

'Well, yes, it was.'

'Do you know anything about a Claude Maddox?'

· Sargent looked blank, and shook his head.

'No. Who is he?' he asked.

'Apparently he was engaged to her – at least, that's what he says.'

'Oh, that's a lie,' Sargent protested, looking very much disturbed. 'I'm sure ... I never heard ... I mean, she would have told me ... I should have heard.'

'Or Mr Beattie?' Mitchell asked.

'Oh, I knew he was running after her,' Sargent answered. 'There were plenty like that. This Maddox was most likely another of them – lots of them, I know. She hardly knew them all herself.'

'She does seem to have been a busy young lady,' Mitchell agreed.

'I don't want you to misunderstand me,' Sargent went on. 'I just took a friendly interest in her, that's all. I wanted to help her if I could. That's why I hit on this idea of a Beauty Contest. I knew she would have a good chance of winning it. I thought it was a good publicity idea in itself, and if she won it she would have all the introductions she wanted. Of course, what she was after was to get out to Hollywood – that's what she was really keen on. Look here,

I don't want any of this to get out. I suppose it needn't, need it? You see, Mrs Sargent ... I didn't tell her about those dinners up West Carrie and I had together – no need to; there was nothing in them. ... Oh,' he added, with a touch of bitterness, 'Carrie knew how to take care of herself – just how to keep you at arm's length.' He paused, and seemed to ruminate in silence on past experiences that had not been altogether flattering to his self-esteem. 'Well, now then, I don't want anything said about it publicly, you understand? Not that it matters really, only it might lead to a little bit of bother at home – cost me a new diamond ring or a new fur coat to put it right,' he explained, with a somewhat feeble grin.

'Nothing will be said that is not necessary, nothing will be kept back that is,' Mitchell assured him gravely; and, after a few more questions, Sargent was allowed to go, though not before he had reiterated once again that his friendship with Miss Mears had been of the most ordinary and innocent type.

'Which I am inclined to think it was,' Mitchell commented, after his departure, 'but more thanks to her than to him, I daresay. I'm beginning to think Miss Mears was a rather remarkable young lady in her way. I wish I knew what was keeping Penfold – have to send an expedition to look for him soon. You had better bring in that door-keeper you were telling me about, Owen. Wood's his name, isn't it? We had better hear what he has to say.'

But Wood merely repeated the story already told – that a rough-looking man had asked for a Miss Quin, and while the list was being consulted for her name, which was not on it, had pushed by into the building.

'Any other night,' declared Wood, 'I'd have been after him like a shot, and had him out before he knew what was happening, but, to-night – well, a pantomime, that's what it's been; same as Mr Sargent said himself – a pantomime, he said, and so it was all the blessed evening, with all them blessed girls all rushing in and out same as they were, all mad together, and all their friends and relatives after 'em, brothers especial. If you ask me,' said Mr Wood solemnly, 'every girl what entered for the competition to-night had ten brothers at the least, and most of 'em a good many more. Brothers – why, they sprout brothers, they do.'

'Well, never mind that,' said Mitchell. 'Did you see this man, you speak of, again?'

'No, sir.'

'Didn't see him go out?'

'No; never set eyes on him again. But that's not to say he didn't go by without me noticing, harassed as I was with brothers and suchlike by the dozen and the score, so as it was all evening just a fair pantomime.'

'So you said,' interposed Mitchell. 'Can you describe him?'

But that was altogether beyond Mr Wood's powers, except for the bare facts that he was elderly, about middle height, was shabbily dressed, wore a cloth cap, and hadn't shaved that morning – or washed either, in Mr Wood's opinion. Also he had been drinking, for his breath smelt of beer, which Mr Wood considered a good smell in its time and place, but not in his little office at a moment and on an evening which was more like a pantomime – –

'Quite so,' agreed Mitchell, and, as there was apparently no more information to be got out of the worthy doorkeeper, dismissed him, with thanks and a cigarette, and then turned to Bobby. 'Penfold must have got lost,' he said. 'I – –'

But then the door opened, and Penfold himself appeared.

'Very sorry to have been so long, sir,' he said. 'I couldn't get any answer at first, and then, when they did open the door, all I could get out of Mr Irwin was that he had nothing to say, and there was no object in coming to see you. He said we could arrest him if we liked, but short of that he wasn't going to stir. He just kept repeating he had nothing to say.'

CHAPTER X

A BOY'S DENIAL

PENFOLD was plainly very angry and disturbed – quite hurt indeed. To him Mr Irwin's attitude seemed simply deliberate insult to law and authority – not to mention Scotland Yard. Had it rested with him, Mr Irwin would promptly have been marched off, in custody, to the nearest police station, and deeply he regretted the pedantry of British law that made inadvisable such prompt handling of the situation.

'That's all I could get out of him,' he repeated, and added darkly: 'Means he knows a lot he doesn't want to say, most like. I put that to him, but I couldn't get a word more out of him, he just stuck to it he had nothing to say. So then I said he had better come and see you, and he said he was going back to bed, and off he went. Left me sitting there and walked off. Told me to stop as long as I liked, but when I did go would I put the light out and be careful to shut the door. "I mean, of course, if you do go," he said, and cleared off.' Penfold paused, ruminating, indignant, and bewildered. 'Jiggered, I was,' he concluded. 'Fair jiggered.'

'Were you, though?' said Mitchell sympathetically. 'Well, I don't wonder. Still, if the mountain won't come to you, I believe precedent is that you go to the mountain.' But, though he spoke lightly enough, he was evidently almost as puzzled and surprised as Penfold himself by this new development. He began again his drumming with his finger-tips on the table, and then, noticing that Bobby was looking at the felt hat apparently identified as Mr Irwin's, he said: 'Well, Owen, what do you make of that?'

'There's evidence Leslie Irwin was seen coming out of the room where Miss Mears was found,' Bobby answered, 'and apparently about the time of the attack on her, though there

doesn't seem to be much to show whether it was before or –
or just after. It seems he was in love with her, and she had
just turned him down. Mr Irwin must have been in the
room some time, as his hat was left there. He is said to be
very fond and proud of his son. After Leslie was seen coming
out of the room, apparently both father and son left here
as quickly as possible.'

'There, now then,' Penfold cried, quite excitedly. 'Just
what I said myself – they know, the two of them.'

'Very likely,' agreed Mitchell. 'Only what? And how
much?' He looked at his watch. 'Not much chance of bed,'
he sighed. 'It's nearly three, and a bit late for a call. Still,
I think I would like a chat with this gentleman who's so
sure he has nothing to say. You didn't see the young man,
Leslie Irwin, did you?' he added, to Penfold.

'No, he didn't show himself,' Penfold answered. 'I asked
if he was in, and the old man said he was in bed, and I left
it at that. You can't,' he protested indignantly, 'do much
with a man you can't get a word from, except that he has
nothing to say.'

'Holding your tongue does make things difficult,' observed Mitchell. 'Lucky for us so few people can manage it.
What did you think of Mr Irwin?'

'Jiggered,' answered Penfold slowly, 'jiggered if I know.
He is the sort you would always look at twice and wonder
who he was. Under fifty, I should say, and well-preserved
at that, very tall and thin, with a thin face and a big nose,
and eyes that – well, that seem to see things, if you know
what I mean. Mouth tight shut all the time – even when he
speaks he hardly opens it, though the words come out clear
enough. Black hair, rather long, a little thin on top, but not
a sign of grey hair. Close beard. Very neat and precise.
Gives you the idea he's watching all the time, only you don't
know what, but all the same he's ready. He makes you think
of a Mills bomb that might go off sudden if you weren't
careful.'

'Sounds as if he were going to be difficult,' Mitchell

mused. 'Very difficult. We had better go and see him, any-how. Perhaps he may be more reasonable now he's had time to think a bit.'

He led the way into the corridor outside. There were still a number of people hanging about, whispering, awe-struck, in corners, or unable to tear themselves from the fascination the scene of so strange and terrible a tragedy exercised upon them. There were still newspaper men, too, waiting in the hope of some further crumb of information they could pick up and announce in enormous letters as, 'Exclusive to Us,' or, anyhow, as 'Amazing Development.' They swooped down on Mitchell the moment he appeared, but long experience had taught him the technique for deal-ing with them. Pacified with the assurance that important clues were being closely studied, and that a successful issue to the investigation was confidently anticipated, the news-paper men departed, and Mitchell, having given Ferris a few instructions and assured himself a constable was in position at the door of the room where the attack had taken place, so as to guard against any risk of disturbance, went out, with Penfold and Bobby, to the waiting car.

'Headquarters,' he ordered, in a loud voice, for the bene-fit of any lurking, listening reporter, but the chauffeur knew that phrase was really an indication to him to stop presently for further orders.

Round a corner or two, and well out of sight, he slack-ened speed accordingly, and Mitchell gave him the Irwin address.

It was not far, and the house proved to be a fair-sized, old-fashioned-looking residence standing by itself in a large garden. In one window above the front door a light still shone, but the rest of the house was in darkness.   .

'Someone awake, anyhow,' Bobby remarked.

'Probably they've been expecting us,' Mitchell said. 'I doubt if there's been much sleep there to-night.'

'The light only shows in one window,' observed Penfold.

'The son probably,' Mitchell suggested. 'If the father's

waiting for us, he's waiting in the dark. Well, we're in the dark, too. Better knock, Owen.'

Bobby obeyed, and this time, within a minute or two, a light went up in the hall. The door opened, and on the threshold appeared the figure of a man, strangely tall and thin between the darkness of the night and the lighted hall behind. He was wearing a dressing-gown and pyjamas, and his bare feet were in bedroom slippers. He said coldly :

'You have come back, then. It was quite unnecessary. I have nothing to say. Could you not wait till the morning?'

'Death did not wait for the girl who has been murdered to-night,' Mitchell answered gravely.

'I suppose you want to come in?' the other said, after a pause. 'But I tell you again, I have nothing to say.'

He led them into the dining-room; an apartment well, and indeed comfortably, furnished, though in the somewhat heavy Victorian style modern taste is apt to find oppressive. The atmosphere of the room was chill and a little damp, as though it were not much used, and everything was not only in its place, but looked as though in no circumstances would it ever dare to be otherwise. Even the droop of the curtains before the window seemed depressed and sad, as if hiding melancholy things, and a text prominent upon the wall above the empty fireplace, 'The Lord Watcheth,' seemed meant for a warning and a threat rather than as a promise of protection and comfort.

Mr Irwin, with a silent gesture, invited his visitors to seat themselves, and himself took his place in an armchair at the head of the long, solid mahogany table.

No one spoke. Mr Irwin waited, calm, impassive, grim, almost as if he had forgotten their presence. Yet his eyes were bright with a kind of burning watchfulness. For a man may control with absolute command every nerve and muscle in his body but never his eyes, where shines his soul. Penfold and Bobby waited for their senior officer. But Mitchell waited, too, for he knew that, so strong and strange a thing is silence, few of the light and chattering race of man can endure it for long. But plainly Paul Irwin was of the few, and Mitchell understood that he would sit there indefinitely with his impassive features and his burning eyes. Mitchell said:

'I take it, Mr Irwin, you are aware that murder has been done to-night in the Brush Hill Central Cinema?'

The old man gave no sign that he had even heard, except, indeed, that he changed the direction of his fierce watchful gaze and fixed it upon Mitchell.

'The victim is named Caroline Mears,' Mitchell went on. 'I understand she was known to you and to your son, Leslie Irwin.' He paused, but he might have been addressing a dead man or one totally deaf for all the impression his words seemed to have made. Mitchell continued: 'In the room where the murder was committed, a hat, believed to be yours, was found.'

Still there was no reply; not so much as a quivering eyelid revealed that what had been said had been heard. Mitchell waited while, as it seemed to Bobby, interminable minutes passed. Then he said:

'I think you heard me. May I request a reply?'

'You have said nothing that calls for a reply,' Mr Irwin answered then, as impassive as before. 'You have made two statements. I do not challenge either. I have nothing to say.'

'I believe you are a solicitor, Mr Irwin,' Mitchell said. 'May I remind you that a solicitor is himself in some sort an officer of the King's justice, and has duties to perform – more so even than the ordinary citizen, who also has a duty to assist the police.'

But to this there was still no reply, only that fixed, unwavering, unchanging gaze that yet seemed somehow to tell of a tumult of fears and passions and desires held tremendously in check.

Mitchell got to his feet.

'You are also a man,' he said. 'Murder has been done to-night – murder on a woman – a young girl. Do you refuse me your assistance?'

'I have nothing to say,' answered Irwin, each word, so

to speak, throbbing with an intensity of suppressed emotion, yet an emotion of which there was still no least, outward sign.

'I think I must remind you,' Mitchell said formally, 'that your adoption of such an attitude gives rise, naturally, to the gravest misgivings.'

'His hat there, and him seen near the door as well,' mumbled Penfold, even discipline unable to keep him silent longer or control his indignation.

To Mitchell it seemed that at this remark of Penfold's old Mr Irwin's tense expression wavered for an instant, into a momentary relief, only to harden again at once into immobility again. Swiftly Mitchell flashed another question.

'Do you agree,' he asked, 'that your son, Leslie Irwin, was seen leaving Miss Mears's room during the evening, that immediately afterwards he left the cinema, and that you followed him?'

This time Mitchell succeeded in obtaining an answer other than the perpetual 'I have nothing to say,' that hitherto had been Mr Irwin's sole response.

'Who told you that?' he asked. 'Mr Sargent, I suppose? If you ask him again, and if he answers truly, he will agree that, at the time, he both said and thought that Leslie was only in the act of opening the door to enter the room. Also he will agree that when my son saw us he closed it again without going in, or even looking in, and after that he immediately returned home.'

'Did you follow him?' Mitchell asked quickly.

But again Mr Irwin, as if regretting his outbreak, fell back upon his formula of 'I have nothing to say,' and, recognizing the uselessness of continuing, Mitchell said:

'I think your son, Leslie Irwin, is in the house and awake. Can we see him?'

'He is in the house, I believe. I do not know whether he is awake,' Mr Irwin answered. 'There is nothing that I know of to prevent you from seeing him. If you call to him up the stairs, I think it likely he will hear you.'

Mitchell thought so, too. He thought it likely the young man, who must have heard their arrival, was not only awake but listening. He muttered an order to Bobby, who left the room for the hall, and at the bottom of the stairs called softly. :

'Is Mr Leslie Irwin there? If so, will he please come down?'

That the young man had been waiting and listening was evident, for at once he appeared, coming with a quick, hurried nervousness down the stairs and across to the dining-room, the door whereof Bobby was holding open for him.

Like his father he was tall and of slender build, and in feature he bore him a strong resemblance, though a resemblance curiously softened. It was as though Nature, in taking the elder man for a model had wished to introduce an element of beauty, but had been able to do so only at the cost of introducing also weakness and indecision. The bright fierce steady eyes of the father were equally bright in the son, but with a soft and gentle, almost timid, brightness, and were veiled by exquisitely long and curling lashes. The nose, equally well-shaped, had lost its aggressiveness. The mouth, in the older man set in such hard, straight lines, showed in the younger yielding curves above a dimpled and receding chin that was almost ludicrously different from old Mr Irwin's; square, determined, and forward thrusting. None the less the likeness was very marked, and if the boy showed none of his parent's grimly resolute air, as of one who would yield not even in trifles, yet still Leslie did somehow in his manner suggest an innate wilfulness, and even obstinacy, that told he would not readily give up anything he wanted. Possibly the essential difference between them was, however, that what the father willed he would always will till he had achieved, but the son's will would be much more fluid, various, and changeable.

And Mitchell thought to himself that the strain they only too plainly both endured showed itself characteristically in each : in the father by a grim and almost sullen silence and watchfulness, in the son by the haggard, worn expression of his features, and in a redness and inflammation of the eyes that suggested recent tears.

It was on Leslie, as he came into the room, that both Penfold and Bobby concentrated their attention, trying to form an estimate of his character, and noting his distressed and haggard look and the extreme nervousness he seemed to show. But Mitchell chiefly watched Paul, and how a glow of tenderness and love and pity seemed for an instant to transform his features, melting momentarily through the mask of his impassivity and then vanishing again.

'Come in, Leslie, my son,' he said, but so softly it is doubtful whether any of them but Mitchell heard him.

Leslie did not. His father's words went, for him, unheard. He stood in the doorway, facing them, for Bobby had gone back to his place and his notebook. Leslie looked at the three police officers in turn with a kind of angry defiance, clenching his fists, squaring his shoulders a little, as if he would have liked to fling himself on all three of them in physical conflict. He stared across at his father with a mingled expression of dread and challenge of which Mitchell could understand nothing. He had seen a man in the dock look at the judge on the bench like that, dreading him, and yet defiant of all he could do. Very loudly, but not too steadily, Leslie said:

'I don't care what you think. I didn't do it.'

CHAPTER XI

OBSTINATE SILENCE

THE words sounded clear and strange in the heaviness of that oppressive room. No one answered, and Mitchell, watching Paul Irwin closely, and seeing that he allowed no sign to show on his impassive, unmoved countenance that he had even heard his son, thought it certain that all this had been discussed between them previously – that the unchanging features of the elder man, the reddened eyes and twitching nervous mouth of the younger, both testified to some scene of high emotion that had recently taken place between them.

'They knew,' Mitchell thought. 'How did they know?'

At the same moment Bobby leaned across to him, and whispered:

'They've been talking it over. They've been getting ready for us.'

Mitchell nodded, and Leslie left his place by the door and flung himself down in an empty chair near the fireplace. He said:

'Well, now then.'

'Mr Irwin,' Mitchell said to him. 'No one has accused you – –'

'What's the use of talking like that?' Leslie snarled, interrupting. 'When a lot of bobbies turn up after ... after – – My God!' – he broke off into a kind of low wail – 'it's awful ... awful.'

'You know what has happened?' Mitchell asked.

'Carrie's been murdered,' Leslie said, staring at him. 'Murdered,' he repeated, as if trying to understand the significance of the word. More collectedly, and even with a certain dignity, he added: 'I loved her, and some day we were going to marry.' Then, in the same jerky manner, he turned to his father. 'Well, now then, it won't happen now,' he said very bitterly. 'So that's all right, isn't it?'

But not so much as the quivering of an eyelash showed that Paul Irwin had heard. Mitchell asked:

'I believe you left the cinema before the discovery was made. Do you mind explaining how and when you heard?'

'Good Lord,' retorted Leslie impatiently, 'all Brush Hill heard within two minutes. I heard some people going by outside here talking about it. Then my father came in and told me.'

Almost simultaneously Paul said:

'I was walking home. Someone passing called out to me – it was someone who knew me; more people know me in Brush Hill than I know. He called out that a girl at the Central Cinema had been killed. I went back. There was a crowd outside, talking about it. I came back here and told Leslie.'

When they had spoken, father and son exchanged strange glances; both Mitchell and Bobby saw, and wondered what might be their meaning. Leslie noticed how they were looking at him, and looked back angrily:

'Well, now then, if you want to run me in, why don't you?' he demanded.

'We are only making preliminary inquiries,' Mitchell answered. 'There is not sufficient evidence as yet to justify action. But I am bound to say that refusal to answer questions, refusal to help – –'

'Who is refusing to help you?' Leslie interrupted angrily. 'I'll help you all I can. I'm perfectly ready to tell you everything. You can believe it or not, just as you like. I don't care. Everyone knows I wanted to marry Carrie. I called for her to-night in a taxi. I took her to the cinema. Heaps of people saw me. I hadn't told father. He thought I was going to a lecture at the Birkbeck. Well, I didn't. That's all. I went to the Central instead. Then I saw dad there. So I thought I had better clear out. I didn't want another row just then, and I rather hoped he hadn't noticed me. I told Carrie, earlier on, I should have to get away quick so as to turn up at home as if I had come straight from the Birkbeck, so I knew she wouldn't be surprised if I didn't stop.'

'Do you mind telling me where you were, and what you were doing, when Mr Paul Irwin saw you?' Mitchell asked.

'I was just opening the door of Carrie's room. I wanted to see her. Some of them were saying things about her.'

'What sort of things?'

'They were all jealous of her; it was all a lot of lies just because of that. But I wanted to ask her about it. They said she had let one of the other girls down somehow. I went back to her room to ask her.'

'You knew which was her room, then?'

'Of course I did. I couldn't have gone there if I hadn't. It was Sargent's own private office. They had managed to forget her somehow when they were assigning accommodation to the competitors, and they had to ask her to make shift with Sargent's office because there was no room anywhere else. The whole thing was a muddle. Sargent couldn't run an afternoon- tea-party without messing it up. I was just going in to speak to her when I saw dad, with Mr Sargent, at the other end of the passage. It was a bit of a startler, because dad never went near places like that, and he and Sargent had been going for each other over the Sunday-opening question. Well, I didn't want a row there, with Carrie and everyone listening, so I cleared out home – that's all. Then dad came, and told me ...'

He paused, nearly breaking down. Mitchell waited till the boy had gained his self-control once more, and then asked:

'I understand that was the first you had heard of what had happened?'

'Yes, it was. Except that I heard some people talking outside here, but I didn't know what they meant. Of course, if I had done it I should have known all about it, shouldn't I? Only I didn't.'

Mitchell took no notice of this outburst, but continued:

'You tell me you hoped Miss Mears would consent to

marry you. Does that mean there was an understanding between you, but no formal engagement?'

'Yes. We were waiting. She said we must wait till I was more settled, and she was, too. She wanted to get a start on the films, and, then, I don't get my money till I'm twenty-five. If she had once got a start she would have made a big hit – couldn't help it, not with her looks. Our idea was I would be her manager, and write things for her and produce them.' He was looking at his father as he said this, angrily and defiantly. Evidently it was the first time he had ventured to tell of such hopes and ambitions for the future, only now that they could no longer be realized. He added : 'I had to wait till I was twenty-five before I got my money, and, besides, she said I must pass my final, too. She thought it would be such a help, when I was manager for her, if I had been admitted a solicitor.'

'No doubt,' agreed Mitchell. 'This money you speak of ... is that a legacy?'

'Yes – two thousand; an uncle left it me – mother's brother. I get it when I'm twenty-five. I haven't a farthing of my own till then. I ought to have had it when I came of age, of course,' he added, still staring defiantly at his father, who neither confirmed nor denied, but remained as before, impassive, unmoved, and attentive.

'There had been some sort of discussion about this legacy?' Mitchell suggested.

'Dad wouldn't let me have it, if that's what you mean,' Leslie answered sullenly, and again his father neither confirmed nor denied. Leslie continued : 'Dad's trustee. There's a clause about my having it "for good and substantial cause, at the trustee's discretion," any time after I came of age. Dad said there was no "good and substantial cause." When I'm twenty-five, I get it all right – only, he can still hold it back for the same "good and substantial cause." Of course, that's all right; no one could call it a good and substantial cause for keeping me out of my money that I want to get married. But it was enough to prevent my getting any advance on it from the bank or anyone. And Carrie said we must just wait, and it wouldn't be fair to either of us to be formally engaged. But we were going to be – she promised that – if she won the competition and was able to go to Hollywood.'

'Was that part of the prize?' Mitchell asked. 'A trip to Hollywood?'

'No,' answered Leslie, hesitating, and uncomfortable in a way Mitchell noticed but did not understand. 'No. But that was the idea. If she went there as the Brush Hill Beauty Queen, she would have been sure of a trial, anyhow – and that was all she wanted. She would have managed it somehow – getting there, I mean.'

Mitchell was beginning to look worried again, and his fingers started once more their drumming, this time upon the arm of his chair. He said:

'Do you know a Mr Claude Maddox?'

'Claude Maddox? Yes, of course – everyone does, the way he splashes his money about. We were at the grammar-school together, and then he went out to Brazil or somewhere. He's got a good job, and he had his money given him all right the very day he came of age.'

'Liberal, extravagant young gentleman?' Mitchell asked.

'I suppose he can afford – all the girls fall for him – the way he stands treat. Carrie didn't, though.'

'No? He wasn't at the cinema to-night, was he?'

'No. Carrie had just turned him down, so I expect he felt a bit sick and kept away. Treated some other girl to a supper at the Savoy, most likely.'

'Is it likely he and Miss Mears were engaged?'

'Good Lord, no! Didn't I tell you she had just turned him down? Of course, he tried to cut everyone else out with her, but it didn't work that time. His office was near where she worked, and he used to see her sometimes in Town. That's all.'

'Miss Mears was a young lady with many admirers?'

'Of course – everyone almost; quite middle-aged, old

chaps sometimes. She used to tell me about them. But Maddox was only one of the crowd.'

'Do you mind telling me what makes you say Miss Mears had just turned him down?'

'Well, she had, that's all. She told me so herself. To-day. She met him in the dinner-hour in Town, and she told him right out she didn't want anything more to do with him.'

'Was Mr Sargent one of her admirers?'

'I dare say. I don't know. Everybody was.'

'Do you know if he had promised to help her get a start acting for the films? Or if they ever had dinner together in Town?'

'No, I'm sure they hadn't. Of course not, Carrie wouldn't – not Sargent. Besides, he's married already. Got kids, too. Someone been telling you that? Well, you can take it from me it's a lie.'

'You and Mr Maddox were at school together,' Mitchell went on, ignoring this. 'Did you keep friendly afterwards?'

'Yes, we were pals all the time till he went abroad for his firm. He used to come here a lot, and do carpentry and so on in the attic. He had no place at home, and I had a workshop upstairs. He used it like his own.'

'I was glad to see the two of them keeping out of mischief,' Paul Irwin interposed now. 'Young Maddox had a key of his own, and used to let himself in and out as he liked. Both of them learnt how to use tools. They did some good work up there – quite first class.'

Mitchell turned to him.

'Mr Irwin,' he said, 'your son has been frank and open with us. Don't you think it would be wise if you were to reconsider your own attitude? If you continue to refuse to answer questions, you must not be surprised if we put our own interpretation on your silence?'

'I have nothing to say,' answered Mr Irwin once again, and then there came, suddenly and rather startlingly, a knock at the door; so absorbed had they been in question and answer, that quiet knock made them all start.

'It'll be Mrs Knowles. She can't stand it any longer. She's wondering what's happening,' Mr Irwin said. 'My housekeeper,' he explained to Mitchell. 'She came to me from a friend three years ago, when he left London, and Miss Temple, who had been with me since before my wife died, felt she was getting too old for the work.'

'Have you other servants?' Mitchell asked.

'Only a daily woman,' Paul answered, and went across to open the door.

An elderly woman, in a dressing-gown, was standing there. Paul told her everything was all right – they wanted nothing – she must go back to bed. She said something about Mr Leslie, and Leslie got up and joined them, saying loudly:

'It's all right; they've only come to run me in for murdering Carrie, only they aren't quite sure.'

Left alone for the moment, the three police officers waited, and Penfold leaned across and said to Mitchell, in a growling whisper:

'What do you think the old 'un's holding back on us? There's something.'

'Shouldn't wonder,' agreed Mitchell, and added: 'He looks older than you said, I think. I should take him to be fifty at least.'

'Yes,' agreed Penfold. 'It must have been the light, or something. I can generally tell a man's age pretty near, but he does look older now than I thought before. I thought his hair was all black, too, but there's streaks of grey showing if you look close. Don't know how I missed them before.'

The two Irwins, father and son, having pacified their housekeeper, came back into the room. Mitchell asked a few more questions of but small importance, and told Leslie that the statement he had made would be written out and brought to him for signature. He added that probably they would have to question him further, but that considering the lateness of the hour they wouldn't trouble him any more just then.

With that they took leave, and, as they were making their way to the waiting car, Mitchell said :

'I almost believe that boy was planning to elope to Hollywood with the girl. Only it seems he has no money, and then Maddox claims she got engaged to him only this afternoon. A pretty tangle to find out where the truth lies.'

CHAPTER XII

DISCUSSION ON INCONSISTENCIES

I T was when they were all three safely in the car that Penfold's smouldering indignation burst forth.

'I tell you what it is, sir,' he said angrily, to Mitchell.
'Old Mr Irwin knows something he doesn't mean to tell.
Deliberate concealment.'

'Yes, that's pretty plain,' agreed Mitchell.

'Defeating the ends of justice,' declared Penfold. 'He
ought to be made – –'

'Difficult,' observed Mitchell, 'to make a man speak when
he doesn't want. Once upon a time they used to put him
on the rack, and then he probably told lies; or else tie him
down on the floor and pile fresh weights on his chest every
day, and then he generally died first.'

'Oh, well,' said, a little doubtfully, Penfold, who had
never heard before of the *peine forte et dure*.

'Because,' explained Mitchell, 'if he didn't talk, then he
couldn't be found guilty, and, if he wasn't found guilty,
then his property couldn't be confiscated, and his wife and
family kept it still. Rummy what a man will do for his wife
he spends half his time quarrelling with, and for his children
he's on bad terms with because they won't do just what he
thinks they ought.'

'Oh,' said Penfold, thinking this over, and Bobby, quicker
to discern what was in Mitchell's mind, said :

'You mean, Mr Irwin's silence is his way of protecting
his son?'

'I'm told,' Mitchell said without answering this directly,
'Mr Paul Irwin is a very religious man. Is that right, Penfold?'

'Well, sir, if you ever heard him preaching about hell on
Brush Hill Common, you would think so,' Penfold answered.
'Seems to think that's where we're all bound.'

'Perhaps, then, with ideas like that,' Mitchell went on, 'he won't actually lie, but thinks he has a right to keep silence. Nothing in the Bible against holding your tongue.'

'Then he knows young Irwin killed the girl?' Penfold cried excitedly.

'He may think he knows it,' Mitchell answered slowly. 'But then he may be wrong all the same. Religious people of the Paul Irwin kind are so jolly sure all the rest of us are vile sinners they're always ready to believe the worst – of other people. Vile sinners are evidently quite likely to be guilty of anything going.'

'You think Leslie may be innocent, even though his father believes him guilty. Is that it, sir?' Penfold asked, after he had considered this in silence for some moments.

'Yes. But then Paul Irwin may not think – he may know. It's quite on the cards Leslie is the man we want. It all looks like what the papers call a love drama. Leslie says he and the girl understood each other and had it all fixed up. But that may be only what he thought himself. Maddox says she was engaged to him. Sargent says she had turned young Leslie down. My own idea is she was keeping all three on the string, and very likely one or two more as well. But suppose she did say something to Sargent about turning down Leslie, and Leslie hears about it and goes off in a rage to have it out with her – won't be played with any longer, sort of feeling. She laughs at him. Perhaps she slips in a word, as women can, that gets him under the skin. He loses his head, as passionate youngsters in love will at times, and lets fly with the knife. Then he bolts in a panic. His father and Sargent see him leaving the room. Mr Irwin doesn't like the looks of it. He gets rid of Sargent, has a look, sees the girl on the floor. Drops his hat on a chair, while he has a closer look to make sure, and forgets it's there – a shock, of course. And then, instead of giving the alarm, he goes off home to find his boy and warn him. He won't lie about it, against his principles. But he'll hold his tongue till kingdom-come.'

'If you ask me,' grumbled Penfold, 'I would just as soon think it was the old man himself did it. He wanted to save his son. He was bitterly opposed to any marriage with the girl – looked on it as ruin for the boy, ruin in this world and the next. Quite sure of that, because, as you said, Mr Mitchell, sir, that kind of religious type is always so sure what's good for other people.'

'We're always, all of us, jolly sure of that if of nothing else,' murmured Mitchell, but Penfold swept on unheedingly:

'He knew more than Leslie thought, and the Birkbeck lecture stunt didn't take him in for a minute. So he had a look in at the Central Cinema, and there the young man was all right. Shock number one. Then he saw Leslie at the door of the girl's room, either just going in or just coming out. Second shock. He's pretty wrought up by now, and he barges in on the girl to tell her what he thinks. She snaps her fingers at him, tells him she has the boy nailed, and that's that, and, what's more, they're off to Hollywood together as soon as they can get the coin that very likely the young man could raise on his expectations. The old man thinks Hollywood and hell are much the same. There's only one way of saving Leslie. He takes it and goes home, and, if you ask me, what it all amounts to is just this – he admits he did it, and what are we going to do about it?'

'His hat was in the room,' Mitchell admitted. 'Many a man has hung on less evidence.'

'It's religion does it,' declared Penfold, pleased to think Mitchell was coming round to his point of view. 'Once a man's got religion, he's capable of anything.'

'Like Habakkuk,' murmured Bobby, but neither Mitchell nor Penfold, neither of whom had studied Voltaire, took any notice, Mitchell continued:

'I think it's more likely Mr Irwin is protecting his son rather than himself. If it was himself, I should expect him to say so. He might possibly persuade himself he had a right to kill, but, if he did, he wouldn't attempt to hide it. At least,

I don't think so, but that's psychology, and the only sure thing about psychology is that it always works the way you don't expect. Then, again, he may not really suspect his son, but feel that his evidence would throw unjustified suspicion on the boy, and so he won't give it. Anyhow, we've no case, so far, to put to Treasury counsel. They would shoot it full of holes at once – lots of points to be cleared up yet.'

'For instance,' suggested Bobby, 'about who it was the girl was actually encouraging?'

'If you ask me, the whole boiling,' put in Penfold.

'Maddox claims an engagement, and seems actually to have bought a ring,' Mitchell observed thoughtfully. 'That must be checked up on. Then young Irwin claims an understanding, and the Hollywood idea he says they talked about is just the thing to attract a girl like Carrie Mears. Mr Sargent admits to a flirtation that may have gone further than he says. He is evidently uneasy about it, and I don't like his story about her having been forgotten when accommodation was arranged for the competitors, so that she had to be pushed into his private office as a last resource. I think that all sounds as if it had been fixed up before. Perhaps only for the chance of a kiss or two on the sly, but perhaps for other reasons. There's that missing handbag to explain, and there seems no reason why either of the Irwins should have taken it.'

'Could that be Sargent?' Penfold asked.

'Someone took it, apparently,' Mitchell said. 'Why? It doesn't seem likely there was anything of great value in it – not money or jewellery, I mean. But there must have been some reason why it was worth taking. We know Sargent had been taking Miss Mears out to dinners and so on. Most likely, then, he had been writing her letters, and letters he wouldn't want other people to see. Suppose she was doing a spot of blackmail – probably not so much for money as for getting a start on the films. You can imagine her saying: "Get me an engagement with a good film company, or what about those letters of yours?" Suppose that, as is very likely, she thought him much more influential than he really is, and he simply hadn't it in his power to do what she wanted, but she wouldn't believe it, and told him straight out she was going to make use of his letters in a way he wouldn't like. He arranges for her to have a room to herself so they can talk unobserved. He makes a final appeal to her to let him have the letters back. She says, my engagement first, or – – He loses his temper, and his head. The knife's handy, and he uses it. He goes off with the handbag, and when Paul Irwin discovers what's happened, he either really suspects Leslie or feels his evidence would go against the boy. So he makes up his mind he won't say anything. All that's only theory, of course, but if anyone else than Sargent is put in the dock, it's a theory defending counsel will exploit, and one we'll have to be ready to answer. So it has got to be tried out as best we can.'

'There's that finger-print of the other girl on the knife that was used. How is that to be accounted for?' Penfold asked.

'That's difficult, too,' Mitchell agreed. 'It's not enough to prove her guilt, but it is enough to prove almost anyone else innocent – unless we can account for it. And, of course, there's the story of the trick played on Miss Ellis – her own admission of the anger she felt, and the history of some sort of violent temper and knife-flourishing she had shown previously. Only what about the handbag again? No reason why Miss Ellis should have taken it.'

'There's the photographer, too – Beattie, I mean,' observed Penfold.

'Yes, we mustn't forget him,' Mitchell said. 'It was he who made the discovery; no bloodstains found, except on him; he admits to having felt strongly about the trick played on Miss Ellis, and to having gone to ask Miss Mears about it. Well, there you are, a plausible case against half a dozen of 'em, but nothing conclusive, and the case against each in turn proving the innocence of all the rest. Talking of bloodstains, Ferris had better make as thorough a search as he can to-morrow of the Irwins' house, just to see if he can find anything.'

'That will give them time to get rid of anything incriminating,' Penfold pointed out. 'Oughtn't we to act at once?'

'They had plenty of time before we got there to do that,' Mitchell answered. 'A little delay may give them time to grow careless, perhaps. Ferris had better check up on their tailor's bills, and see if any suits or trousers are missing, and have a look in the dustbin, too, to see if anything of that sort has been burnt recently. Another point to be cleared up is that story about the suspicious-looking character said to have been asking for a Miss Quin who wasn't there. There's just the chance he was a crook on the prowl, asking for someone by name as a blind, but really wanting to get admission to see what he could pick up. It might be that Miss Mears caught him in the act of lifting her handbag, that she tried to give an alarm, and he – silenced her. Not likely of course – sneak thieves seldom commit murder. But we must have that door-keeper up at the Yard and see if he can identify any of our collection of photos. People can sometimes recognise where they can't describe. The picture in their mind is clear enough, but they can't put it into words. Of course, if it was like that, then the handbag being missing is accounted for at once. Plenty of promising lines to follow, if only they didn't all contradict each other.'

'Speaking of contradictions, sir,' observed Bobby, who, as befitted his junior rank, had been silent during most of this discussion. 'I thought there were one or two inconsistencies in the story Mr Maddox told. I made a note of two.'

'I noticed two myself,' observed Mitchell. 'What were your two?'

Bobby handed over his notebook, and Mitchell nodded approvingly.

'Exactly,' he said. 'Not very important, perhaps, but you never know. They must be checked up on.'

'Meaning,' asked Penfold, 'that both Maddox and young Irwin say they are engaged to her?'

'No, that's not an inconsistency, that's a contradiction,' answered Mitchell. 'Owen means – –'

He showed the inspector Bobby's notebook, but Penfold did not seem impressed.

'Don't see they amount to much,' he said.

'The first is pure psychology – always deceptive, psychology,' Mitchell admitted. 'Young Irwin confirmed, though. The second might be merely a guess – a thing taken for granted. Interesting points, both. To-morrow – this morning, I mean,' he added, with a rueful glance at his wrist-watch, 'Ferris and Owen had better call at Miss Mears' address and make a thorough search of her room. There may be letters – there should be some from Sargent. If they are there, that washes out the idea that they might have been in the missing handbag. You can check up, too, on Maddox's story of his buying an engagement-ring this afternoon – I mean yesterday afternoon,' he corrected himself with another, and even more rueful, glance at his wrist-watch. 'Oh, and, Owen, try to make an opportunity to have a confidential chat with Miss Mears's aunt. She may have more to tell than she thinks. Tell Ferris to let you handle that end – you being young and beautiful, while Ferris is neither. But don't tell him I said so,' Mitchell added hastily, 'or his feelings might be hurt.'

CHAPTER XIII

THE ENGAGEMENT-RING

BOBBY'S rest that night consisted solely of a bath and a shave. So refreshed, he settled down to his notes, and then, on his way to headquarters, where he was due at noon, he called at that Regent Street shop where Maddox said he had bought the engagement-ring given to the murdered girl.

The assistant, to whom Bobby introduced himself and explained his errand, remembered the transaction perfectly.

'Oh, yes,' he said. 'That's all right. We've got it. The gentleman can have it any time he likes to call.'

'Got it?' repeated Bobby, puzzled. 'I mean an engagement-ring – seed pearls and a small diamond – Mr Maddox bought – –'

'That's right,' interrupted the assistant. 'One of my own sales – five pounds, it was. Thought I was going to bring off something good at first. He was wearing one himself -- a ring, I mean; fine sapphire, worth fifty pounds of any man's money – and when a gent, wearing a fifty-pounder piece, comes in and asks for an engagement-ring, you do expect him to splash a bit.'

'I suppose you do,' agreed Bobby thoughtfully, remembering that young Leslie Irwin had used the same expression in speaking of Maddox as liking to 'splash his money about.'

'Wasn't even,' pursued the assistant, 'as if he were shy about it – some of 'em pretend it's for a friend, you know, or some other fairy-tale, but you can always tell – they give themselves away every time. Makes it easier in a way; you can say right out: "Can't be mean or stingy on an occasion like this," and then they generally fall for anything in reason you care to sell 'em. But this gentleman – Mr Maddox, you said? – he wasn't like that. Said right out it was for the young lady he had just got engaged to. He looked the sort that's ready to spend, too. Generally I can tell 'em at sight. There's something about the man that looks twice at a shilling before spending it quite different from the man who'll throw a pound note down and never notice hardly – different in the way they wear their hats or carry their gloves. Goes deep, it does ; and I always thought I could tell which was which at a glance. Well,' confessed the assistant, with the smile of the man contemplating the ridiculously impossible suddenly become fact. 'I was wrong. Just clean wrong,' he repeated, savouring the rare, the incredible, strange experience. 'Showed him a fifty-hundred range first of all, thinking to lead him on. He wasn't interested. Showed him a ten-twenty range next. He asked for something cheaper. As near as nothing I advised him to go to Woolworths. I got out a five-ten range instead, hoping to shame him. Believe me, or believe me not, he took one of the fivers.'

'Dear me,' said Bobby, feeling something was expected of him.

'You can take it from me,' said the assistant, 'either he don't think an awful lot of his girl – or else he isn't too sure of her. Only if it's that way,' added the assistant shrewdly, 'there'd be more sense in getting something really good she would know she might have to turn up again if they parted, and so she wouldn't want.'

'Yes, there would be that,' agreed Bobby, in whose head some strange thoughts were buzzing.

'Gentleman did ask,' the assistant added, 'if we would mind changing it, supposing he wanted something more expensive, which, if his young lady knows what's what, as most of 'em do,' said the assistant, with some show of feeling, 'something more expensive is what she'll want and quick about it. Unnatural, I call it, wearing a fifty-pounder sapphire yourself, to put your *fiancée* off with a small pearl-and-diamond fiver.'

'Unnatural does seem the word,' agreed Bobby.

'And then to go and lose it,' the assistant went on. 'At least, if it was him lost it. Shouldn't wonder, myself, if the

young lady wasn't so mad and disgusted she just up and
flung it at his head, and that's how Mr Quin came to find it.'

Bobby fairly jumped. A detective should not show surprise
too easily, nor too easily be taken aback, but this name came
in so unexpectedly it was almost like a blow.

'Quin? Quin?' he repeated. 'But who? But how?'

'Gent,' explained the assistant, wondering a little at the
excitement Bobby seemed to show, 'who found it lying in
the street, and brought it back here this morning – our name
and address being on the cardboard box it was packed in.'

'You mean,' Bobby asked, very puzzled, 'that someone
picked it up in the street and brought it back to you this
morning?'

'That's right,' said the assistant.

He went on to explain in detail. A rough-looking man had
come into the shop almost as soon as it opened that morning. He had produced the ring purchased by Maddox the
afternoon before, and had explained that he had picked it
up, and, seeing the shop's address on the box containing it,
had brought it back to them on the assumption that they
would know their customer's name and address.

'Which we didn't,' said the assistant. 'Not even his name
till you mentioned it just now – Maddox, didn't you say?
It was just an ordinary counter transaction, paid for in
pound notes on completion.'

'Honest of Mr Quin to bring it straight here,' Bobby observed.

'So he thought,' answered the assistant, 'and he let us
know it, too. Kept on saying some would have put it in their
pockets and kept it there, but he wasn't that sort, which, to
look at him,' the assistant added, 'you would have thought
he was. Second time,' declared the assistant, frankly bewildered, 'I've been wrong in two days. Wrong yesterday,
thinking Mr Maddox was a spender, wrong in thinking Mr
Quin wasn't the sort to bring straight back any little bit of
jewellery he happened to find in the street. Of course, he
may have some game on.'

'Did he leave his address?' asked Bobby.

'I asked him, but he said it didn't matter,' the assistant
explained. 'All he wanted was for us to take charge of the
ring for our customer. I told him there ought to be a bit of
a reward, and if we didn't know his address, how could we
let him have it? Besides, if it isn't claimed, he had the best
right to it. But he said he wasn't out for a reward; all he
wanted was to be honest and run straight. Said he had
always believed honesty was the best policy, and no one
could say anything else or anything against his character.
You can take it from me there was something behind. Being
honest wasn't so natural to him as all that, or why did he
talk so much about it? And he looked as if there was something upsetting him pretty bad – scared, he looked to me.
Shouldn't wonder if he hadn't pinched the thing, and then
got the jumps. Thought someone saw him, perhaps, and he
had best bring it back here so as to prove *bona fides*.'

'Perhaps there was something like that,' agreed Bobby.
'We should like a chat with Mr Quin, I think.'

Before he left the shop, he arranged that if Quin called
again he was to be detained, and that if Maddox called to
claim the ring he was to be referred to Scotland Yard.
Bobby arranged, too, that an appointment was to be made
for the assistant to visit the Yard and see if he could identify
any of the photographs of criminals kept there as that of this
mysterious Mr Quin, who seemed to be hovering on the outskirts of the case in so peculiar a manner.

'Though what he can have to do with it, it's difficult to
see,' Bobby said to himself thoughtfully.

For one thing, why had he been so anxious to emphasise
the honesty of his action? Was it simply because he was a
gentleman to whom honesty was a rarity, and therefore a
quality to which too much attention could not be drawn?
Or was there some hidden motive? And was it true he had
simply picked the ring up in the street? If so, an odd coincidence indeed. Or had he come into possession of it in some
manner? Had it been in the missing crocodile-skin hand-

bag, for example? If so, was Quin the thief responsible for its disappearance? But, if he had stolen it, why should he have taken the trouble to return the ring, and why in so elaborate and marked a manner, even leaving a name that, whether his own or not, certainly hinted at some other connection with the case?

Could Quin be the murderer, Bobby wondered, and was this return of the ring part of some elaborate scheme to establish an alibi? It seemed unlikely, nor when he made his report at the Yard was anyone there able to suggest any probable explanation, even though they all seemed to feel, like Bobby, that somewhere in this odd incident lay a hidden and important clue, if only it could be discovered.

'Seems likely to turn out important, a key-piece, perhaps, to fit into the puzzle,' Mitchell commented. 'But I think we shall have to wait a while before we can guess where it ought to go.'

'May not be the same Quin at all,' suggested Ferris. 'Plenty of Quins – not such an uncommon name as all that.'

'I never much care for coincidences,' Mitchell remarked. 'They do happen, but they're rare, or else they wouldn't be coincidences. We'll have to check up on all the girls in the Beauty Queen competition to see if any of them have any friends or enemies called Quin. Mr Sargent will have a list of their names and addresses. All the staff connected with the cinema had better be questioned, too, and if necessary every Quin in the directory. The fellow has got to be found somehow. Maddox had better be seen, too, to find out what he has to say about the ring, and whether he knows, or has ever heard of, Quin, especially if Miss Mears has ever mentioned the name. His story was that he had given the engagement-ring to Miss Mears, I think?'

'Yes. He said he met her as she left her office, and gave it her before he saw her into the train. She travelled by train from Cannon Street every day.'

'Have a talk with young Irwin, too, in case he knows anything about Quin. Make the same inquiry of Sargent, and tell him we want a list of names and addresses of his staff and of all competitors. Then go on to Miss Mears's flat. Ferris is making a search of her room this afternoon. She may have left letters or papers that may help. Try to get on good terms with the aunt, and see what she can tell about the girl's love-affairs. If you've any time to spare – –'

'Sir?' Bobby could not prevent himself from interposing, nor control the pained indignation in his voice, but Mitchell swept on unheedingly:

'Report back here for further instructions, but whatever you do don't hurry the aunt – let her talk as long as she wants. Get her to give you some tea, if you can, and don't ask too many direct questions. Most people will tell far more if you let them ramble on than if you try to cross-examine them. They get scared and flustered, and won't mention trifles, because they don't seem important, and it's trifles that'll most likely tell us most in this case. It's the trifles that help you to understand people, and the better we understand people in this case the more likely we shall be to get an idea of what they were all doing. We don't know whether it was a lover's quarrel that led to jealousy and death. Or theft, if the Quin person, the missing handbag, and the restored ring mean that. Or resentment and revenge for an injury, if the Ellis girl is responsible. Or the same sort of thing if it was Beattie, and we mustn't forget he is the last person known to have been in the room with Carrie Mears. Or self-protection, for I think it seems clear the girl was pressing Sargent pretty hard. Or something else we've no hint of yet. Difficult to know how to set to work till we've a clearer idea of the motive.'

'Love and passion,' mused Ferris, ticking off on his fingers. 'Love, that's one. Theft, that's two. Revenge, that's three. A sort of protecting-your-girl idea, if it was Beattie, and that makes the fourth possible motive. Blackmail, if it was Sargent, and that's the fifth possibility. Plenty of lines of approach, but, if you ask me,' declared Ferris, with energy, 'it's just one of those love dramas.'

'Likely enough,' agreed Mitchell. 'Young people lose their heads sometimes, and think of nothing else till it seems to them there is nothing else. Only we've got to clear up all these other possible lines before we go any further, or it'll be just waste of time making an arrest. Treasury counsel wouldn't even prosecute. And it'll be as well to remember there are more kinds of love than one.'

But what Mitchell meant by this last remark neither Ferris nor Bobby had any idea.

CHAPTER XIV

THE CHALLENGE CUPS

THE tube took Bobby swiftly to Brush Hill, and there, at the Central Cinema, the first thing he did was to arrange with the door-keeper, Wood, for him to call at Scotland Yard, to see if he could pick out from the photographs kept there of various criminals one that in any way resembled the man who on the night of the murder had inquired for the non-existent Miss Quin. It was with enthusiasm that Wood fell in with this proposal.

'Take it from me,' he announced. 'You're on the right track there. It was him did it, sure as nuts in May.'

'Well, we haven't got quite as far as saying that,' laughed Bobby, 'but we would like to have a talk with him.'

Then he went on to Mr Sargent, whom he found in a very depressed, nervous condition.

'Reserved seats all sold for I don't know how far ahead,' he announced without joy – almost, indeed, as if this statement, the idle, happy dream of every exhibitor in his most after-dinner mood, were but the added blow of a remorseless and malignant fate. 'People come along and tell us we ought to shut down after what's happened, and how surprised they are we haven't that much good feeling, and then they ask for seats giving a clear view of the exact spot where Carrie stood last night, and may they have just one peep at the room where it happened? I've told Wood he gets the sack if he lets anyone else go behind to look. Made him turn up some of the tips he's had, too – made him send them on to the hospital.'

'But isn't the room locked?' Bobby asked. 'I thought we had the key?'

'Yes, I know,' answered Sargent, 'but they can look at the outside of the door, can't they? And then sometimes

Wood lets them rattle the handle. I made him turn up thirty bob – I expect he's had twice that.'

'Anything like this happening always means a lot of trouble and worry to everyone,' observed Bobby sympathetically.

'If it was only that,' groaned Sargent, looking more melancholy than ever, 'I wouldn't mind. People are pointing,' he burst out suddenly.

'Pointing?' repeated Bobby, slightly puzzled.

'At me,' explained Sargent. 'Whispering, too. Do you know what I caught some of the pages up to this morning?'

'Mischief?' suggested Bobby, playing for safety by suggesting the obvious.

'Staging a hanging,' said Sargent miserably. 'My hanging,' he explained. 'I sacked the lot. On the spot. Without a reference.' He looked up sharply, and Bobby understood that in part at least this story had been told to test official opinion. 'A lot of people think it was me,' he said. 'Do you?'

'We are trying to get enough to go on to think that about someone or another,' was Bobby's non-committal reply. 'Of course, you've told us yourself you were on friendly terms with Miss Mears.'

'The only thing the fools think of is that it happened in my private office,' Sargent said moodily. 'I wish to heaven I had never thought of letting her have it.'

'Mr Sargent,' Bobby said gravely, 'probably you will be asked if that really was entirely an afterthought; and if it was entirely by accident that her name was overlooked when the other competitors were being given their places. I'm not suggesting anything, but you will certainly be pressed about that, and, if you don't mind my saying so, it's always the best plan – and much the safest' – Bobby lingered a little on this last word, and Sargent wriggled uncomfortably in his seat – 'to be entirely frank and open, and absolutely accurate about every detail.'

Sargent took a cigar from a drawer of his desk, and offered it to Bobby, and then, without waiting for either acceptance or refusal, proceeded to light it himself. Then he put it down again, and let it go out, forgotten. Then he said:

'Oh, all right. It was fixed up beforehand, why not? I made sure she would be the winner – certain to be with her looks; besides I knew the committee of judges would be favourable to her type. I fixed that, too, if you want to know. I thought it would be better if she had a room to herself, for congratulations and all that sort of fuss. And then,' he added, seeing that Bobby was still waiting, still expectant, 'if you must know, though it's nothing to do with it, I wanted to have a chance to talk to her without all the rest of them all buzzing round.'

'I understand,' Bobby said, persuaded that now at last he had the truth on at any rate one point. 'Was there anything special or important you wished to see her about?'

'I only wanted to tell her it was no good her expecting too much. I was doing my best for her all right, but she never quite got the difference between an exhibitor and a director or a producer. I suppose a director or a swell producer could have had any girl he fancied given a real serious test right off. All I could do was to tell her to apply in the usual way, with name, address, experience, and photo, and I would write in at the same time. Unluckily she didn't take too well – her photos never did her justice. When all she got was a printed form to say her name had been put down and she would be communicated with in due course, if occasion arose, and not a word about me, she thought I had let her down. Didn't believe I had been trying.'

'Did she show anger openly, do you mean?' Bobby asked.

'Well, depends what you call threatening to go round and tell my wife; asked me how I would like Mrs Sargent to know all about our little dinners up West when I was supposed to be looking after things here – not that there was any harm in them, only I wasn't keen on Mrs Sargent hearing it like that. She's interested on the financial side· here, for one thing – put all her money in when we started, on debenture.'

'On debenture?' repeated Bobby thoughtfully.

'Yes, a mortgage – safer, of course, as I told her,' said Sargent, though just a little uncomfortably; and added: 'Much safer, and then she hadn't to attend meetings or be bothered with voting.'

'Quite so,' agreed Bobby, rather inclined to suspect that the fact that the debenture holders had no right to attend the general meeting or vote at it was one reason why Mrs Sargent had been advised to invest her money in a debenture holding.

'I don't deny,' added Sargent, 'it would be a bit awkward if she chose to call her money in.'

'But the company could pay?'

'Oh, yes. But I should be left high and dry.'

'Did you think it at all likely Miss Mears would do what she said?'

'No; not for a moment. She was only a bit excited and hysterical. Besides, I should have denied the whole thing. She had nothing to show – no letters, for instance.'

Sargent paused and looked cunning – and unpleasant.

'I wasn't born yesterday,' he said. 'I always phoned.'

Bobby went away, convinced that Sargent had been in fact more troubled and alarmed by the girl's threats than he now cared to admit. All the same, from being alarmed and disturbed to committing murder is a long step – especially to murder in circumstances and surroundings bound to cast suspicion on oneself.

Then, too, Sargent had made more admissions than might have been expected from a guilty man, though that might be due to his perception that sooner or later the facts he acknowledged were bound to become known.

On the whole, Bobby thought that an interesting case against Sargent was being slowly built up, but hardly one that at present justified action. Too many loose ends, he told himself, still lying about – loose ends that in a trial counsel for the defence would thoroughly enjoy trailing before a jury.

Still, he felt satisfied with the results of his interview. He went back to the Yard, deposited there the list of the names and addresses of the Beauty Queen competitors Sargent had provided him with, and knew that very shortly a polite plain-clothes man would call on each in turn to inquire if anything was known of any person named Quin, just as a good many people of that name entered in the directory were likely to be asked presently if they knew or ever had known anything of Carrie Mears. Not that Bobby felt it likely that these inquiries would have much result, as in fact they had not. They were, indeed, merely a part of the slow, dull, laborious, careful routine of which detective work almost entirely consists, since to meditate deeply and arrive at deep conclusions is of little value when what a jury asks for is quite commonplace proof.

Bobby's next visit was to Maddox's office in the City. The young man held apparently a sufficiently important position with his firm to have a small room to himself, and Bobby, left alone in it to wait, while Maddox, somewhere else in the building, was sent for, examined the apartment with a keen, intent interest.

Personality is so strong and strange a thing there is nothing so insignificant we use we do not leave on it our own private stamp, though it may be in signs little easy to read. Bobby, now looking about him with the concentrated attention he had learnt from Mitchell, thought he could perceive enough to deduce a character flamboyant, pleasure-loving, self-indulgent, a little careless and even reckless, yet dominating, self-confident, and successful. The fountain-pen lying on the office table was of the most expensive make on the market, and heavily banded in gold, and there was a five-pound note near by, under a paper-weight representing a running greyhound. Only a somewhat careless, even reckless, individual would leave money and a pen of so valuable a make lying on the desk in a room to which access was evidently easy, just as only a flamboyant, pleasure-loving personality would use such a pen in business, or smoke the expensive and heavily scented cigarettes in the silver-mounted box near by. Yet the room had at the same time a business-like and efficient air. On another smaller table near by were several financial journals, neatly folded and laid together, and a list of what seemed Stock Exchange securities with the latest quotations carefully marked.

'Does a bit on the Stock Exchange,' Bobby thought, and reflected that perhaps the running-greyhound paper-weight was another indication of another form of gambling.

On each side of the fireplace stood a bookcase, containing what seemed solid works of reference, and on the top of the one nearest the window, and facing the chair that a caller would naturally occupy, was a row of seven silver challenge cups. There were several photographs, too, all of Maddox himself – even one of what seemed to be the firm's premises in Buenos Aires showed Maddox standing at the entrance as though he were the sole owner. Another photograph showed him in what Bobby thought at first was fancy dress, and then recognized as the traditional gaucho costume – hat and spurs and leggings, all complete. In another similar photograph Maddox was in the act of throwing a lasso, and in yet another he was sitting a rearing horse with a great appearance of skill and mastery. But Bobby knew enough of horsemanship to guess that the rearing was not quite spontaneous. A set piece, Bobby thought, staged so that an effective picture could be taken.

'Must have got on well to have a room like this to himself at his age,' Bobby thought, 'but not quite so well as he wants you to think, or he wouldn't take such pains to impress himself.'

The door opened, and Maddox himself came in. He looked pale and heavy-eyed, as was only natural after what had occurred, but seemed brisk and self-confident as ever.

'Thought some of you chaps would be along,' he said. 'I've been expecting you all day. Have a cigarette – help yourself. Those are rather good in that box, but I've some gaspers, too, if you prefer them.' He produced some that, if not exactly 'gaspers,' were less expensive and unscented, and, when Bobby politely declined, helped himself to one from the first box. 'Bulgarian,' he explained. 'Always smoke them. Of course, anything I can do to help ... Sure you won't have a cigarette?'

'We're not supposed to – not on duty,' Bobby explained. 'I was admiring your photographs, Mr Maddox. South America, aren't they?'

'Brazil and the Argentine chiefly,' Maddox answered. 'We've big interests in both places. Used to get a lot of riding out there. Missed it when I got home. I did try trotting round the Park for a time, but that seems so infernally slow when you've been used to a gallop over pampas that stretch away for hundreds of miles.'

'I see you are throwing a lasso in one,' remarked Bobby.

'Yes, I got quite good at it – came in second in a competition once. Only amateurs allowed to compete, though,' he added smiling, 'the genuine gaucho article was barred. Wonders some of those chaps are, but they thought me quite good for an amateur – and an Englishman.'

'I noticed you have some challenge cups there,' Bobby observed.

Maddox turned quickly as if to look at them. There were seven of them, three on each side of one very big one that appeared to be a rowing trophy, as it was supported on crossed oars. To Bobby there came irresistibly the impression that his mention of these cups had startled Maddox considerably, had even alarmed him, though how that could be, Bobby could not even imagine. Yet when Maddox turned again he was very pale, his eyes were uneasy, his hands not quite steady. It was as if some swift danger had shown itself to him, as when on the road at night a sudden obstruction appears.

Bobby told himself crossly that he was letting his imagination run away with him. How, in the name of all that's reasonable, could a sudden danger show itself in a row of challenge cups won probably years ago, and apparently all of them in South America, many hundreds of miles away in distance, and in time long before Carrie Mears and Claude Maddox had met.

'No sleep last night, that's what it is,' Bobby decided.

He went on to explain that he was trying to trace a man named Quin. Quin, Bobby explained, had paid a somewhat mysterious visit to the cinema shortly before the murder, and the authorities would like to find him. Probably he had nothing to do with the case, but he ought to be found and questioned. Maddox could give no help. He did not much think he had even heard the name before. He was quite certain he had never known any person called by it; he was equally certain he had never heard it mentioned by Miss Mears.

Bobby felt fairly certain that in this Maddox was speaking the truth. Then he asked about the engagement-ring Maddox had spoken of buying in Regent Street. Maddox repeated what he had said before. He had given it to Carrie, after having met her as she was leaving her office at the conclusion of work, and while walking to the station with her. He had seen her into the train, but had not accompanied her as he had a business appointment to keep. He repeated, too, his previous story that after disposing of this business he had gone straight home, had his supper, and then, feeling nervous and agitated, had gone out for a spin on his motorcycle, finally proceeding to the cinema when, on ringing up to inquire about Carrie's success, he had been informed of the tragedy.

When he had repeated all this, he added, somewhat petulantly:

'You had the whole thing the other night, why do you want it again? Trying to catch me out?'

'We have to check everything,' Bobby answered.

'It's the ring being missing that's worrying you, I suppose,' Maddox said. 'If it can't be found, someone must have pinched it – the murderer probably. I suppose you'll keep an eye on the pawnshops and so on. I expect poor Carrie had it in her handbag. You said that had been stolen, didn't you?'

'I think all we know for certain,' Bobby said, 'is that there didn't seem to be one anywhere about, and yet every woman carries a bag. So we rather assumed it must have been taken away by somebody.'

Maddox agreed, adding, again, that it was an expensive one, worth stealing, even apart from the question of whatever it might have contained. So then Bobby departed, still a good deal worried in his mind over the swift agitation Maddox had shown at the reference to his array of the seven challenge cups.

'Only that's cracked,' Bobby told himself once more. 'What can challenge cups, won long enough ago, thousands of miles away, have to do with it? Keep your head screwed on a bit tighter, my boy,' he adjured himself.

CHAPTER XV

AN OLD WIFE'S TALE

IT was Inspector Ferris who was to make the formal examination of the room Carrie Mears had occupied in the flat
rented by her aunt, Miss Perry, that was still under the
lock and seal of the authorities. But in order to carry out
Mitchell's idea that Miss Perry would be more likely to give
useful information during a friendly chat than under direct
question and answer, Bobby had instructions to arrive first,
and, during the interval of waiting for his superior officer,
to do his best to get the old lady into a gossipy and communicative mood.

'Because what we need,' Mitchell explained again to
Bobby, 'is to get as clear a notion as we can of all these
people. We are groping in the dark till we can establish motive, and we can't even make a guess at that till we know
what sort of people we have to deal with. The more you can
get Miss Perry to tell you about the girl, the better idea we
shall have of where to look for her murderer.'

Bobby had been a little afraid that he might find the old
lady had entirely collapsed under the weight of so terrible
and so unexpected a tragedy impinging on her placid, un-
eventful existence. A little to his surprise, and even more to
his relief, its chief effect seemed, however, to have been to
galvanize her into a more alert and livelier mood. But there
had never been much sympathy or affection between her
and her niece – they had found each other mutually useful,
and that had been about all.

Miss Perry, therefore, in her rickety, comfortable old
chair, with her medicine and her knitting, and her picture
paper on the small table by her side, was in just the excited,
communicative mood Mitchell had hoped Bobby would be
able to turn to account. But the idea, though a good one,

worked out in an unexpected way, as sometimes happens
with good ideas.

Bobby began by asking permission to wait there the arrival of his superior officer, who was to come to look through
Carrie Mears's papers and possessions in the hope of finding
useful clues. Miss Perry had no objection, but repeated her
previous warning that it was little likely anything would be
found of any use.

'Carrie was always a close one,' Miss Perry wheezed
between two fits of coughing. 'She never told you anything.'

Bobby was aware of a possibly unjust suspicion that in time
past Miss Perry herself had done a little private examining
on her own account of her niece's belongings and had not
found much to reward her curiosity. He said carelessly:

'Well, one never knows. Sometimes even an old bill or a
picture postcard gives us a hint where to look. Or you might
be able to help us. Even the most trifling detail might turn
out important. But I don't suppose it's likely there's anything much you can tell us.' Leaving this remark to sink in,
he added: 'I'm admiring that picture of Hamlet over the
mantelpiece. Oil, isn't it? is it a portrait?'

'My father,' Miss Perry explained. She named an actor
well known in his day, but forgotten now – Bobby, for instance, had never heard of him. 'He toured his own company,' she went on, with nicely adjusted pride and regret.
'Lost every penny he had doing it, too. The Perrys – of
course that wasn't the name he used on the stage – and the
Irwins are both Brush Hill families. Leslie Irwin's grandfather was a member of my father's company at one time.'

'Really?' exclaimed Bobby, interested. 'That's peculiar
– an odd coincidence.' He did not see that the fact could
have much bearing on the recent tragedy, but it seemed
strange. 'Curious to think of their grandfathers – Leslie
Irwin's and Miss Mears's – being colleagues so long ago.'

'If you call it being colleagues,' said Miss Perry, a little
stiffly. 'Of course, it was father's own company, and he

always played leads while Irwin only took small parts – very small parts.'

'He wasn't a very successful actor, then?' Bobby asked.

'No talent whatever,' pronounced Miss Perry. 'I've heard father say so himself – he always said that was the difficulty that wrecked him, finding any supporting talent. And Irwin had less even than most. But all the Irwins are like that. They've all got the theatre in their blood, but none of them can act.'

'I thought Mr Irwin – Leslie Irwin's father, I mean – was very strict in his views. I was told he had never before even been in a cinema, and never in a theatre since he was a child and his father took him.'

'He didn't dare,' said Miss Perry.

'Really? Do you think it was that?'

'I do. He didn't dare. I've never been in a theatre for years – I wouldn't go if you paid me. But that's because I know it too well – sickened me, it has. But Paul was afraid. He knew what the theatre did to his father.'

'That's extraordinarily interesting,' Bobby said. 'But wasn't he – the father, I mean – wasn't he the founder of the Brush Hill Building Society?'

'He was,' agreed Miss Perry, 'but that was after he left the stage, because no one would have anything to do with him any more.'

'Was he as bad as all that?'

'It wasn't his acting. It was because one of the ladies of the company – well, at the inquest they brought it in accidental death. She was found at the bottom of some steps with her neck broken. Stone steps and slippery, and so they brought it in an accident. Only there was talk – a lot of talk. He had to give evidence – Paul's father, I mean. Accidental death, the verdict was, but after that no one wanted him any more.'

'So he had to give up acting?'

'Yes. And started the Brush Hill Building Society. But he always hankered after the theatre, and, though he had no

chance of an engagement after what had happened, he could
still take an interest in new productions and so on. Find
money to back them sometimes.'

'He still had some money, then?'

'Not a penny.'

'Well, then ... ?'

'Ah,' said Miss Perry, and was taken by a violent fit of
coughing. When she recovered, she said slowly: 'There were
stories got about. Not so much in Brush Hill itself. In Brush
Hill they don't know much about theatre business. But
people in the profession wondered. In Brush Hill they didn't
know he was even interested in stage affairs, but the profession knew he was secretary and manager of a building society. After a time Brush Hill people did begin to get a little
uneasy, but he was clever with figures, and he had a stock
of funny stories and a way of telling them. They used to say
in Brush Hill a general meeting of the Building Society was
as good as a play – he kept the shareholders and depositors
laughing all the time, and, if anyone asked an awkward
question, he didn't answer it, he just told another funny
story and everybody laughed and the question was forgotten. Then he took a chill, walking home in the rain after
a first night he had put money in that was as bad a flop as
could be. He was dead from pneumonia in twenty-four
hours, and Paul had to take his place. Paul was only twenty-
two, but there was no one else to do it, for there was one
else could understand the books. They had been kept in
what was almost a kind of shorthand, but Paul said he could
straighten them out – and so he did, only it took time. Some
of the committee backed him and some didn't, but he hung
on, fighting all the time, and the more those against him
tried to down him, the harder he fought back. Once they
all turned on him and told him to resign. He refused flatly.
He said they had the power to dismiss him, but if they used
it they would be in bankruptcy in twenty-four hours – and
there wouldn't be much left for the sweeping up, either. But
he told them he could save them, and he would, though only

if they left him alone. So they did. Every night I could see his light burning in his office – that was in the old place, before the new building was put up. He was secretary, manager, cashier, clerk, office-boy – everything. He wouldn't have anyone else in the office – not then. It's different now – a big staff they've got; but the first time I knew he had won through was when he told me they were engaging two new clerks. There's many living yet in Brush Hill still remember how he worked like the tides that never rest or are still – twenty hours a day, often enough – until at long last the society was safe again.'

'You think when his father died there was a deficiency?'

'I think there was nothing else,' Miss Perry retorted. 'I think it was all one huge deficiency. But he fought it out – dear Lord Christ, how he fought! Day and night, day after night, year after year – any little slip, any awkward question almost, any unsatisfied curiosity, and there was his father known-for a thief and a forger, and the Building Society bankrupt, and half Brush Hill ruined – and gaol for himself, most like, though I don't believe he ever thought of that, but only of his father's name and all the little people in Brush Hill with all their savings for their old age all swept away. That's why he married.'

'Married?'

'Yes. There was one man who suspected – at least, perhaps others suspected, only they were willing to wait, and this man wasn't. The others hoped to save their money, and knew Paul was their only chance. But this man hadn't any money of his own in the Society, he was only a trustee for a fund he didn't care much about. Most likely he more than suspected. He had a daughter. She had no looks, a pasty face and flat hair, and one shoulder higher than the other, and a tongue like a snake's. Nagged her father fit to drive any man to drink, and, what with her tongue and her looks, he had long ago given up any hope of ever getting her off his hands. Paul – Mr Irwin – I called him Paul then – Paul knew this man was going to insist on an investigation and he knew he had figures ready. Paul knew he was going to post a letter with them on the Wednesday to the chairman, ready for the committee meeting on the Thursday. That Wednesday evening Paul called and asked the girl to marry him. Jumped at him, she did. Her only chance, and she knew it, and she wasn't going to miss it, either. The chairman never got that letter, it was never posted.'

She lapsed into silence, and Bobby, profoundly interested as he was, was silent too, making no comment. He was wondering what part in this strange tale had been taken by the commonplace-looking old woman who had told it and sat there in her chair, wheezing, rheumatic, her bottle of medicine and her knitting by her side, looking as if none of the storms of life had ever troubled her dull repose, as if nothing but her medicine and her knitting had ever interested her.

'That Wednesday,' she said abruptly, 'before he proposed to the girl he married, he came and saw another girl. He told her what he was going to do. It was the last time they ever saw each other.'

She picked up her knitting and began to work at it. Bobby was still silent. She said:

'They had one boy. When the child was seven or eight the wife died. Twenty years they had been married then. There had been another child before, but it died when it was a baby, Paul Irwin had strong feelings always – he loved, he hated, as he worked, with every ounce of energy and being that was in him. He hated – ah, hate's a little word for what he felt – he hated the Building Society. He had made it, sweated his life and more for it to make it what it is to-day, and, by all that he had given it, he hated it. He hated the theatre – hate's a tiny word, but there's no other – for what it had done to his father. You see, he had loved his father. His wife he neither loved nor hated – she was just a convenience, a useful gag to stop a babbling tongue. His son he loved – but love's a tiny word to use. For men like Paul, love and hate are words that are only shifting shadows of what they feel. Leslie's like that, too, the same kind, only

as yet he doesn't know where his feelings belong – he's just
a mass of unrelated feeling.'

'You must have thought a great deal about all this,'
Bobby said.

'Young man,' she answered, 'when you have nothing else
to do by day and by night – by night above all – but think
and think, then presently you come to understand.'

Bobby did not answer. He was musing on this strange,
tragic tale of passion stifled, of love compelled, of a whole
life controlled and forced to one determined end, of all that
huge effort hidden behind what seemed the ordinary suburban life of a successful business man here, and there a commonplace calm domestic existence bounded by knitting and
a picture paper and medicine from the doctor at the corner.
How many, he wondered, of those one meets passing to and
fro upon the daily routine of their affairs, could tell such
tales of such fierce, prolonged endeavour, of such unending,
desperate battle? How many old women wheezing in their
armchairs by the fire as if they had never known life, as if
the storms and trials of existence had passed them by entirely, had yet known such flame of thwarted passion as this
one had endured?

He seemed to see behind the dull and commonplace façade
of ordinary, everyday life, a seething tumult of passion and
of lost endeavour. He said presently:

'Did your niece, did Leslie Irwin know all this?'

'No. Only that there was some kind of family connection.
It was that brought them together in the first place. But Paul
wouldn't hear of Leslie's marrying Carrie. He had suffered
so much, he had endured so much, I think he felt he could
not bear that as well. Besides, we should have had to meet
again.'

'You think that was the reason ...'?

'It wasn't only that. I think he was afraid Carrie would
get Leslie into the theatre, and there was nothing he wouldn't
have done to stop that. He thought the theatre meant ruin
and destruction – body and soul and everything. He knew

what the theatre had done to his father, and he thought it
might be the same with Leslie. You see, he had lived all his
life in fear, never knowing what the next moment might not
bring. No wonder, I think, he preached always a God of
fear and anger.'

Bobby looked at her.

'You understand so well,' he said.

'Young man,' she answered, 'it is time I had my medicine. The glass is there just behind you, if you'll pass it.'

CHAPTER XVI

FINANCIAL CONSIDERATIONS

THERE was not much more passed between them before there arrived Inspector Ferris, very bustling and efficient. With him, at first, Miss Perry seemed inclined to be more reticent, as if she had exhausted her emotions in outpouring to Bobby her memories of the past. To Ferris's questions her answers were brief, serving merely to confirm what was already known. On one point she was very clear. She knew nothing of the supposed engagement to Claude Maddox, and did not much suppose Carrie had ever really intended to marry him, though it was quite possible she had accepted attentions meaning more to him than to her.

'Carrie was like that,' Miss Perry said. 'She kept her own head so well she thought everyone else was the same.'

'What about young Leslie Irwin?' Ferris asked. 'Anything between him and her?'

'Couldn't,' Miss Perry answered shortly. 'She knew Leslie was dependent on his father, and she knew there was nothing he wouldn't have done to put a stop to that.'

'Nothing, eh?' repeated Ferris, and somehow that one word served to invest Miss Perry's sentence with a strange and sinister significance. When she had used the same words before, they had seemed merely a conventional expression of extreme dislike, and so Bobby had accepted them. But now they seemed to mean much more as Ferris uttered his solitary word of comment, and Bobby looked startled and Miss Perry more than startled.

'Oh, I didn't mean that,' she said. 'Of course, I didn't mean that.'

'Ever heard the old gentleman use threats? Or heard tell he had?' Ferris persisted.

'No. Yes. No. Not like that. I haven't seen Paul – Mr Irwin I mean – not for twenty-nine years next March.'

Ferris looked a little surprised at the precision of this statement, but did not comment on it. Miss Perry, a little flustered, went on talking rapidly, as if by a flow of words to wipe out all recollection of the unlucky phrase she had used.

'I don't believe,' she declared, 'Carrie meant to marry anyone – not just yet, that is. She knew what she wanted – Hollywood. A star she meant to be. Thought with her looks it would be easy. Thought I was a jealous, spiteful old maid when I told her looks and talent, yes, and opportunity, too, all together may lead nowhere. She wouldn't believe all that's merely the least you must have to join in the gamble, and whether they win for you or not depends on the card that turns up. She thought what qualified you for entry meant you were sure to win, and it don't. It only gives you the right to try. But she didn't believe that -- they never do, not the young ones. And it wasn't any man she wanted, but just two hundred pounds to pay for her fare to Hollywood, for a few smart frocks to take with her, and a little over to keep her in style while the fat contracts were being drawn up.'

'She was a good actress, then?' Ferris asked.

'She didn't even know what acting was,' Miss Perry retorted. 'She thought it was wearing a smart frock and turning up her nose at the audience. But she might have done well – she couldn't act, but so few actresses can. She had looks, but she thought a winner in Brush Hill must still be a winner in Hollywood, where they tell me even the kitchen-maids in cheap restaurants have all been beauty queens at home. What would have counted, perhaps, is that she knew what she wanted and could keep her head – and that's as rare as genius. None of the boys here ever got a thing from her – not so much as a kiss – nor would have till they had paid for it, cash down. And then as likely as not she would have bilked them – and never thought twice about it, either, for all she ever thought of was herself.'

In answer to further questions Ferris put, she agreed that Leslie had called for Carrie, in a taxi, on the night of the Beauty Contest.

'Must have cost the boy a pretty penny,' she wheezed. 'I don't know how he got enough to pay for it the time she kept him waiting. And then, when she was ready, she came back for her crocodile bag, because she thought it would hold her things better than the little bead one. That took her another ten minutes.'

Ferris made a careful note of this detail, and Miss Perry went on:

'I always thought Leslie was the one that cared the most. But he hadn't a chance with her. He doesn't come into his money till he is twenty-five, and Carrie wasn't going to wait that long. When you are young, three years seem like three centuries, but when you're old they pass like three weeks or less.'

'Then you don't think Mr Maddox really cared much about her?' Ferris asked, sharpening his pencil to make another note.

'Yes, he did, but not like Leslie – not the same way. And it was Claude who was in the biggest hurry. Leslie loved her the best, but Claude desired her the most. Only, once Claude had got her, he would have tired of her and gone off, while Leslie meant it for life.' She was musing again now, talking more to herself than to them. 'Leslie was slow combustion,' she said, 'burning slow but burning steady, and Claude was a fire in dry grass, blazing sky high while the fuel lasted – the fuel being always a failure to get just what he wanted just when he wanted it.' She took up her knitting again. 'A spoilt boy,' she said. 'Never denied anything either by himself or by anyone else, wanting what he wanted just when he wanted it, and for just as he long as he wanted it. A spoilt boy, that's Claude Maddox, but he wouldn't get what he wanted from Carrie, not till he had paid for it – and perhaps not then, unless he watched out very careful.'

'There is Mr Beattie, too,' Bobby observed.

'A nice boy,' she said. 'I liked him best of all the three of them. He's the artist type, like the men I used to know in father's company – sudden and temperamental and generous, nothing mean or calculating about them. Do it first and think afterwards. But he was running after Miss Ellis. Carrie didn't like that. Not that she cared two pins for Roy Beattie, but she hated to lose him or any boy. Insulted she felt when a boy looked at any other girl, because that meant she wasn't quite all she thought.'

'There's not much against him,' reflected Ferris, 'except that he was on the spot – and someone had to be. Mr Sargent seems to have been a bit smitten, too. You knew Mr Sargent?'

'A nasty little man,' Miss Perry said. 'The real stage-manager type. But he didn't know Carrie. He was working up for a surprise. She was beginning to suspect he was just fooling her, and you weren't safe with Carrie if she thought that. Play her a dirty trick and she would play you a dirtier. Spirit all right, she had – lots of spirit. Never cared what she did to get even.'

Ferris thought that by now it was getting time to make his examination of Carrie's room and papers. So he disappeared on that task, and soon, for it did not take him long, came back with some letters in his hand.

'She was busy booking her passage to Hollywood all right,' he said. 'I found these put away in a drawer she had locked. One letter from one of the travelling agencies says they can complete all arrangements if she will call with remittance as arranged, when a berth will be reserved on the next steamer. All cut and dried, apparently, and there's a rough note of her reply saying she would bring the money next day – that's next day after she was murdered. So she evidently had the cash.'

'But she hadn't,' protested Miss Perry. 'I'm sure she hadn't. How could she? She had it all worked out – two hundred pounds was what she needed, and where was she to get it from? She said as much to me herself only a week ago.'

'Two hundred pounds?' Ferris repeated, glancing at another paper he held. 'Yes, that's the figure jotted down here – at the bottom of the copy of the note to the agency, saying she was going to call with the money.'

'But she hadn't got it,' Miss Perry persisted. 'She can't really have sent a letter to say she had. Why should she, when she knew she hadn't?'

'If she was really engaged to Mr Maddox, couldn't he have promised it, or given her the money?' Ferris suggested.

Miss Perry began a scornful laugh that ended in a bad bout of coughing.

'Not likely,' she said, when she had recovered. 'Give her two hundred pounds for her to go off to the other end of the world with? Not him – not Claude Maddox. Leslie Irwin might, but never Claude. Besides, he hasn't got two hundred pence, let alone two hundred pounds, to bless himself with.'

'I understood he came in for some money when he came of age?' Bobby said. 'And then he seems to have a good position in his firm.'

'Yes, and a good salary,' agreed Miss Perry, 'but he's in debt all round. The money he got when he came of age he spent long ago, making a splash,' and Bobby remembered that was the third time he had heard this expression 'making a splash' used with reference to Claude Maddox. 'Anything he has left is locked up in shares he couldn't sell now except at a dead loss – he has the real gambler's instinct, and he'll never admit a loss because he is always so sure the luck will turn. So he always hangs on right to the end. No, he would never have given Carrie money to go and leave him, and, if he would, he couldn't, for he hasn't got it. Though he might have raised it by hook or crook to stop her going. It would have driven him half mad to think of her there, doing just what she liked, and him obliged to stop here. But not a penny would she have had to help her go.'

'This young Leslie Irwin, could he have raised the money?' Ferris asked.

'Why, he hasn't a penny,' Miss Perry answered, quite

E

amused. 'As articled pupil, he gets no salary. He's to follow
his father as manager and secretary of the Building Society,
but he isn't even one of the staff yet. People think he is,
because he is there so much and sits in his father's office.
But that's only so he can get to know all the ins and outs of
the business. The idea is if he was given a regular post, then
it would have to be a junior appointment, and when Paul
retires there would be others on the staff senior to Leslie
who might try for the managership. But if Leslie's brought
in quite fresh, then it's an outside appointment and not a
promotion in the staff over seniors. And, to make sure, Paul
sees to it Leslie has all the confidential books in his charge,
and all the threads of the concern in his hands, so if they
try to appoint anyone else, they'll never get straight.'

'Or Mr Beattie – could he have provided this money
Miss Mears must have had from somewhere?'

'He might,' agreed Miss Perry doubtfully. 'I don't know,
but it's hardly likely, is it? – now he's taken up with Lily
Ellis?'

'Or, Mr Sargent?' Ferris asked.

'Sargent?' Miss Perry repeated. 'Well, now you mention
him, I expect he might have been willing to pay that much
or more to get rid of Carrie. Carrie could be nasty when she
wanted, and I know she was ready to let fly at him as soon
as she was sure he had only been fooling her when he promised to get her an engagement. Yes, he might have raised
the money – or promised it; he's better at promising than
doing.'

'That might be a good line to follow,' Ferris remarked
thoughtfully. 'It might be this way: Sargent promised her
the money to keep her quiet. But he hadn't got it. So he
knew there was bound to be a row, and that's why he arranged for her to have a room by herself, so he could have
a chance to quiet her down, or anyhow they could have it
out by themselves. But, when the money wasn't there, she
rounded on him worse than he looked for, told him straight
out she would give him away to his wife, and perhaps other

threats as well – when a woman goes it,' said Ferris profoundly, 'she goes it. And he got mad, and the knife was lying there on the table same as that Ellis girl said, so he up and slung it at her, just to scare her, most like, and the point took her in the throat, and that was that, and murder done before you knew it. Take it from me, that's how the whole thing happened.'

'I don't quite see why, if it was like that, her handbag should be missing,' Bobby objected.

'He thought there might be something in it compromising, so he grabbed it before he ran.'

Bobby looked unconvinced. It was possible, of course. Even if there were no letters, Carrie herself might have written out a statement of their connection Sargent might not have wanted anyone to see. Yes, that was possible. He said :

'What about the knife? Why should a knife like that be lying there? The staff have been questioned, and no one has ever seen any sort of knife in Sargent's office or in his possession.'

'No, we've got to trace the knife,' Ferris admitted. 'If we can, and if it's Sargent it's traced to, then, take it from me, it's a case.'

CHAPTER XVII

THE KNIFE TRACED

MISS PERRY was a good deal impressed by this declaration. She evidently disliked Mr Sargent, and was quite ready to believe ill of him.

'Nothing of the artist in him,' she said. 'The pure manager type.'

Then, too, the personality of Inspector Ferris had its effect – his brisk and confident manner, indeed, persuading her to that offer of some tea before they went which Bobby's youth and supposed good looks had, contrary to Mitchell's expectations, not succeeded in obtaining.

Neither Bobby nor the inspector himself had had much time for rest or refreshment that day, nor any sleep the night before, but there was so much to do that Ferris was already phrasing a refusal when Bobby managed to whisper a reminder that Mitchell had said they were to try to get the old lady into as talkative a mood as possible. So Ferris turned his refusal into an acceptance, and Miss Perry, lifting herself with some difficulty from her chair, pottered about making the necessary preparations. While she was out of the room in the little kitchen across the landing that once had been a dressing-room when the house in more prosperous days had been occupied by a single family, Bobby repeated to Ferris the gist of the long story Miss Perry had told him. But Ferris was not much impressed.

'Wasting our time listening to her, if all she can tell us is things that happened thirty years ago,' he grumbled. 'If I had known that was all, we wouldn't have stayed. What we're up against is what happened at the Brush Hill Central Cinema. You keep that in mind, my lad, and don't go off on side-tracks about things that's been stale thirty years.

Stale and dead – dead,' repeated Ferris, with a comprehensive wave of the arm.

There is a phrase 'Being dead, yet liveth,' that at this flashed into Bobby's mind. But prudently he did not utter it. Instead he went on to tell of his interview with Maddox, of the curious incident of the engagement-ring found in the street by someone giving that name of 'Quin' which had already appeared once before on the outskirts of events, and of the equally curious, but apparently unrelated, incident of the evident agitation Maddox had shown over Bobby's interest in his display of challenge cups.

That this was curious, Ferris admitted; but no more than Bobby could he see any possible connection between that agitation and the subject of their investigation.

'Unless, of course,' he suggested, 'there was something Maddox kept inside one of the cups he didn't want you to see. And that don't seem likely. But it isn't hardly possible for a sports cup won in South America some years ago to have anything to do with Carrie Mears's murder. I think we can wash that out – got to keep inside sense and reason. But this Quin business is a bit more than funny. It may mean something, though I don't see where it fits in. Nothing even to show Quin was the name of the party who was asking for Miss Quin before the murder happened. Lots of loose strings in this case that don't none of them connect,' he said, shaking his head gravely.

Miss Perry returned, a little exhausted, wheezing more badly than ever, but triumphant with the tea. In honour of the occasion she had produced her best china and her solid silver spoons, as well as some seed cake, preserved in careful wrappings for visitors, but that had, nevertheless, not entirely escaped the effect of the slow passing of the days. However, Ferris did not seem to mind; and, if Bobby practised a sleight of hand that transferred most of his share of the cake to his pocket instead of to his mouth, no one noticed. Once, it is true, he was nearly caught when Miss Perry, recovering with unexpected rapidity from a fit of

coughing, turned round to offer him some more milk. He
was only just able to avoid detection by displaying a sudden
interest in the tea-spoons.

'Fine old silver,' he pronounced, the first adjective being
quite conventional, for there was nothing specially fine
about their very ordinary make and workmanship, and the
second being fairly obvious for long usage had worn them
nearly smooth. He looked more closely at the one in his
hand, trying to make out the hallmark and failing, so nearly
erased was it by constant polishing. All at once he stiffened
with sudden attention. 'The initial,' he said, 'is it a "Q"?
It looks like a "Q".'

'They belonged to my sister's second husband,' Miss
Perry explained. 'Good-for-nothing scamp he was, too. It's
a wonder they never went to the pawnshop, but I suppose
Aggie saved them somehow.'

'Was his name Quin?' Bobby asked, making his voice
sound as indifferent as he could.

'How did you know?' asked Miss Perry suspiciously. 'He
left her after he had spent all her money – a sponger if ever
there was one. Got it all from her, every penny, and then
left her to face all the other people he had got money out
of. I've heard people say that if you stopped Quin in the
street to ask the way he would borrow half a crown from
you before he told you. A good-for-nothing if ever there was
one, and up to all kinds of tricks. Why, once Aggie came
home and found him on the stairs with a rope round his
neck. Just done to frighten her into giving him more money,
but she couldn't see it.'

'Where is he now?' Bobby asked.

'Dead,' Miss Perry answered. 'He went to Australia and
then Aggie got a paper with a notice of his death : ''Deeply
regretted by numerous friends.''' She sniffed comprehen-
sively : 'True enough,' she commented, 'if friends meant
them he owed money to. After that Aggie came to live near
here, and when she died Carrie came to me. A good thing
Quin did die,' she concluded, 'or he would have been back

here before long, trying to sponge on Aggie – at least, if he hadn't been too afraid of his creditors, for there were some had said they would take it out of his skin if they couldn't out of his purse. He wouldn't have got much after Carrie had grown up, though, she would have been a match for him and all his tricks.'

'Did she ever go by the name of Quin?' Bobby asked.

'Always till she came to live with me. Then I said Mears was her proper name, and Mears she was going to be so long as she was with me, and Mears she always was after that. And to do the girl justice, willing enough. She remembered enough of Quin to know the kind of good-for-nothing he was.'

Bobby asked if she could give a description of Quin's appearance, but it seemed she had never seen him or even a photograph of him – he had had no taste for being photographed – 'had his reasons, most likely,' snorted Miss Perry – and any description she had ever heard from her sister, she had long forgotten. In fact she knew little or nothing of him except his name, his talent for borrowing, as exemplified by his successful extraction from her sister of the few hundreds left by her first husband, and his departure to Australia and opportune death there.

'All very interesting,' commented Ferris afterwards, as he and Bobby were making their way back to headquarters, 'but I don't see that it takes us much further forward. If Quin's dead, it can't be him was making inquiries at the cinema that night, or who found the engagement-ring, and anyhow there doesn't seem any reason why he should want to kill his step-daughter, supposing it was him.'

'I should think it quite likely the announcement of his death in the paper was a fake to put off any specially pressing creditors,' Bobby observed.

'Likely enough,' agreed Ferris. 'Anyhow, I suppose it means another line to follow up, though we weren't exactly short of lines before. Nothing to show, though, that the man at the cinema is the same as the man who returned the engagement-ring to the Regent-Street shop, or that either

of them has any connection with the step-father. Of course,
it's quite possible it was the same man in both cases, and
that he is the step-father come to life again and back from
Australia.'

'We shall have to try to find him,' remarked Bobby.

'As if we hadn't enough on our hands already,' grumbled
Ferris. 'Of course, he may come forward on his own account,
but he sounds more like one of your shy birds.'

'It might turn out he is the murderer himself,' Bobby suggested, though a little doubtfully. 'Miss Perry called him
a sponger. Suppose it was Quin himself, and suppose he was
trying to get money out of his step-daughter. She refused,
there was a quarrel, the knife was lying there, and it was he,
and not Sargent, who slung it at the girl. Only, that theory
leaves the knife unexplained still.'

'Take it from me,' said Ferris, slowly and thoughtfully,
'it's the knife that counts; it all depends on who we can
trace it to. If it ever is traced at all,' he added, somewhat
despondently.

Mitchell was not at the Yard when Ferris and Bobby returned. They made out their reports, and then, both having
been continuously on duty for a very considerable time, were
allowed to go home.

Bobby went straight to bed the moment he got in, and
never woke till his alarm-clock went off with a bang next
morning. At headquarters he found more tasks awaiting
him, though they did not prove of great interest or value,
and also a special order to report to Mitchell at three in the
afternoon.

'The old man,' explained someone confidentially to
Bobby, 'won't be turning up much before then – seems he
was out all night. Something in the City.'

'In the City?' repeated Bobby, slightly surprised, for the
City police look after their own area.

'Seems so,' said the other. 'We thought he had cleared
out all his other work to concentrate on this beauty queen
affair. But last night he came in late, read the day's reports,

and then went off – and next thing we heard was when the City police rang up with a message from him. That was about three this morning. He had been out with them all night – some fresh case turned up, but Lord knows what!'

Bobby wondered, too, and since one of the tasks assigned him necessitated a visit to the City, he took occasion to go round by the building wherein were situated on the first floor the offices occupied by Claude Maddox's firm. Nor was Bobby greatly surprised when discreet inquiries revealed that there had been a burglary alarm there during the night, that the building had, in consequence, been thoroughly searched from cellar to roof, but that nothing had been found in any way suspicious, neither burglar nor any trace of one.

'False alarm,' Bobby's informant pronounced. 'Police wanted something to do for a change – they must get jolly tired of dawdling about the streets all day with nothing to do but stare in the shops and tell old ladies the time.'

Bobby gasped faintly at this view of police work. When he had slightly recovered, he said, with tremendous, but entirely and completely unnoticed irony:

'I expect that was it. Do you know if they took long over it – made a close search, I mean?'

'Went into every room in the building,' asserted the other. 'Looked under every table and inside every waste-paper basket.'

'Well, it would be a change from staring in shops and telling old ladies the time,' observed Bobby bitterly, and went away, wondering a good deal why Mitchell had gone to all that trouble, for he could not doubt but that the reason why the co-operation of the City police had been invoked in order to search this building was that Claude Maddox worked there.

'Only, even if he thinks Maddox is guilty,' Bobby wondered, 'what could he expect to find? The missing handbag? But, even if Maddox has it, surely he would never hide it where he works?'

Bobby was careful to be punctual in keeping the appointment given him for that afternoon. When he reported himself, he was sent for almost immediately to Mitchell's room, where he found Ferris deep in consultation with the superintendent.

'Making progress?' Mitchell was saying, somewhat irritably, as Bobby entered. 'Oh, yes, we've got quite a good case against some of 'em – only a much better case against the rest. One snag is the older Irwin won't tell us what he knows, and he certainly knows something.'

'One of the Brush Hill men pointed him out to me this morning,' Ferris remarked. ' I saw a report yesterday described him as looking young for his years, but I thought he looked his age all right and a bit more, too. A feeble sort of way with him somehow.'

'You thought that?' Mitchell asked, though half to himself.

'Yes – quite breaking up. Of course, it's partly his hair and beard being all streaked with white the way it is.'

Mitchell and Bobby glanced at each other. Neither of them spoke, but Ferris seemed to divine something in their looks. He said sharply:

'Well, what about it? At his age ...'

'Yes, at his age,' Mitchell agreed. 'Perhaps in time he'll tell us what he knows. Owen, I think you had better make it part of your job to keep in touch with both the Irwins. Don't try to question them. Just try to be on the spot. It may all come out with a rush. That happens sometimes. People get to feel they simply can't keep it to themselves any longer. But I don't think it will ever be like that with Paul Irwin – he is a stronger type.'

'Do you think it can be him did it, sir?' Ferris asked. 'Miss Perry did say there was nothing he would have stopped at to prevent his boy marrying Miss Mears. His hat was in the room, too.'

'I think the case against him is so strong,' Mitchell said slowly, 'I think we could proceed to arrest, if it wasn't just as strong against half a dozen others.'

'He's very religious,' Ferris mused. 'Highest character and all that – leader in Brush Hill church and chapel circles. But sometimes these religious people feel so sure everything they do is right, they'll do almost anything.'

Mitchell nodded an agreement. He would have thought the observation one of unusual penetration for Ferris's somewhat slow and pedestrian but always trustworthy mind, had he not recognized it as almost word for word a repetition of what he himself had said to Ferris only the day before. But that sometimes happened with Ferris, though always quite unconsciously; for if he could not originate, he could at least repeat, and that is a rarer gift than is always thought. Mitchell turned to Bobby:

'Owen,' he said sharply. 'How many silver challenge cups did you see in Maddox's room?'

'Seven, sir,' answered Bobby at once.

'Sure?'

'Quite. A big one mounted on oars in the middle, and three smaller ones on each side.'

'Well, there are only six now,' Mitchell remarked. 'The big one you speak of, three smaller, on the side next the fireplace, and two towards the window.'

So that was what the burglary alarm had been staged for! Mitchell had not seemed to pay much attention to Bobby's report of the apparent agitation Maddox had displayed at the reference to his collection of challenge cups. Yet he had thought it of sufficient importance to investigate – and to stage all that elaborate business of the supposed burglary, so that his real purpose might escape observation; and Maddox, when he heard that a search had been made, have no reason to suppose it was in any way connected with himself. That meant, then, that Mitchell's mind was moving, so to say, Maddox' way, but was that because of definite suspicion, or merely because every line of inquiry must be followed up with equal close attention, nothing forgotten and nothing neglected?

And yet, once again, what possible connection could there

be between a silver challenge cup, won years ago in South
America, and the recent murder of Caroline Mears?

Impossible, Bobby told himself, to suppose that any such
connection did in fact exist. Yet apparently Maddox had
taken the precaution to remove one sports cup from any risk
of such examination as Mitchell had so elaborately attempted to carry out. Or was it all mere coincidence, and had
Maddox taken the cup away for some quite other reason?

Bobby put his hand to his head with a gesture of complete
bewilderment, and his look at Mitchell was almost piteous
in its entreaty. But Mitchell had turned to Ferris, and was
speaking to him:

'Oh, yes,' he said. 'The knife. Yes, that's been traced; the
report's just come in. It's been identified at a shop in Brush
Hill as having been sold to Wood, the door-keeper at the
Central Cinema.'

CHAPTER XVIII

WHITENING HAIR

FOR the rest of that day, and for most of the day following
– a Sunday – Bobby found himself assigned to no more oner-
ous duty than to hang about Brush Hill, apparently, only
that it was a Sunday and therefore all the shops were closed,
in order to conform to that opinion of police work expressed
by the gentleman who held that it consisted of staring into
shop windows and telling old ladies the time.

He was expected, he knew, to keep in touch with the
Irwins, both father and son, and yet, also, his instructions
were that he was to take no action to that end. Everything
was to come about quite naturally and inevitably, as it
showed at present absolutely no sign of doing.

Wandering about, idly and dismally, between the residence of the Irwins and the old-fashioned, substantial
dwelling Claude Maddox shared with his mother, a lady
approaching her seventies and old for her years, and an
elder sister married to the first officer of one of the Australian liners, Bobby spent most of his time trying to guess what
Mitchell really had in his mind, and what he himself was
really expected to do.

Be on the spot, apparently, if anything happened, as it
probably wouldn't, and that was all. A nice tedious uninter-
esting sort of job, Bobby thought resentfully, and one little
to the taste of an ambitious young detective, avid for every
chance for earning distinction.

It was, of course, quite in harmony with Mitchell's general
theory. Once before, in the first case in which Bobby had
ever been associated with him, Mitchell had remarked that
the really successful detective was the man who sat and
waited for people to come and tell him things. So now it

seemed he expected enlightenment simply through setting
Bobby to stand and watch.

'They also detect who only stand and stare,' Bobby murmured to himself, wickedly parodying an august line of
English poetry.

Probably that really was what Mitchell aimed at – the
making of as complete a picture as possible of the actions
and reactions of all concerned, so that presently there might
appear the motive pointing to the actual perpetrator of the
deed.

The incident, so elaborately staged, of the pretended burglary in the building where Claude Maddox worked seemed
to suggest that it was he who occupied in Mitchell's mind
the position of chief suspect, and that the missing challenge
cup was considered an important element in the case, but,
then, why was Bobby set to dawdle about Brush Hill with
nothing to do, apparently, but wait for some vague possible
development affecting one or other of the Irwins? – or both
of them? – or, if not both, then which? – and was it the
father or the son who was to be regarded as the principal?
That the knife used in the murder had been traced to the
door-keeper at the Central Cinema showed every line of
inquiry was being carefully followed up, just as, as Bobby
was well aware, intensive efforts were being made to trace
the mysterious personage who had asked on the night of the
murder for a Miss Quin. But probably this unknown was
now to be identified with the finder of the engagement-ring,
who had given his name in the Regent Street shop as Quin,
and who might easily turn out, also, to be the dead girl's
step-father. For the notice in the Australian paper of Mr
Quin's death did not strike Bobby as being in the circumstances sufficient evidence of the fact.

Only, supposing that this stranger did prove to be Carrie
Mears's step-father, was he just hovering on the outskirts of
the affair, little concerned in its development, or was he one
of the central figures? Roy Beattie and Lily Ellis seemed,
Bobby reflected thankfully, to have faded away out of the

picture. But at any moment, in a business so bewildering as this they might be prominent again, and anyhow, what had become of Miss Mears's handbag, and why had it disappeared? Why had the murderer taken it – if, that is, it was the murderer who was responsible for its disappearance?

So round and round, to little purpose, went Bobby's thoughts till, tired out with putting to himself unanswerable questions, a little despondent, indeed, of ever seeing the sequence of events made clear in all their tangled interaction, he turned into a public house when presently opening time arrived. In more than one of these establishments in that district he had recently acquired a reputation for incipient lunacy from the fact that, having ordered a drink, he would sit or stand with it before him for long enough, listening to, and sometimes taking part in, the chatter going on around that was so seldom, for his purposes, either interesting or enlightening, and then presently departing again, leaving his drink still untasted. For Bobby, though no teetotaller, believing fervently, indeed, that all good things are for use, had no more intention, while engaged on such a problem as this, of taking off the fine edge of his mentality by the use of the soporific, alcohol, than he would have had of lessening by it his nervous reactions when about, for instance, to compete at a Bisley shooting range, or drive a motor-car through crowded streets.

Brooding over his glass, Bobby still listened intently to the talk going on around. There was naturally a good deal said about the recent murder that had given Brush Hill a sudden notoriety on the contents bills of the evening papers. But there was also a good deal about greyhound racing at a track recently opened not far away, and in this connection Bobby was interested to hear casually mentioned the name of Wood, the Central Cinema door-keeper. Wood was apparently regarded as a knowledgeable man in greyhound-racing circles. Once indeed, a twelvemonth or so before, a tip he had given regarding an outsider had been justified by the event, and this was so strange, so rare, so unusual a fact, that it had established his reputation for ever.

This piece of information set Bobby wondering again why Mitchell had as yet apparently made no attempt to follow up the success achieved in tracing the knife used in the murder to the possession of this man. True, Wood's character was good; he had the reputation of being a steady, trustworthy person, but greyhound racing sometimes leads hitherto steady and respectable men into difficulties from which their very dread of losing their position and their reputation may lead them to take strange ways of escape. It was at least conceivable that Wood had thought to take advantage of the confusion and excitement due to the Beauty Competition to see what he could pick up in the dressing-rooms. Suppose it was like that, and Wood, knife ready to rip or force any troublesome purse or handbag, had been caught in the act by Carrie Mears? Then instant exposure might have been averted by an instant, instinctive blow, and Wood could be back at his post without his absence having been remarked.

A possible theory, Bobby thought, as he wandered out of the public house, leaving, to the bewilderment of all, his drink untasted behind him; and one that seemed to cover all the circumstances of the crime.

He was still deep in thought, weighing one theory against another and that against a third, when presently he found himself in the neighbourhood of the Maddox residence, between which and the Irwin house he had been alternating at intervals all day long. He turned a corner into the street where the Maddox house stood, and then, as he dawdled past it, he saw the door open and a man's figure appear on the threshold. To his astonishment, he recognized not Maddox, but young Leslie Irwin.

He seemed to be letting himself out, more as if he were an inmate of the house than a visitor. Interested, even a little excited, for this was the first hint that between the two young men there had been any intercourse of any sort or kind since the crime, Bobby drew back into the shadow of one of the trees that here lined the road. Leslie came down the steps of the house and along the garden path to the gate. There he seemed to hesitate for a moment. Then, one hand thrust deep into the pocket of the light raincoat he was wearing, though the day had been fine and dry, he pushed open the garden gate and walked straight towards where Bobby was standing. It was growing dark now, and Bobby drew back into the shadow made by the tree under which he was standing. He hoped to remain unseen, but Leslie stopped in front of him.

'I called to see Claude Maddox,' he said, with a kind of excited defiance. 'Anything wrong in that? He wasn't in, anyhow.'

Bobby thought it best to make no answer, partly because he didn't quite know what to say, partly because he saw that the young man was in an excited, wrought-up mood and needed careful handling.

'I knew you fellows were following me,' Leslie gabbled on. 'All day long I've seen you. Well, what have you found out, eh?' He began to laugh, a high shrill laugh with a note in it that Bobby did not like. 'All day I've seen you,' Leslie repeated, 'always there – not that I care.' He laughed again, or rather uttered a harsh and threatening sound that was but the caricature of a laugh. 'But you don't know what I came for, in spite of all your peeping and watching. And you don't know what I've got in my pocket, either.'

'What have you in your pocket?' Bobby asked quietly.

'Find out,' Leslie retorted. 'Some day you'll know,' he said, and swung away, and then came back again. 'Going on following me wherever I go?' he demanded.

His voice ran up and down the scale. He seemed not to have it under proper control. Bobby was half afraid, so threatening, so excited, did the other's manner seem, that a physical assault was coming. And to have to report to headquarters that he had got mixed up in a tussle with one of the suspects would not do him any good. Discreet and competent detectives are expected to avoid such mischances. But he braced himself for a possible attack, as he said, as soothingly as he could :

'Oh, well, come now, Mr Irwin, you aren't very complimentary, are you? If you had seen me following you all day, I should have been making a mess of my job, shouldn't I? As a matter of fact, I haven't been following you at all, and I don't think anyone else has been, either.'

'Just a coincidence, your being here, I suppose?' Leslie sneered.

'Well, hardly,' Bobby answered. 'I take it you realize we are pursuing inquiries in this neighbourhood? But no one has been following you, so far as I know. I certainly have not.'

'Expect me to believe that?' demanded Leslie, though in a quieter tone. 'Every detective's a liar – that's his business.'

'Yet it is the truth that is his business in the end,' Bobby answered gravely. 'If we are liars, though that is a hard word, we are liars only as and because we are servants of truth.'

'Truth? The truth? That's what father's always preaching,' Leslie cried, and again his voice had changed and grown wild and uncontrolled once more. 'Do you know why his hair's going white?' he asked. 'Going white every day – more white every day ?'

Now there was a kind of deep horror and amazement in his manner, as if he looked on things beyond belief, and Bobby made no answer. Indeed, for the moment he had the impression that he dared not speak.

'That's your truth,' Leslie said then – whispered rather, so low had grown his tone. 'That's your truth done that !'

'What truth?' Bobby asked, moistening his lips that had gone dry, so dreadful seemed the horror and despair in the young man's words. 'What truth?' he repeated, and his voice, too, he sank unconsciously to little above a whisper. 'What is it making his hair go white?'

'Yes, you would like to know, wouldn't you?' Leslie re-

torted, with his harsh cackling laugh – or, rather, caricature
of a laugh. 'Well, find out.'

He turned, and began to walk away. Bobby followed, the
thought in his mind that the boy was in no mood to be left
alone. Leslie did not seem to resent his company. Bobby
asked presently:

'What did you say you had in your pocket.?'

'That's my affair,' Leslie retorted. He added: 'Nothing
to be surprised at – about my going to Maddox's place, I
mean. We used to be always in and out. He had a key to
our door, so he could come in and mess round in the attic
when he wanted to. We turned out some jolly fine work, too.
I never had a key to his place, though. Our workshop was
in the attic, at home, you see. We did everything there.
That's years ago. I don't know why I'm saying all this. I
expect you think I'm mad. I'm not.'

'I don't think you're mad,' Bobby answered. 'But I do
think you're a bit nervy. It's no wonder. Been sleeping all
right?'

'Sleep?' Leslie answered, and again there came that harsh
cackle that seemed to mock the very name of laughter. 'I
just lie and listen while dad walks up and down his room.'
Suddenly Leslie paused and took off his hat. 'Is my hair
going white like his?' he asked. 'It might be.'

'Look here,' Bobby said, 'you take a tip from me – go and
see a doctor, and ask him to give you a bromide, or something else, to make you sleep.'

'No need,' Leslie answered, chuckling, and in the darkness where they walked, between the feeble glimmer of two
street-lamps, this chuckle that he uttered had a dreadful
sound. 'I've something already that'll make me sleep sounder
than any bromide. It's in my pocket now.'

'What do you mean?' Bobby asked, sharply and uneasily,
but now when Leslie answered it was in an entirely different
voice – soft and slow, as though a new man spoke. 'I loved
her, you know,' he said. 'We were going to get married –
Carrie, I mean, you know. It's funny to think the girl you

loved is dead – dead like that. Funny that you loved her; funny that she's dead; it's all funny, isn't it?'

'This is your street, isn't it?' Bobby asked. 'I think I remember there's a doctor at the corner. How about dropping in to see him? Wouldn't take a minute. A good sleep would make you a different chap altogether.'

'I know, but if I slept I should dream, and that's much worse. You haven't got a cigarette, have you? Thanks. Every morning his hair is a little more white than it was before – father's, I mean. Could you see that every morning and keep quite sane, do you think?'

'Not unless I had had a sleep,' Bobby answered. 'After a good sleep, a bromide – –'

'If you say "bromide" again, I'll slog you one,' Leslie announced, though quite without emotion. 'It's because he knows – that's why every morning – –' He paused, and, with a slow horror in his tone that shook Bobby to the depths, he said: 'To-morrow, most likely, it'll be white all over – white as snow.'

'Why?' Bobby found himself asking.

'I expect he's back home now,' Leslie said, paying no heed to this question. They went on a few steps in silence, and then halted opposite his home they had now reached. 'There's no light,' he said, staring up at the house. 'He can't be back. Mrs Knowles is out, too – her sister's ill or something; she goes to see her; just as well, too. Father's been somewhere preaching – hell fire and the wrath of God, most likely. Only there's things you'll risk it for. But I never heard of anything else. I had a grandfather dad was always scared I should turn out like. You know, dad always thought everything of me – I wonder why? But he did – nothing he wouldn't do.' The young man broke off what he was saying, and then, with a fresh note of horror in his voice, he muttered: 'I don't know what I'm saying. That's because his hair's going white the way it is. You watch it day by day, every morning whiter than it was before. And you know why.'

'Why?' Bobby asked, once more, letting the word slip dreadfully between his half-closed lips.

'Yes, you want to know, don't you?' Leslie snarled, with a sudden change of tone. 'Well, you won't – not from me. ... Trying to find out, aren't you? ... Well, I would put a bullet through you right away if I thought that would stop it ... only I know it wouldn't ... only make it worse. You want to know why? Well, because of me ... it's all through me.'

Bobby did not speak. He did not understand the young man's mood. It was plain some emotional crisis had him in its grip, and yet of the cause he could not be sure. Leslie went on, more quietly now :

'There's something dad knows – something he's found out. I can see it when he looks at me. He hasn't said a word yet, but he will some day – at least he will if I'm there still. Now he's found out, he is more sure than ever I'm my grandfather all over again. But he knows all the time, and you would like to know, too, only you never will.'

'Do you mean about Carrie Mears?' Bobby asked.

'I loved her, you know that?' Leslie said, still in the same quiet, abstracted tone that was such a contrast to his previous excited, almost hysterical manner. 'She had a way of looking at you that made you near crazy – quite crazy; only it was worse when you saw her look at other chaps just in the same way. I could have killed them – I felt like it. I expect they felt the same. She used to laugh when she saw us – she used to see how near she could go to making us lose our heads. Power, that's what she liked. That's why I felt I had to make sure, and I didn't care about anything else so long as I made sure – so long as I didn't lose her. Very likely that's what Maddox felt, too. Only, what would make him mad would be the idea of anyone else having her – he was always like that; it isn't so much he wants things himself, but he can't stand another chap having them. That's why she and I – – I don't know what I'm telling you all this for. I expect you think I'm drunk. Well, I'm not.'

'Mr Maddox told me he and Miss Mears were engaged,' Bobby said.

'That's just a lie – a silly lie,' Leslie answered. 'Just one of Claude's lies – if he couldn't get there first, he would always pretend he had, and lie about it, too, if he got the chance. How could he be engaged to her?'

'Was she to you?' Bobby asked.

Leslie leaned forward. He spoke with a suddenly renewed vehemence, though a vehemence more controlled than before.

'I didn't care what I did,' he said, 'so long as I made sure of her – you can't understand, no one could. I didn't care about anything else so long as it made me sure of her. Only then ... afterwards ... well, you know what happened. Trying to find out who did it, aren't you? You never will – never!'

He turned away sharply, pushed open the garden gate, and hurried through towards the house, banging the gate behind him as if to intimate that Bobby was not to follow. Bobby hesitated, not knowing what to do. He felt profoundly that the young man was in no fit condition to be left alone, and yet he himself had no right or power to thrust his company upon him. The tall, dark, silent house into which Leslie was now entering seemed to take on, to Bobby's excited imagination, a sinister and threatening aspect, and he made up his mind he would ask the doctor at the corner if he could possibly manufacture some excuse to call, even at this late hour. He turned away to carry out this intention and then he was suddenly aware of a movement in the shadow of the wall close by, between it and one of the trees that here bordered the road. Some man, it seemed, had been standing there and listening, and, as Bobby turned sharply towards this unknown, first he heard a soft, long-drawn sigh, as of an infinite relief, and then a low, uncertain voice that said:

'I thought you were arresting him. You aren't, are you?'

'Is that you, Mr Irwin?' Bobby asked, recognizing the voice.

Paul came forward – an old, stooping, shaken man, bare-headed – and Bobby's startled glance perceived that in his right hand, gloved in black kid, he held, incongruously, a brick lifted from the wall near by, where it had been lying loose.

And Bobby saw, too, that, where the light from the street-lamp near fell on his uncovered head, his hair showed white – white as snow.

CHAPTER XIX

FRESH CLUES

F OR a moment or two Bobby felt too bewildered to speak, nor could he keep his eyes from the brick Paul Irwin had been holding, or his mind from questioning what use it had been meant to serve. Unutterably changed, also, did the old man seem, as if he had passed, in these last few days, from a hale and sound maturity to extreme old age. And yet, in spite of his bowed form and silvery hair, there was still a smouldering fire in his eye that seemed as if it yet had power to turn to momentary flame; there was still a hint of power in his bearing, as though all was not yet decay. He said, almost childishly:

'I've lost my hat.'

But in Bobby's voice there sounded a touch of terror, of horror even, as he muttered, half to himself:

'What's changed you so?'

A moment or so later he added, this time aloud:

'Your hat's there – just behind you, on the ground.'

'Oh, yes, so it is,' Paul said, and stooped and picked it up. He continued, his voice no longer childish or shaken, but charged with an intense emotion: 'I thought you were arresting Leslie. I thought you were arresting the boy.'

'Why had you that brick?' Bobby asked. 'What were you going to do with it?'

'Brick?' repeated Paul, as if puzzled. 'Brick?'

'Yes. What were you going to do with it?'

'God knows,' Paul answered sombrely. 'I found it in my hand. When I saw you together, I thought you were going to arrest him.'

'Was that why you grabbed the brick?' Bobby repeated, quite convinced now that he had had a narrow escape of getting his head smashed in.

'I've been preaching to-night,' Paul said, 'at the chapel in East Street. They said they would get someone in my place, but I would not let them, for I needed help myself. Now they tell me I have never spoken with more conviction than to-night – never made them fear more God and His damnation.' He flung out his hand, and took Bobby by the shoulder with a grip that seemed as though it must make the bone crack. With a kind of fierce anguish, he cried out : 'What do I care what he's done? He's still my son ; my son.'

'What has he done?' Bobby asked, whispering a question whereto he in his turn dreaded the reply.

Paul stared at him without replying, then turned and walked a step or two away and back again . Once more his mood had changed, and now he spoke quite calmly.

'Nothing at all,' he said, 'that I am not to blame for. Nothing that is not my fault – all my fault.'

'What is it you mean?' Bobby asked again, but Paul shook his head.

'I told you before,' he said, 'didn't I? I have nothing to say – nothing.'

'Not even why you had that brick in your hand?' Bobby asked, pointing to it.

'I thought, at first, you were arresting him,' Paul answered. 'You see, he is my son – my son Leslie – and nothing makes any difference to that, does it?'

'So you were going to smash my head in if I had been going to arrest him?' Bobby asked again. 'Well, if you had, what good do you think it would have done?'

But at that Paul laughed, suddenly and harshly.

'You don't think,' he said, 'you only feel. Afterwards, you find something's happened. That's often the way things do happen.'

'Oh, is it?' grumbled Bobby. 'I suppose you mean that's how it happened at the Central Cinema the other night?'

'No, I don't,' Paul retorted. 'I don't mean that at all, and Leslie's innocent – innocent.'

'There's not much doubt you know he's guilty,' Bobby

countered, 'or why do you talk like this? Why did you think
I was arresting him?'

'That was because I saw you with him,' Paul replied. 'I
know you think he's guilty, but he isn't. He is innocent. I'll
swear that before God Himself, by any oath you like.'

'You aren't going the way to make us think so,' Bobby
said. 'Especially not by grabbing bricks to argue with.'

'That won't happen again,' Paul said gravely. 'It just –
well, something came over me; it won't again.'

Bobby grunted. He wasn't so sure of that, and, besides, he
could not help wondering if once before 'something had
come over' Paul Irwin – at a time when he was alone with
a girl in the office of the manager at the Central Cinema.

'If you want us to believe you,' he said, 'you had better
tell us what you know. It's quite certain you know something you haven't told us. That means you are hiding the
truth. So long as you do that – well, you must take the
consequences, and you mustn't wonder if we draw certain
conclusions. I wasn't arresting your son to-night, but I tell
you quite clearly that's likely to come – so long as you refuse
even to answer questions.

'Look,' Paul said, ignoring this, to which, indeed, he did
not seem to have been listening, and pointing to a window
above the house door, where a light had just appeared.
'That's Leslie's room. He is going straight to bed. Do you
know why? Because he daren't stay up – because we sit and
stare and never speak for fear of what we know.'

'Mr Irwin,' Bobby said, 'you're saying too much, or too
little – much too much, or else much too little.'

'I've been giving an address,' Paul explained, 'down there
in the little chapel in East Street. That started me, I suppose. Then seeing you with Leslie, thinking he was going to
be arrested – something seemed to go then. Leslie's innocent
– quite innocent – but you may have found out things
making you think he isn't.'

'Mr Irwin,' Bobby said again. 'You lost your hat to-night,
if you remember, when you picked up that brick you meant

to use if I had really been making an arrest. And I think there was another time when you lost your hat, wasn't there?'

'Yes,' Paul answered deliberately. 'That's right. I did. At the Central Cinema. And you found it. Well?'

Bobby did not answer. They stood there, still and silent in the dark night, for some minutes. Then, with an abrupt motion, Mr Irwin pushed open the garden gate.

'As I told you before, I've nothing to say,' he said. 'Good night.'

He went on towards the house, and for some time Bobby stood there, staring after him, thinking deeply, or rather with his mind so possessed by such a medley of dancing, changing, incoherent ideas as made him almost dizzy but hardly deserved the name of thought.

'Of course, they may be both of them mad – Leslie and the old man too,' he thought, catching at a theory he felt might help to convince him of his own sanity he was on the verge of beginning to doubt. 'Only, the old man knows something – something that's made his hair turn white.' In spite of himself Bobby shivered as he stood there with one hand on the garden gate, for he had been half-minded at one moment to follow Paul to the house. Indeed there was something strangely terrible in that mute witness of his whitened hair to an old man's agony, so that the very latch rattled again as the garden gate shook under Bobby's shaken hand. Frowningly Bobby moved away, resolutely turning his mind from that thought of terror – an old man's snow-white hair that had shown so short a time ago not so much as a streak of grey. 'The boy knows something, too,' Bobby muttered to himself. 'Something that's driving him half crazy. Does that mean one or other of them is the murderer and the other knows it? But then, what about Maddox, and why was Mitchell so keen on that silver challenge cup, and why has it disappeared, and why has the knife been traced to Wood, and what has Quin got to do with it?'

Growing only more and more confused the more he tried

to see reason and coherence in this whirling chaos of events, he went back to the local police station, and there, while the memory of them was still fresh in his mind, wrote out as full a report of these two strange conversations as he could contrive. By the time he had finished it was late, and he was given permission to go off duty and home to bed.

Night brings counsel, say the French, but morning found Bobby still as helpless as ever to pick out any meaning or significance from the chaos of conflicting evidence in which the case seemed so hopelessly entangled.

Only one point seemed to him quite clear – namely, that if he had in fact been about to place Leslie Irwin under arrest, then the papers this morning would have had another mysterious tragedy to record in telling of a certain promising young detective having been picked up with his skull smashed in by a brick from an adjacent garden wall.

'The old boy meant that brick right enough,' Bobby remarked, later on, to Ferris, who had just been reading his report. 'There's not much he would stick at where his boy's concerned – talk about a love drama, it would have been one all right, though no one would have called it that.'

Ferris was searching his memory.

'Didn't Mitchell say something about there being more kinds of love than one?' he asked. 'Perhaps that's what he meant.'

'Shouldn't wonder,' said Bobby. He added: 'I've heard of mother love, but this – this is father love.'

'Looks to me as if it accounted for the whole thing,' declared Ferris. 'Looks to me as if he wanted to stop his boy marrying Miss Mears, and that's how he did it. Anyhow, it's sure they both know more than they mean to tell if they can help it. If we could trace the knife to either of them it would be good enough.'

'Only,' Bobby pointed out, 'it's been traced to the door-keeper at the cinema instead.'

Ferris agreed, with a gesture of mingled despair and bewilderment.

'I know,' he said. 'Nothing sticks together in this business. I'm to see what Wood has to say to-day about that,
though. You're to come along.'

That Monday afternoon, therefore, Inspector Ferris,
Bobby accompanying him, appeared at the Brush Hill cinema, where they found Wood on duty as usual.

Cautiously, Ferris, a cautious and a patient personality,
approached the subject. Had, he asked, the mysterious seek-
er for a Miss Quin, by whom it was now probable had been
meant Carrie Mears, been seen again? Wood answered in
the negative – classic phrase indicating exactly the involved
and roundabout reply actually made by the door-keeper.
But he was keeping a sharp look-out, he declared, and he
was quite sure he would know him again anywhere, at any
time. But this assurance was not one that carried much
weight with Ferris, who knew that when shown the Scotland
Yard collection of photographs of criminals, Wood had
picked out two, of entirely different types – one of a man
known to have been dead some years, and the second of a
man who for the last three years had been enjoying the
hospitality of the country in a south-country gaol.

'Looks as if he was keeping out of the way on purpose,'
Ferris commented.

'Take it from me,' said Wood impressively, 'he's the man
you want. That's what I've said from the very start.'

'Well, go on looking out for him,' Ferris directed. 'By
the way, were you ever shown the knife the murderer
used?'

Wood shook his head. He had been asked about the knife
– he had given his assurance that he had never seen any
sheath knife in the possession of anyone employed at the
cinema, and certainly never in Mr Sargent's office. But in
the general excitement and confusion reigning that night he
did not think he had ever actually seen the weapon used.
At any rate he had had no more than a passing glimpse
of it.

'Bought a sheath knife yourself, a little while ago, didn't

you?' Ferris remarked. 'At Sadler's, round the corner, in
the High Street.'

Wood seemed a little startled, but agreed at once that he
had done so. He had purchased it for a nephew, due presently to join a ship in London, but at the moment staying
with his parents in Devon. It was a sheath knife of a type
much used by sailors. After buying it, he had put a good
edge on it, and then had locked it up in a drawer ready for
the nephew when he called for it.

'Let's have a look at it, will you?' asked Ferris casually.

Wood, very pale now, very uncomfortable, made some
pretence of searching in various drawers, but finally, under
questioning from Ferris, grown sharper and more imperative, admitted that it was missing. But he had only discovered that fact quite recently, and till then it had never
occurred to him to connect his knife with the murder. Indeed he still protested vehemently that, though he could not
account for its disappearance, he was certain it could not
be identical with the one that had been used. Ferris demanded sternly why he had not immediately reported a fact
of such importance, and Wood, stammering and by now
badly frightened, protested that at first he had simply never
thought of it – it had never entered his mind to mention a
knife he believed safely locked up in a drawer of his own
table, indeed he had not even remembered it. And when
he discovered it was missing, then, though he would not
actually make the admission, he had evidently been too terrified to say anything.

But he asserted passionately that it could not possibly be
the one used in the murder. How could it be, when he kept
it safely locked up? Ferris retorted that if it had been in fact
kept locked in a drawer, locked in a drawer it should still
be. But it wasn't. So where was it?

Desperately seeking for corroborative evidence, Wood remembered that on the night of the murder he had shown the
knife to a friend, who now kept a small shop near, but had
at one time been at sea. He rang up this friend, whose name

was Abbott, and when Mr Abbott appeared he confirmed
that the knife had been in a drawer Wood had unlocked to
show it to him.

'Asked me if I thought it was the kind of thing would be
useful on shipboard,' said Mr Abbott, 'and I said it was.'

'Why didn't you tell us all this before?' demanded Ferris
angrily.

'Wasn't none of my business,' retorted Abbott sturdily.
'What was the good, anyway? I suppose you don't reckon
it was Mr Wood did the girl in, do you? Him and me was
talking here, in this very room for that matter, when it must
have happened.'

It was pretty clear he had kept silent because he had not
wished to seem to throw suspicion upon Wood – a suspicion,
too, that no doubt he had felt quite convinced had no foundation in fact. But Ferris glowered at them both.

'Keeping back information,' he growled. 'Ought to be an
offence. What do you suppose we can do if people keep
things back? Serious, I call it.'

But Wood was recovering his courage now he found his
neighbour supporting him.

'Never entered my head,' he protested, 'it could be anything to do with the knife I bought for Steevie. If it is, then
it must have been pinched without my knowing. The chap
that was in here asking for Miss Quin, most likely. You remember?' he appealed to Abbott. 'He asked for a Miss
Quin, and I told him there wasn't any name like that on the
list – the fellow that said he had come by motor-coach.'

'Not much to go on in that,' observed Ferris, at whom
Wood had looked as if he felt he was offering a valuable
clue. 'Any number of motor-coaches. Now, if he had said
where it came from – –'

'He didn't say anything about that,' Wood answered. 'All
he said was – when I told him if he had wanted to see one
of the young ladies he ought to have been earlier, before
they started doing themselves up – that he would have been
earlier only the coach got in a bit late.'

'Not much help there, either,' grumbled Ferris. 'Lots of 'em come in a bit late.'

'I suppose,' asked Bobby, speaking for the first time, 'he didn't say what made it late?'

'Ran over some lady's pet dog, just as it started,' answered Wood. 'The chap said he thought they were never going to get off, along of the fuss she made.'

Ferris, a reserved and patient man, became eloquent. Bobby listened with sympathy, and now and again, when Ferris seemed to hesitate for a word, which was seldom, he supplied one. Wood gaped and cowered under the storm he had aroused. Abbott edged towards the door, but on the threshold paused to listen with an awed admiration.

· 'Heard nothing like it,' he said, in a thrilled aside, 'since a deck hand on the old *Eutropus* dropped a bucket of tar on the old man's shore-going togs the day we docked in New York.'

'What's the matter now?' Wood demanded, in an injured voice, when presently the storm showed signs of abating.

'Can't you see,' demanded Bobby, Ferris being still slightly hysterical, 'that gives us just the clue we want. It's a million chances only one motor-coach ran over a lady's pet dog that day, and you say it was just as the coach started. It ought to be quite easy to find out where it happened, and then we'll know what district to look in for this man you talk about. I expect we shall want you to go there for a day or two, to see if you can see him.'

'What about my work?' asked Wood, somewhat sullenly.

'I think, for your own sake,' observed Ferris significantly, 'you had better do all you can to help us now.'

His meaning was evident, and Wood went slightly pale again as he hurriedly promised to do all he could to help.

'Why on earth couldn't you tell us before?' Bobby demanded.

'Well, no one asked me,' explained Wood.

'It's like Mitchell says,' lamented Ferris. 'The things people know and don't tell is just about as bad as the things they don't know and do tell.' Then he turned sharply on Wood again. 'Anything else,' he demanded bitterly, 'you're keeping up your sleeve and never saying a word about?'

'I've never kept anything up my sleeve I knew mattered,' asserted Wood sullenly.

'About that knife of Mr Wood's,' remarked Abbott, from the door. 'It can't have been the fellow you were talking about that took it – I remember now. After he had gone, Lily Ellis came in to ask about a parcel she was expecting from a shop in the High Street. A boy brought it in just then, and she wanted to open it to see if it was right, so I picked up the knife, from where it was on the table, and give it her to cut the string with.'

'Did she give it you back?' Ferris asked quickly.

'I don't think so; I don't remember,' Abbott answered. 'The phone went just then, and I answered it, and then I had to call Mr Wood to speak. But after that I don't remember seeing either Lily Ellis or the knife.'

Ferris made a gesture of a new despair.

'That means,' he almost wailed, 'that now we've traced the thing back to Lily Ellis. This isn't a case, it's a nightmare.'

CHAPTER XX

THE HANDBAG FOUND

HOWEVER, Mitchell did not seem unduly impressed when this new development was reported to him.

'We knew already Miss Ellis had handled the knife,' he pointed out, 'as her finger-print is on it. What we need is proof who used the thing. As the case stands, it is still riddled with doubt. Half Brush Hill is whispering about the way Mr Irwin's hair has turned white since the murder, and the other half about Sargent's connection with the girl – it seems to have got about now they had been seen together in restaurants and places like that. Then there's Miss Perry's statement. It gives us valuable pointers, of course, though a good deal will depend on a cable I'm expecting to-day or to-morrow. And we've no idea yet what became of the missing handbag, or who took it, or why. Meanwhile, as soon as we can be sure what motor-coach ran over a dog that day, and where it happened, it must be followed up for all it's worth. It may mean a good deal if we can get in touch with step-father Quin Miss Perry told us about.'

'He must be lying low on purpose, that's certain,' observed Ferris. 'And why? – unless he's the murderer himself. That's what I'm coming to think. Miss Perry says he staged a sham suicide to try to get money out of his wife. Well, suppose he staged a sham murder, threats and all that, to try to get money out of his step-daughter, and went just a bit too far – so the sham turned into the real? There was a case the other day where a woman tried to stage a sham accident to get money out of a motorist, and it went too far, turned into a real accident – and a fatal one, at that.'

'It's a possibility,' agreed Mitchell, 'though still only one among a whole lot of others, and possibilities aren't good enough for Treasury counsel, let alone juries. For the present

we must just carry on. Owen, you had better stand by ready
to follow up as soon as there's a report comes in about any
place where a motor-coach ran over a pet dog the day of the
murder.'

'Very good, sir,' said Bobby, and, after he and Ferris
had left the room, he remarked to Ferris:

'Sounds as if Mr Mitchell were following up some fresh
line. I hadn't heard of any development abroad, but there
must be if he is expecting a cable.'

'It's all fresh lines in this affair,' grumbled Ferris. 'Give
me a nice simple straightforward case where a burglar pots
a householder, or a wife gives hubby a dose of poison to
teach him to keep his eyes in the boat. Then you know where
you are, but in a business like this – well, where are you?'

Bobby felt himself unable to answer this question, and so
made no attempt to do so.

'Mr Gilbert,' he remarked, 'you've heard of him, of
course – Mr C.K.Gilbert, I mean – said in one of his broad-
casts that a detective's first need is to put himself in the
criminal's place, so as to understand his motives, and then
he'll understand his actions, too. But how can you do that
when there's any number of different motives suggested,
and any of them may be the true one – jealousy, panic,
anger, theft, revenge, preventing a marriage, a quarrel,
blackmail, goodness knows how many more?'

Ferris only shook his head without answering, and departed on his affairs, while Bobby found a quiet corner
where he could sit and try again to form some coherent
theory of events that would fit the facts, and all the facts so
completely as to exclude all other possibilities.

He failed entirely in the effort, but fortunately had not to
spend much time on so fruitless an occupation, for soon a
report came in that one of the motor-coaches of the indepen-
dent Blue-Yellow line had on the day of the murder run over
a dog just after leaving the garage at Lowfields. Luckily the
animal had not been much hurt, but its indignant owner
had protested so volubly, and it had taken so long to pacify

her, that the coach had run late all through that journey.

To Lowfields accordingly, to pursue the investigation there, Bobby was promptly dispatched. It proved a small isolated village, consisting of a few cottages clustered about the twin foci of the community, the church and the pub, that ministered to man's two essential needs, the spiritual and the physical, and of an outer fringe of villas whereof the masculine inhabitants disappeared gloomily to London during the week (Tuesday to Thursday), but came joyfully to life during the week-end (Friday to Monday), when, with enormous gravity, they drove little balls round and round what once had been bits of the local common, a flourishing poultry farm, a field or two of grain or pasture, till all had been turned to nobler uses.

As Lowfields could proudly boast that the nearest railway station was five miles distant, and as the Blue-Yellow coach service was neither frequent nor rapid, the district had been spared that invasion from London which has done so much to spoil the countryside – at least, saved from all save those who could afford a car, or preferably two, the six-cylinder for the head of the family, and the little runabout held in aid. So during the week (Tuesday to Thursday) one saw a long procession of these little runabouts, conveying their drivers to those mysterious offices in the City whence flowed, in equally mysterious fashion, that stream of cash which permitted the soul-shaking activities of the week-ends (Friday to Monday); this stream of little runabouts being presently followed by another stream of stately six-cylinders, directed, for their part, towards those once-again mysterious operations known as 'shopping' or 'calls.' But, for the aboriginal inhabitants, means of communication were still infrequent, slow, and a trifle uncertain.

Indeed Lowfields occupied so remote and hidden a position, most probably even the Blue-Yellow coaches would never have found it out but for the fact that a friend of the private secretary of the managing director had had for sale a piece of land in the village extraordinarily suitable for

the building of a garage for the company's coaches. The
private secretary had so discreetly and so skilfully crabbed
all other suggestions that in despair the managing director
had suggested Lowfields as a possible, but unlikely, alter-
native, and, finding considerable opposition expressed, had
thereupon developed his well-known strength of character
– 'pig-headed obstinacy,' it had been called – that by sheer
immovability of disposition had bullied success itself into
acquiescence. So his worn-out colleagues on the Blue-Yellow
board had also acquiesced, and at Lowfields a garage and
offices were duly established.

They had proved inconvenient and a cause of delay and
waste of time, so that other garages and offices had to be
established elsewhere, but they still functioned, and to
these Lowfields offices – now in part used as store-rooms –
Bobby forthwith proceeded on his arrival in the village on
the motor-cycle the paucity of means of communication had
enabled him to secure permission to employ.

The office was in charge of two young ladies, neither of
whom, however, could provide him with any information
concerning any person named Quin. Six months' residence
in Lowfields had given them jointly and severally an intimate and comprehensive knowledge of the affairs of all
the inhabitants of the village, and also a knowledge still
more intimate and comprehensive of the inhabitants of the
outer fringe where was practised the double life divided
between the City and the links, but neither the name itself,
nor the somewhat vague personal description that was all
Bobby could offer, awoke in them any response.

'No one like that here,' they declared, in turn.

The incident of the run-over dog, however, they both
remembered clearly. It seemed, indeed, a landmark in
recent Lowfields history, and they agreed that the driver
and conductor of the coach might possibly remember something about their passengers on that special trip. No doubt
the accident had produced much comment and converse,
and it might even have established sympathetic relations

between the worried conductor and passengers equally annoyed by the delay caused by the dog owner's loud protests. Fortunately the coach in question was due back soon in Lowfields from its morning trip, and so Bobby repaired to the village inn for refreshment, and in a further judicious search for information that produced only confirmation of the fact that no one named Quin was known in the neighbourhood.

But Bobby's luck proved better when presently the coach came in, for the conductor, a man named Dickson, remembered the incident perfectly, and remembered, too, that one passenger had seemed specially impatient over the delay. On arrival in Town he had complained again that he had been made late for the business that he had come up on. And not only did the vague description Dickson gave tally more or less with the vague descriptions Bobby already possessed, but also Dickson remembered that this passenger had inquired the best way to get to Brush Hill, and had been advised what bus to take.

'He came back with us on our last trip,' Dickson added casually. 'I remember that special, because he gave me a lady's handbag he picked up under one of the seats; quite a swell one it was – crocodile leather – only funny, because there hadn't been any lady with us that trip, and, of course, the car had been swept out as usual. But there it was. He wouldn't give me his name and address, because he said he was going to France and then to Australia, so it wasn't worth while.'

Bobby fairly jumped, and he marvelled how often, when there seemed in front merely an impenetrable wall, suddenly a door would open. Of course, if this mysterious personage had in fact gone abroad on his way back to Australia he might have passed finally out of knowledge, but the reference to a lady's handbag he had found might well refer to that of Carrie Mears, to the recovery of which Mitchell evidently attached so much importance. But then that seemed to prove the unknown was certainly a thief, since the

story of the find in the coach was pretty evidently invented ;
and, if he were thief, was he not most likely murderer as
well? Only, then, for what reason had he handed the bag to
the conductor with his story of having picked it up in the
coach? It seemed an odd, indeed an incredible, way of
disposing of so incriminating a piece of evidence.

Feeling that he might be on the verge of the most important discovery so far made in this baffling case, Bobby
asked :

'What did you do with it – with the handbag, I mean?'
'Handed it in at the office,' Dickson answered. 'May be
there now. They keep things a day or two to see if they are
claimed locally, and then forward to head office.'

Bobby hurried off to the office, where the two young
ladies smiled him a bright welcome, wishing that every day
brought a chat with a good-looking young man as a change
from entering and adding dull, interminable figures. They
agreed at once that they had had a handbag, of crocodile
leather, certainly of some value, in their charge, handed in
by Dickson as found by a passenger in his coach. No, it
had not been opened. It had been forwarded that very
morning, as being still unclaimed, to the head office. There
it would be inspected, and, if it contained any clue to owner-
ship, that would be acted on.

'They don't let us open packages here,' one of the young
ladies explained. 'Afraid of what we might pinch.' She
giggled. 'Of course, when it's a handbag, we could open it
all right and no one the wiser, couldn't we, Tots?'

'Tots' agreed that they could, but added, seriously, that
they never did. Forgotten handbags were so common an
event, much traffic with them had killed all interest, and no
one ever wanted to open the things.

'Nothing ever in them,' she explained in her turn, 'except
just what everyone's bound to have -- cigarettes, make-up,
comb, and a little money they can't pretend you've helped
yourself to if you say it's the rule never to open anything
here.'

'Always as well to be careful,' agreed Bobby, and asked
leave to use the office telephone so as to inform headquarters that this might prove the lost handbag of Carrie
Mears they had all been so anxious to trace.

He was told, in reply, that immediate steps would be
taken to obtain possession of the bag and examine its contents, and there was even added a dry word of congratula-
tion on his discovery. Then, feeling rather pleased with himself and his luck, Bobby went across to the village inn for a
little more refreshment before starting on his return journey.
There he found the conductor of the coach, with whom he
shared a friendly glass in the hope that his recollections of
his passenger might grow clearer under the influence of
beer and further thought. But the conductor's memory was
not of a type susceptible to much improvement, and then the
barmaid serving them, who had heard part of their con-
versation, remarked :

'You mean the gentleman who was so cross because you
didn't start to time that day you ran over Mrs Hoskins's
pom? I heard him say he had walked in from Clement's.'

'Clement's,' she explained, was a small poultry farm
where they also took in visitors – 'did more with them than
with hens, if you ask me,' said the barmaid. They were on
the telephone, she added, and the gentleman could ring
up, if he liked, to find out if a Mr Quin was staying there.
Bobby did so, and was informed that no one of the name of
Quin was known. The only recent visitor was a gentleman
named Greggs, who had now left. Yes, they had his address.
He had asked for letters to be forwarded to him to a number
and a street in Brush Hill, London, and it was in a voice
trembling with emotion and excitement that Bobby first
thanked them for this information and then, ringing up the
Yard, repeated it to his superiors.

CHAPTER XXI

THE DEAD GIRL'S LETTER

Bobby's orders he had received over the phone in the Lowfields office of the Blue-Yellow line of motor-coaches were to report as quickly as possible to the Brush Hill police station.

Thither, therefore, he repaired, with such speed as traffic conditions permitted, and on his way he wondered much if at last a solution of the mystery was in sight.

Yet strange and suspicious as the tracing of the murdered girl's handbag to her step-father seemed to be, it was difficult to conceive that he could have had any motive for committing such a crime. There could be no outstanding cause of enmity between two people who had not met for years; there seemed no way in which their interests or desires could have clashed; it was unlikely that the girl had taken anything of value to the cinema that night with her in her handbag; the theft of it seemed, indeed, as aimless as the handing it over to the conductor of the coach appeared inexplicable.

Then, too, there was the further complication of the engagement-ring returned to the Regent-Street shop where it had been bought by Maddox. If that had been in the handbag, why had it been selected for removal and subsequent return to the shop, though the handbag itself had been given to the conductor of the coach? And if it had not been in the bag, how had it come into the possession of this man who called himself Greggs, but was probably, though even that was not certain, identical with the Quin Miss Perry talked about?

Bobby began to think his discovery had merely darkened counsel further, and told himself gloomily there was jolly little chance of finding the self-styled Greggs at the address left at the Lowfields poultry farm.

Absorbed so deep in thought he was, wonder must be he reached his destination without accident. But so it happened, possibly that special providence which is said to look after drunken men extending its protection this time to one drunk only with perplexity and wonder.

Superintendent Mitchell was there in person, he was told, on his arrival, and waiting to see him in Inspector Ferris's room. Thither, therefore, Bobby proceeded, and found talking earnestly round the inspector's desk, whereon lay a lady's handbag in crocodile leather, Mitchell himself, Ferris, and Penfold.

'Oh, there you are, Owen,' Mitchell said, as Bobby presented himself. 'Well, this looks like a step forward, even if only into a worse puzzle than before. The Blue-Yellow people had the handbag all right, and there was a package in it of two hundred pounds in banknotes – tens, fives, and ones,'

'Two hundred pounds,' repeated Bobby. 'Why, that's the amount that was mentioned before. Is it certain it is Carrie Mears's bag?' he asked.

'Got her name and address written in on the lining,' Mitchell answered, 'and a letter from her as well. We'll get it identified, as a matter of form, to make sure it's not been changed or anything. Miss Perry might be able to do that for us. But there's no real doubt.'

'Does that mean this Greggs or Quin is the murderer?' Bobby exclaimed. 'And robbery the motive?'

'If it was robbery,' Mitchell observed, 'Quin would hardly have deposited the thing as lost property, quite intact. It would have been bound to go back to Miss Mears in the end, with her name and address in it.'

'He may have got frightened, lost his head, in a panic, when he realized what he had done,' Penfold suggested. 'Then he played the fool. Murderers do sometimes; that's why they get hanged – sometimes. I suggest he tried to bully her into giving him some money, she told him to clear, he was flashing the knife around, to frighten her, and slipped her one in a temper. Then he grabbed the handbag and ran, and afterwards got into a panic and rid himself of it the first way he could.'

'If it was panic,' Mitchell observed, 'you would expect him to throw the thing away at any dark street-corner ; or, if he wanted to leave it in a bus, let somebody else find it. Can you imagine a murderer in a panic handing over the evidence of his guilt to the conductor of the coach he was travelling on?'

'He wouldn't give his name or address,' Penfold persisted, 'and, anyhow, he had the bag somehow, and that's the way he did get rid of it.'

'There's another thing,' Mitchell went on. 'Where did the two hundred come from? We know it was the amount she is said to have been trying to get, and apparently expected, but who gave it her? And when did she get it? Did she take it along with her to the cinema? Or did she receive it on the way? Or at the cinema after her arrival there?'

'Put it this way,' suggested Ferris, interposing suddenly, 'that Sargent gave it her. It's not likely if she had the money already she would bring it along in her handbag. It's not likely anyone gave it her on the way. So probably it was someone at the cinema. That looks like Sargent. We know she was trying to squeeze him. He had the money ready and passed it over. But perhaps he didn't get the equivalent he expected – written promise to leave him alone, or something like that, or letters – or perhaps they just started a fresh quarrel. He outed her, took the handbag, got what he wanted from it, left it in some corner out of the way where he hoped it wouldn't be noticed.'

'Leaving the two hundred in notes in it – if he knew it was there and had given it her?' interposed Mitchell.

'Never thought of the notes – too excited,' persisted Ferris. 'Just wanted to push it out of the way for the time. But Quin spotted it, knew it belonged to his step-daughter, opened it, found the money in it, and bunked off, and then had a scare fit and got rid of the thing the best way he could.'

'In my humble opinion,' declared Penfold, 'it's much more likely Quin did the job himself. Good enough to arrest him on, if you ask me.'

'It's always been good enough to arrest any one of the lot, if only it hadn't been equally good enough to arrest them all,' answered Mitchell. 'Only there it is; the evidence against one cancels out the evidence against another.'

'There's that letter,' Penfold remarked. 'Means a lot.'

'Yes. Only, what exactly?' asked Ferris; and Mitchell, seeing that Bobby was looking both eager and puzzled, picked up a scribbled sheet of paper from the articles on the table and handed it to him.

'It was in the bag, with the girl's other things,' he explained.

Bobby took it and read:

'DEAREST LESLIE, – Everything's ready, and I shall call for the ticket to-morrow. It's just wonderful to think I shall be in Hollywood in a week or two, and then you'll be able to come too, as soon as I'm a star and be famous as well. It won't be long, so you mustn't be impatient, because I only want the chance, and now I've that, everything will be easy. Don't worry about the pig thing. He's not a gentleman, and I'll tell him so now, too, and he's most awfully mean as well, and now I don't care any more I mean to tell him off proper. He's a beastly temper, but he never frightened me, and I don't mean to take any more lip from him, either.

'Ever so gratefully and lots of love,

'CARRIE.'

Bobby read it over carefully, and saw that Mitchell was watching him. He folded up the note and gave it back.

'Does that mean,' he asked, 'that the two hundred came from Leslie Irwin?'

'That's what we want to know,' Mitchell said; 'and, if it did, where he got it from.'

'Two hundred's a lot of money,' Ferris said. 'Where could young Irwin get it? Sargent, I say.'

'Who does she mean by "pig thing"?' Bobby asked again, and once more Ferris repeated:

'Sargent – fits him to a T.'

'What about Maddox?' suggested Penfold. 'Suppose she meant him?'

'It might be anyone – nothing to show,' observed Mitchell.

'Anyhow,' Bobby said thoughtfully, 'it shows she was on good terms with Leslie Irwin – that seems to let him out, doesn't it?' And he always remembered afterwards, as a strange coincidence, that even as he spoke a motor misfired under the window of the room where they were, so that they all started, and Mitchell said, with an unusual show of irritation:

'Those things ... just like a pistol shot.'

Bobby glanced at his wrist-watch, and noticed that it was exactly half-past seven. He said again:

'So far as I can see, that lets Leslie Irwin out all right.'

'If he really did give her the money, and that's what her "gratefully" refers to,' Mitchell remarked, 'I still want to know where he got it from. He had no money of his own, no salary, and apparently his father kept him pretty short.'

'That's what makes me think it was Sargent,' Ferris persisted. 'Of course,' he admitted, 'the letter seems proof she and young Irwin were on good terms, but it doesn't prove the money came from him. How about the money coming from Maddox, and his finding out she meant to double-cross him with Irwin? That would give Maddox a motive.'

'So far as it's a question of Leslie Irwin's innocence of the murder, I don't see that it matters where the money came from, or who provided it,' protested Bobby. 'That letter seems proof he had no motive for murder when she was inviting him to join her in Hollywood. I don't see that the money question is relevant.'

'It may be relevant to other things, or even to the murder

itself, as regards someone else,' Mitchell answered, slowly. 'I've been in touch with Mr Hansum, the manager of the local branch of the City and Suburban Bank, and he's coming along here if there's anything he can tell us.' He added: 'The Brush Hill Building Society banks with him.'

It was only a moment later when there was introduced into the room a tall, well-dressed man. He had, in fact, arrived by the car which had just announced itself by that loud back-fire one could so easily have mistaken for a pistol shot. Mitchell seemed to know him, and, greeting him as Mr Hansum, apologized for disturbing him so long after business hours, and Mr Hansum explained that by good luck he had chanced to be staying at the office, and so had been there when Mitchell's phone call came through and been able to have it attended to at once.

'These are the numbers of the banknotes,' he said, 'and this is the actual cheque on which they were paid out.'

Mitchell took the list of the numbers of the notes, and compared it with the numbers of the notes found in Carrie Mears's handbag.

'They correspond,' he said briefly. Then he picked up the cheque. 'For two hundred, payable to bearer, signed by Paul Irwin,' he said. 'Is the signature all right, do you think?'

'In my opinion, distinctly unsatisfactory,' pronounced Mr Hansum. 'The I, for instance, is much thinner than normal. Mr Irwin's I's almost cut the paper. There are other points as well. But they only show on close examination, and as I believe the cheque was presented by Leslie Irwin in person, it was quite naturally accepted without any very special attention. I have no doubt that I should have accepted it myself – from young Irwin, that is,' and Mr Hansum evidently felt that now he had cleared his staff from all suspicion of carelessness or lack of attention. He added: 'At the bank we all knew Leslie Irwin quite well.'

'Of course,' agreed Mitchell. 'Am I right in believing a special audit of the books of Mr Irwin's society is taking place?'

'So I am informed,' answered Mr Hansum cautiously, for he was of those who, by never running a risk, arrive at a sure and comfortable eminence. 'There is some question of amalgamation with another society, and a certified statement of assets is required.'

'Would Leslie Irwin have known that was going to take place?'

'I hardly think so. Mr Paul Irwin, the chairman, myself, and one or two others knew. But we were all pledged to secrecy, and Mr Irwin is very strict in his views, he never interprets any undertaking lightly. I think we may be sure Leslie Irwin would know nothing about it.'

'If this cheque is a forgery – of course there's no proof yet – but if it is, would it be likely to be discovered by this special audit?'

' I think that may be taken as certain,' declared Mr Hansum. 'Unless, of course, there is gross carelessness on the part of some of the staff engaged,' he added, as one only too wearily accustomed to take that possibility into continual consideration. 'Mr Irwin's attention would be drawn to it immediately.'

Mitchell asked one or two more questions of less importance, and then expressed profuse thanks for the valuable assistance given, and Mr Hansum expressed, on his side, his readiness always to do his utmost to assist the authorities. Then he departed, and, when he had gone, Ferris said:

'Well, now we know where the money came from, and how Leslie Irwin got it, but I don't see that it helps us much to know who did the murder.'

'It clears one suspect, I think,' Mitchell said, slowly and gravely.

'Clears him of murder by proving him guilty of forgery,' Penfold remarked. 'You know, that's a bit funny.'

'Nothing's proved yet,' Mitchell reminded him. 'We can't say it is actually proved till we know if Paul Irwin acknowledges or denies his signature.'

'He won't deny it, he'll acknowledge it,' Bobby said abruptly.

Mitchell nodded.

'I expect so,' he agreed, in the same grave tones. 'We must hear what he has to say as soon as we can. We had better see if he's at home. The sooner he knows his son is innocent of murder the better. Is he on the phone?'

Penfold said he thought so, and went to ring up, and, while the others were waiting, Ferris said:

'I suppose it's knowing about this forgery business has been making his hair go like it has?'

'If he knew about the forgery,' Bobby remarked, 'it might make him all the more afraid Leslie was the murderer, too.'

'Miss Perry told us,' agreed Ferris, 'the old man was always afraid the boy would turn out like his grandfather. Seems to have been some sort of suspicion of murder in his case, too. It would make the old man nervous, naturally – like grandfather, like grandson, so to speak.'

'He's made fear his master all his life,' Mitchell said. 'That's why he's been so strict with himself and everyone else. He's so fond of texts, pity he didn't remember there's one that says, "Fear not." The more you're afraid, the more the thing you're afraid of is likely to happen.',

'Put it this way,' said Ferris. 'He's dotty on the boy – these kinds of strict, bullying fathers often are. He finds out the boy has done a spot of forging, and he thinks he's still tied up with the girl and there's only one way of saving him from her – so he takes it. After all, his hat was there, in the room, and no explanation how it got there.'

He looked inquiringly at Mitchell as he said this, and Mitchell answered slowly, and with some reluctance:

'I expect Treasury counsel would think that good enough to proceed on. They could build up quite a strong case on all this – especially if Mr Irwin still refuses to answer questions.'

'He will,' observed Bobby, under his breath.

Penfold came back into the room. He had dialled Mr Irwin's number, but had been unable to get any reply.

'Well, we'll have to call round ourselves,' Mitchell decided. 'Better get in touch with him as soon as possible.'

'What about this Quin or Greggs, sir?' Penfold asked. 'It won't do to let him slip through our fingers again, and he seems a slippery customer.'

'He'll have to do a bit of explaining,' agreed Mitchell, 'but you'll have seen to that, Ferris?'

'As instructed, sir,' answered Ferris. 'Sergeant Jones is waiting at the address given Owen, and has orders to report as soon as Quin returns. Jones has rung up once, to say a man giving the name of Greggs, and coming from Lowfields, took a room there yesterday, slept there last night, and has been out on business all day. Jones has his orders to take all steps necessary.'

A car was in waiting, and therein they all now proceeded to Paul Irwin's residence. When they arrived, Bobby remarked, as they were alighting:

'Leslie Irwin must be in, anyhow. That's his room over the door, and there's a light in it.'

'Well, why couldn't he answer when I rang up?' grumbled Penfold.

The light Bobby referred to was the only one showing in the house. They went up the path to it, their feet heavy on the gravel in the quiet of the evening. They knocked, but there came no answer.

Again they knocked, and still there was no answer. Penfold kept his finger on the electric-bell push, and they could hear it filling the house with its shrill, insistent clamour, to which still there was no heed paid, though in the window above the front door the light still showed. Bobby went round to the back. The door there was locked, too, and there, also, he got no answer to his knocking. He even tried one or two of the accessible windows on the ground floor, but found them all securely fastened. He rejoined the others, and reported his ill success, and Penfold said crossly:

'Well, there's a light. They must be drunk or dead if they can't hear us.'

'You'll have to tell off another man to wait here till some-one comes, Penfold,' Mitchell said, when still more loud knocking produced no reply. He stepped back and looked up at the window. 'The light's still there,' he said.

'I think this is Mr Irwin coming,' Bobby said, who had heard the garden gate open.

They all turned, and saw a slow, stooping figure coming towards them up the garden path, and the light from a street-lamp near shone in the evening gloom upon a bent and silvery head. More slowly still, as if with an infinite reluctance, the new-comer crept nearer, and now it was a ray of light from the lighted window above that fell upon that old white head.

'Good evening, Mr Irwin,' Mitchell said, as the new-comer approached. 'We were hoping to see you. We've been knocking, but we couldn't get any answer.'

Paul Irwin offered no comment or reply. He might not have heard – he might not even have been aware of their presence. He passed through them and among them as though they were not there. In silence he opened the door with his key, and, except that he left it open behind him, he still showed no knowledge of them. He went across the hall, never so much as glancing back to see what they were doing, or if they were following, and entered the room, opposite, he used as his study. That door, too, he left open behind him, so that they also could come in, if they wished. He turned on the light, and sat down on a chair by the empty grate.

'I'm very cold,' he said, 'but there's no fire here.'

CHAPTER XXII

NEW TRAGEDY

MITCHELL, and the others with him, followed Paul Irwin into the room, and there stood for a moment, grouped and silent and a little puzzled. But Mitchell's face was very grave, and Bobby felt heavy upon him a dark expression he scarcely understood.

'Mr Irwin,' Mitchell said; and then again, since it seemed he had not even been heard: 'Mr Irwin.'

But the words might not have been uttered for all the effect that they produced. No sign came from Paul Irwin; no least movement did he make, but sat silent and utterly immobile. Penfold muttered impatiently: 'Drunk – that's what it is. He's been drinking.'

Ferris said: 'He's dazed – all in a daze. Something's happened.'

Mitchell moved forward, and laid a hand lightly on the old man's shoulder.

'Mr Irwin,' he said slowly. 'We wanted to let you know as soon as we could that new facts we've discovered seem to clear your son, Leslie, of all suspicion of any connection with the murder of Carrie Mears.'

Paul looked up slowly. It was as though the name of his son, and that alone, had penetrated his consciousness.

'Leslie?' he said. 'Leslie? ... You'll find him in his room at the top of the stairs.'

Mitchell glanced at Bobby and nodded. Bobby understood, and left the room quietly. Mitchell turned back to Paul:

'Mr Irwin,' he said. 'You refused to answer our questions before when I saw you, or to give us any information. That has hampered our investigation a good deal. Will you change your mind now we are able to tell you we are fairly well satisfied that your son is innocent?'

'Innocent? Who? Leslie?' Paul repeated vaguely, and then, with more vigour: 'What does that matter?' he asked. 'What do I care?'

The three men looked at each other in astonishment, and Penfold could not prevent himself from exclaiming loudly:

'You don't care ...?'

And Paul answered:

'He was my son. ... What do you care, innocence or guilt, or what he does, when he is your son? ... My son, Leslie.'

His voice had sunk almost to a whisper as he pronounced the last three words, yet to his listeners they sounded as though there cried aloud in them all the sufferings of all the fathers of the ages since the world began. So, as they listened, they were afraid, and they stood silent, looking at each other, till soon Bobby came back into the room. He had a pale and shaken air, nor did this surprise the others, for they thought it natural. He said quickly, and in a low voice, to Mitchell:

'Leslie's there ... dead .. .on the floor ... there's a bullet through his head ... he's been shot.'

Mitchell listened gravely. He appeared to hesitate for a moment, and then again laid his hand on Paul's shoulder.

'I think you knew that, didn't you?' he asked softly.

Paul made some sort of gesture that might have meant anything, and then sank again so deep into his own thoughts as to appear once more completely oblivious of his surroundings.

'Better leave him alone for the present,' Mitchell said. 'The shock's been a bit too much for him. Owen, you stay here with him for the present. Don't try to make him talk. Of course, if he says anything – but I don't think he will.' He added: 'You say young Irwin has been shot?'

'Yes, through the head – the back of the head,' Bobby answered, shuddering slightly as there presented itself again to his mind the picture he had seen on opening the door of that room at the head of the stairs.

'Did you see any weapon?' Mitchell asked. 'Was he holding anything?'

'I didn't go into the room,' Bobby answered. 'The light's burning, and I stood in the doorway. I looked, but I couldn't see any weapon of any kind.'

Mitchell and his two companions went into the hall, closing the study door behind them so that Bobby was left alone with Paul Irwin, who seemed still quite indifferent to, or unaware of, his surroundings. In the hall, Mitchell gave brisk orders. Penfold was directed to search the house and make sure there was no other inmate, and as soon as he had examined them to lock the doors of all rooms of which he could find the keys. Over the phone Mitchell gave more orders, and summoned the help he needed, and then he and Ferris ascended the stairs to the room where Leslie's body lay.

Help soon arrived – a doctor, photographers, finger-print experts, and so on – and all the routine of such an investigation was soon in full progress, and still Bobby sat silently by the side of the equally silent Paul Irwin, still lost, as it seemed, in the immensity of his own thoughts. Then at last Mitchell and Ferris came back into the study, both of them looking pale and tired.

'A bad business,' Mitchell said to Bobby. 'There's no sign of any firearm of any kind up there. The doctor says the muzzle must have been touching the head, just behind the ear. There was only one shot fired. It was enough. The doctor found the bullet. Point twenty-two.'

'That means murder,' commented Ferris. 'When there's no weapon found, what can you think but that it's murder?'

Paul, who had remained till now so silent, aloof, and still, it might well have been that his spirit had fled and only his body remained, inert and dull, turned with a sudden start, half lifting himself in his chair as he spoke.

'Murder,' he said. 'Yes, that's the only word. ... I made

him think God's forgiveness was hard to get ... he thought his father's would be the same ... as if I should have changed to him whatever he had done.'

'Mr Irwin,' Mitchell said. 'When did you find out what had happened?'

But Paul, sinking once again in the strange and dark abstraction of his thoughts, had no word of answer.

'Mr Irwin,' Mitchell tried once more. 'The doctor thinks death occurred about three hours ago. Is that right?'

Paul roused himself for just one passing moment.

'I have nothing to say,' he cried, loudly and clearly, and then, as if the effort had been too much for him, he suddenly collapsed into unconsciousness.

Mitchell was just in time to catch him and support him gently to the ground as he toppled forward from his chair. The doctor who had been sent for was still in the house, and Mitchell told Bobby to fetch him. Ferris, helping Mitchell, was aware of something hard in Paul's pocket. He felt in it, and brought out a small automatic pistol, point twenty-two calibre.

'One cartridge fired,' he said, examining it. 'Looks like it was murder all right, and the old man did it ... he believed the boy was guilty and shot him himself rather than see him hanged.'

'The boy was almost certainly innocent – innocent of murder, that is,' Mitchell said.

'Looks like his father didn't think so,' Ferris repeated. 'It's just what you've been saying all along, sir,' he added to Mitchell. 'People whose religion is two-thirds vanity, thinking how good they are themselves, and how bad everyone else, are ready to believe the worst of everyone, just as Mr Irwin was of his son, till he got to think shooting was better than hanging – thought it was a sacrifice probably, like Abraham and Isaac.'

'There's one thing to remember,' Mitchell said. 'Leslie Irwin was probably innocent of murder, but equally probably guilty of forgery. And most likely his father knew it.'

Bobby came back, accompanied by the doctor. He applied some simple remedies, saying he thought it was no more than a faint. Soon Paul began to show signs of recovering.

'He'll be better soon,' the doctor said. 'It's just the result of shock and strain. But I don't think he ought to be left alone to-night.'

'We'll get him to come along with us,' Mitchell said. 'We'll make him as comfortable as we can.'

'Meaning you are going to arrest him?' the doctor asked. 'You know, that poor boy upstairs ... with that wound he could easily have done it himself.'

'We've just found a small automatic in Mr Irwin's pocket,' Mitchell explained. 'One cartridge has been fired. I think, for his own sake even, we must keep him under observation for the present. But we'll do our best to make him comfortable.'

Paul himself raised no difficulty. He was still weak and dazed, and quite passive in their hands. The doctor, who seemed a little anxious in spite of his reassuring words, undertook to go with him and to make him up a soothing draught.

'He wants a good sleep,' the doctor explained. 'Sleep and rest, they'll make all the difference.'

They went off together, in the care of one of the Scotland Yard men, who had private instructions on no account to let Mr Irwin out of his sight, and when they had gone Mitchell turned again to a close examination of the pistol found in Paul's pocket.

'I wonder where he got it from,' Mitchell mused. 'Where's Penfold? Oh, there you are. Penfold, do you know if either of the Irwins held a firearms licence, or had ever applied for one?'

Penfold thought not, but went to the phone to make inquiries. He came back to say that no licence had ever been issued to either of the Irwins, or, so far as was known at the moment, had any application been made. He added that while he was at the phone the report had come through that

Mr Greggs had just been brought in by Sergeant Jones, that he had already acknowledged that his correct name was Quin, that he seemed in a frightened and communicative mood, and was he to be detained for examination?

'He is,' said Mitchell emphatically. 'All happening at once now, isn't it? Tell them I'll be along as soon as I possibly can. He was still examining the pistol, now with the help of a strong magnifying glass. 'There are some scratches here,' he said. 'Look to me like initials. Looks to me like "C.M.".'

'"C.M.",' repeated Ferris. '"C.M." But that's – –'

'Have a look yourself. See what you make of it,' Mitchell said. 'Claude Maddox's initials,' he remarked.

'Can it be his? Perhaps Mr Irwin got hold of it from him,' Ferris suggested. '"C.M." is what it looks like all right.'

'We shall have to see if he identifies it,' Mitchell observed. 'If it belongs to him, though, how does it come in? How does he come in for that matter?'

'Can it be Claude Maddox did the shooting?' Ferris asked. 'Mr Irwin knew his son was dead, and yet he had been out of the house and was coming back when we saw him. Do you think he knew Maddox did it, and had been out looking for him?'

'Anyhow, only one cartridge of that clip has been fired,' observed Mitchell. 'All the same, we'll go round to Maddox and see what he has to say. But, first, you had better ring him and make sure nothing more has happened there, since so much seems to be happening to-night. Don't let them know it's a police inquiry. Just ask if Mr Claude Maddox is at home, and if there's any truth in a rumour he met with an accident to-night.'

Ferris went off on this errand, and then Bobby appeared. He had been otherwise occupied, and had only just heard of the discovery of a pistol marked with what were believed to be the initials of Claude Maddox. Thereon, remembering his meeting on Sunday night with Leslie Irwin, and how he had seen him leaving the Maddox residence, he came to tell his story to Mitchell, repeating it now with an emphasis on some details that he had not at the time thought necessary for his report.

'It strikes me as possible now, sir,' he explained, 'that Leslie Irwin knew Maddox possessed an automatic, and had been to his house in an attempt to get hold of it – and had succeeded.'

'If that's so,' observed Mitchell, 'that makes it look like suicide again.'

'That's my idea, sir,' Bobby said. 'That night Leslie was in a very excited, hysterical sort of mood. I think one thing coming on top of another has been too much for him. There was the murder of the girl he was in love with just when he thought he had made sure of her, and then he knew he was suspected, and yet couldn't clear himself without confessing to the forgery by which he had got that £200. He felt that was bound to come out, and he couldn't face up to the idea of owning he had forged his father's name.'

Bobby paused, and said slowly, though more to himself than as continuing to urge his theory upon his superior :

'He had no trust in his father's love ; he did not believe he could be forgiven ...'

They were both silent for a little, and then Mitchell said :
'Your idea is that Leslie shot himself?'

'Yes, sir. I think, too, it is just possible he in his turn suspected it was possible his father had killed Carrie Mears. I imagine that idea was in his mind. I think he knew there was not much his father wouldn't have done to stop him from marrying Miss Mears, and I believe that thought was in his mind all the time he was watching Mr Irwin's hair going white with every hour of the day. Most likely he got the automatic that night I saw him, and, when the strain got too much, he broke under it and took what he thought was the best way out. When Mr Irwin discovered to-night what had happened, he picked the pistol up and put it in his pocket. The shock would be so great he hardly knew, very likely, what he was doing. He wandered off out of the house, and then he saw us arrive and he came back, still in the same dazed condition.'

Mitchell was evidently thinking deeply.

'It's very likely that's how it all happened to-night,' he agreed, 'but, if Leslie Irwin suspected his father was the murderer, I'm wondering if he was right. I'm wondering if that's what really happened, and if it is really Paul Irwin who killed Carrie Mears to save his son from marrying her.'

CHAPTER XXIII

MR QUIN TALKS

It was with a certain relief that – their work completed so
far as was possible for the time; the body removed to the
mortuary of the unfortunate Leslie, who so soon had followed
to the grave the girl whom he had loved; a constable placed
in charge of the house – they left behind the scene of this new
tragedy.

Mitchell, indeed, paused and looked back as they came
to where their car was waiting for them. For a moment or
two he stood still, staring, as though he challenged it, as the
dark indistinguishable shadow in the night to which now
the house had shrunk.

'More may be coming,' he muttered to himself, and to
Bobby, too, it seemed that the building stood there, tall and
straight and silent, like some sentinel of evil, bearing witness
of ill to come. Even Ferris felt something of the same influence, as of threat or menace that its dark loneliness
seemed to throw out.

'Just as well we didn't leave the old man there,' he said.
'Or most likely he would have done himself in before morning – enough to make anyone want to finish up.' As the
car started, he added to Mitchell: 'I phoned them your
special instructions that Mr Irwin was to have every care
and attention, but I couldn't quite say myself whether he
was under arrest or detained for inquiry or what.'

'Well, I suppose chiefly the last, so far,' answered Mitchell.
'I don't see my way very clearly at present.'

'No denying it looks bad,' Ferris went on, half to himself.
'Finding that automatic in his pocket the same way we
found his hat in the room where Carrie Mears was. That
would weigh a lot with any jury.'

'So far as this business to-night is concerned,' Mitchell

said slowly, 'I'm inclined to think it was suicide. There's
Owen's evidence that he had been to Maddox's on Sunday,
and it seems likely he got the pistol there. There is motive:
the shock of the girl's death; his knowledge he was suspected
and couldn't clear himself without confessing forging his
father's name; his dread of his father mixed up with another
fear that it was his father himself killed the girl to stop their
marriage; the emotional effect of watching the old man's
hair turning white and not being sure of the cause. I don't
think it's much wonder he crashed in the end. It's all such
a tangle of love of father and son, love of boy and girl,
doubt, fear, suspicion, theft, murder, all together. But what
I would like to know – what's worrying me, is, was the boy
on the right track if he really believed his father killed Carrie
Mears?'

'Miss Perry told us how afraid the old man was his boy
would turn out like the grandfather,' Ferris remarked. 'And
once a man gets religion, especially when it's fear that drives
him to it, well, anything may happen.'

'You mean,' corrected Mitchell gently, 'when he thinks
he has got religion, and made his God from it, instead of
his religion from his God.' After a time, he added: 'After
all, there's no real evidence except opportunity and a possible motive, plus a hat.'

'Men have hung for less,' grumbled Ferris, 'and what
made his hair go the way it did?'

'Can't put that into the witness-box,' Mitchell said, and
then, after a pause, both his seniors being silent, Bobby
said:

'I remember once hearing Maude Royden say, in a sermon, that when a member of her congregation came to her
and said: "God is telling me to do something," her first
thought was always: "Now what crime or folly are you
going to commit?"'

'It works that way sometimes with some people,' Mitchell
agreed. 'It's so easy to take your own wishes for divine –
and so convenient, because then you know you're right,

you and God against the world. If it got to be like that with
Paul Irwin, the whole thing's explained. Only, was it?
What do you think, Owen?'

'I think it might be that, sir,' Bobby answered, 'though I
hate the idea. Only, religion is such a big force, it may twist
you almost any way.'

'Perhaps because it was always fear that was behind him,
and fear is only another word for weakness,' Mitchell mused.
'I hope this fellow Quin will be able to tell us something.'

'My experience of religious folk,' commented Ferris, 'is
that there are some of them who are always sure they're
right, and never are – like my mother-in-law,' he added,
somewhat bitterly – 'and some who are never sure they're
right, but generally are.'

'You're saying the same thing as I did in another way,'
Mitchell told him. 'I don't like religion in murder cases –
complicates things so. Here we are. We'll have to see what
Quin can tell us, and then it'll be us for knocking Claude
Maddox out of bed to see if he can identify that automatic
– he won't like being disturbed so late one bit, but I think
we are going to do it all the same.'

Bobby knew Mitchell well enough to be fairly sure that
this determination not to wait for the morning to get the
automatic identified had some deeper reason than a mere
impatience. He wondered if it had anything to do with the
cable Mitchell had spoken of, since, so far as Bobby knew,
no one connected with the case, except Claude Maddox,
had ever lived abroad. As they were alighting, he managed
to bring in some reference to this cable, and Mitchell looked
at him.

. 'Don't mind asking questions, do you?' he observed, with
a touch of rebuke in his voice. 'Well, yes, it came all right,
but what it's worth now this has happened, I'm not so sure.'

They all went into the inner office, where Quin was waiting, with the evening paper, a good cigar, and a glass of
whisky and soda – all thoughtfully provided by the station
sergeant. With the appearance of Mitchell he seemed in-

clined to put himself more upon the defensive, but Mitchell knew well how to handle such moods. Mr Quin had heard of this fresh tragedy? No? Mitchell described it briefly, enlisted the other's sympathy and interest, and then went back to the earlier case. Not that Mr Quin was to imagine he was under arrest in any way. But he was known to have been on the spot when the murder occurred, and his inquiry for a Miss Quin must be taken to have referred to the victim. Further, the missing handbag had been traced to his possession, and it was known that he had returned a certain ring to the shop in Regent Street from which it had been purchased. In his own interests, therefore, it might be desirable for him, if he wished to do so, to furnish his no doubt satisfactory explanations that it was hoped would throw also light on this new tragedy. Naturally he was quite free to consult a solicitor before making any statement, or he would be perfectly within his rights if he preferred to say nothing at all, but in that case Mitchell feared it would be necessary to detain him in custody while further inquiries were made. If, however, he wished to make a statement, Sergeant Owen, an expert shorthand writer, would take it down in his own words.

Quin, who by now had admitted that that was his correct name and that Greggs had been adopted in the hope of avoiding the too-pressing attention of certain creditors, interrupted with the assurance that he was only too willing and eager to tell everything he knew. It had all been troubling him greatly. More than once he had been on the point of coming forward to tell what he knew. But then he had an innate dislike for all kinds of notoriety or publicity, or for any attempt to push his nose in where it wasn't wanted. Besides, he was engaged in certain very important and delicate business negotiations that might be prejudiced by any association of his name with a notorious murder (incidentally these important and delicate negotiations proved to be a somewhat hopeless attempt to float a company to engage in pearl fishing off the Australian coast). And, thirdly, it did happen that certain unreasonable people who considered that he owed them money might, if his name appeared in the papers, take steps to render themselves unpleasant – indeed, one of them had even gone so far as to make references to a horse-whip and a good kicking, and other such vulgarities. Fourthly, finally, and conclusively, he had no new light whatever to throw upon the problem of his step-daughter's death.

Mitchell made no comment upon the sufficiency or otherwise of these reasons, and Quin continued with what amounted to a re-telling and a confirmation of Miss Perry's story. Then he explained that when making inquiries about his wife, of whose death he had not been aware, and from whom he had evidently hoped to borrow more money, he had heard that his step-daughter, now living with her aunt, was competing in a beauty show she was expected to win, with the prize of a possible engagement at Hollywood. Since to Quin, as to many others, the mere whisper of the magic word Hollywood suggested ready, immediate, unlimited cash, the opportunity had instantly seemed heaven-sent for the securing of a much-needed pound or two – a born borrower, Quin had in his time turned far less favourable opportunities, in circumstances of far less desperate personal need, to profitable use.

'I knew she might turn out a hard case,' Quin explained, with the tolerance of one aware that it takes all kinds to make a world. 'Her ma was like that. Often she wouldn't turn up a penny till I showed I meant it – why, if you'll believe me, more than once I've had to put my razor to my throat to get as much as the price of a glass of beer out of her. But I hadn't thought of her changing her name – Quin being what she always went by. The porter at the door said there wasn't any Miss Quin there, and while we were talking a young lady came in to ask for a box she was expecting. A boy brought it along while she was asking, and she wanted to open it to see if it was all right, but couldn't get the string undone. So, as there was a knife lying handy on the desk near, I used it to cut the string for her, and afterwards, without thinking, I slipped it in my pocket, just as anyone might. Well, the porter stuck to it there was no Miss Quin, and I knew there was, so I thought to have a look round for her on my own.'

He paused for a moment to take a sip of his whisky and soda, and Bobby took the opportunity to make a note on a separate slip of paper:

'Probably means he wanted to get away with the knife before Wood discovered it was gone.'

Quin continued:

'It wasn't long before I spotted Carrie and the room she had. I can't pretend she showed any natural feeling at see-ing her daddy again – as she always called me when she was a kiddy. She did get as far as opening her handbag once, when I told her a single one-pound note might stand be-tween me and the river. But then she shut it again, and gave a heartless sort of snigger, and said: "Right-oh, make it the river, then." Her very words, gentlemen, I assure you, spo-ken to one who was as good as father to her, and had guided her baby steps and guarded her infant cradle, and the way she snapped her handbag made me sure there was more in it than she wanted to be seen – there's a lot in noticing little things like that. So when she said that about the river, I said: "Perhaps you would rather I cut my throat this min-ute," and I got out my knife and put it to my throat. Now, her mother, she could never bear that – never. If you were driven to the razor, it was good for something every time, no matter how little she had. But Carrie – you'll hardly believe it – hard as nails she was, and what do you suppose? I give you my word she snatched up a ruler from the desk and cracked me with it on the elbow-joint! I had to let the knife drop, and then she had the face to tell me all she wanted was to save a mess on the carpet, and if I didn't clear out right away she would call the manager and have me put out.

'Well, when a girl can be that hard to practically her own daddy, there's no good talking. So I took the dignified line

and told her it was all right, but she mustn't blame me for
the consequences, and I retired without another word, and
her with her hand on the bell, if you'll believe me. But I
made up my mind I would see what she had in that handbag made her shut it so quick when she remembered, and
when she came out to do her bit on the stage I just slipped
in to see if it was there still. It was on the table, and, for fear
of being misunderstood if anyone happened to come in, I
took it outside to have a good look; and there, first thing
that happened as I was crossing the road was that some fool
of a motor-cyclist nearly as possible ran me down. We had
a few words, but I must say in the end he did the gentleman
and gave me a pound note.'

'Would you know that motor-cyclist again?' Mitchell
asked quickly.

'Anywhere. You don't forget a man who gives you a
pound note when you're as hard up as I was that night.
Besides, there was a rummy thing happened after, with the
same man. I had had a shock with such a near escape, and
I felt I needed a little drop of something to put my nerves
right. There was a pub round the corner, so I popped in to
have a drink, and as I was coming out there was that same
cyclist chap pelting off down the street the way they do,
and as he passed I saw him, plain as could be, throw something into a dark doorway across the road. A bit funny, I
thought, and I went across to look, though thinking very
likely it was only an empty cigarette-case. But it wasn't.'

'What was it?' Mitchell asked, when Quin paused for
dramatic effect. 'The ring you took back to Regent Street?'

'That's right,' Quin answered. 'At the time I thought it
queer, chucking away a thing like that, only I thought perhaps he hadn't known what it was. You do chuck away
things without meaning to at times. Well, I thought what
to do, and then I took a peep inside Carrie's handbag, and
– well, I couldn't hardly believe it, a great fat wad of notes
there was. No wonder she had been in such a hurry to snap
the bag up again. Very awkward position for me, you'll

G

understand. That girl was every bit capable of declaring I
had meant to steal her bag, and I made up my mind at
once I would simply give it her back again, just as it was.
Besides, I could see some of the notes were fivers and tenners
that are easy traced. And then if I put it to her I had saved
her bag for her, which practically I had, and but for me
she would have lost it, I didn't see how she could turn up
less than ten per cent on that two hundred – you would do
as much for any perfect stranger who brought you back your
bag you thought you had lost. But when I got it settled clear
in my mind what was the right thing to do, and went round
the corner back to the cinema to do it, there was everyone
running about and excited, and crowds rushing up, and
people telling each other one of the competitors, Carrie
Mears, had been murdered.

'Gentlemen,' continued Mr Quin impressively, 'you can
see at once what a very awkward and unfortunate position
I was in, through no fault of my own – pure bad luck, and
all the worse for that. I admit I was scared so bad my nerves
got the better of me. Anyone would have felt the same. I
wanted to help, but I didn't feel I was called on to put my
head in a noose through acting too precipitate. There was
the girl murdered, and me with her bag with two hundred
in it in notes. Shivery, it made me, and my nerves the way
they were, and, acting on the impulse, before I knew what
I was doing, with my mind all a blank, so to speak, there I
found myself in the motor-coach going back home again.
But my nerves were all anyhow still, and there was a big
fellow sitting opposite looking at me in a curious sort of way
that made me go all cold. I was in such a state I was carrying poor Carrie's handbag under my arm instead of having
the sense to wrap it up, which just shows what my nerves
were like. I suppose he thought it queer to see a man carrying
a lady's handbag, especially one that was worth money –
crocodile it was. Anyhow, I lost my head a bit more, and,
seeing the way he looked, like a fool I told him a lady must
have lost it and I had just picked it up. One of the inter-

fering sort, he was, and he nodded to the conductor. A pity some people can't mind their own business, but most likely he wasn't honest himself and couldn't believe others were. Anyhow, up came the conductor, and I had to hand the thing over, and, to tell the truth, I don't know that I was so sorry to get rid of it, now my nerves were a bit calmer. And the ring the motor-cyclist chap had thrown away, I took back next day to the shop it came from, according to the name on the box. I felt it would be just as well to let people understand I was straight and honest through and through, even if, thanks to that interfering meddling fellow in the coach, I hadn't had the chance to prove it by taking back Carrie's two hundred same as I had meant to. And where the girl got all that money from, is another thing I should very much like to know.'

CHAPTER XXIV

ESCAPE

QUIN was now allowed to depart on his promise to return on the morrow to read over and sign the statement he had just made and that by then would be written out in due form.

'Probably, too,' Mitchell told him, 'we shall have to ask you to see if you can identify the motor-cyclist you told us about. Do you think you will be able to?'

'Know him anywhere,' asserted Quin, with confidence, and, since it was as well to keep him in good temper, he was driven back to his address in a police car. Then, when he had gone, Mitchell looked gravely round at the grave faces of his companions.

'It looks to me as if we had come to the end at last,' he said slowly. 'For what else can Quin's story mean, but that Maddox murdered Carrie Mears?'

'If he can identify him,' Ferris put in. 'If he does, at any rate that's proof positive Maddox was lying when he pretended afterwards he had only just arrived at the cinema.'

'What was the motive?' Penfold asked. 'Jealousy?'

'There may have been a quarrel, too,' Mitchell said. 'She was flinging him overboard for Leslie Irwin, whom Maddox had always rather looked down on. In her letter she said she was going to "tell him off." She may have sneered at him for not having been able to help her or get the money she wanted, and the knife was lying there, ready to his hand. It would be quickly done, and then what a magnificent bluff – to come straight back to the cinema, back to where the dead girl lay, as if he knew nothing. He didn't attempt to prove an alibi, he just let us infer it – nerve that took, but I think he over-strained it a bit perhaps. And he made mistakes. He told us Miss Mears had her crocodile handbag with her, though on his own showing he had not seen her since lunch, and there was no reason why she should have brought that special bag rather than any other. Miss Perry, you remember, said she was hesitating up to the last moment whether to take it. It was only a small point, and a jury might easily have accepted the view that it was a kind of unconscious guess that merely happened to be right. All the same, I saw it struck Owen, too, as one of those little inconsistencies that often mean a lot. Also it seemed inconsistent with Maddox's vain character and fondness for showing off that, if his story was true and he was really engaged to her, he should buy so comparatively cheap a ring – and a little inconsistent with her character that she didn't go with him to choose for herself. Even the shop assistant who served him was a little surprised. But if already the thought of murder was in his mind – if he had already made up his mind that, if he couldn't have her, no one else should, and certainly not the Leslie Irwin he had always looked down on – then the purchase of the ring, and the claim to an already existing engagement, would help a lot to ward off suspicion. And then, again, Owen reported that Maddox seemed nervous and uneasy about his display of challenge cups in his office; and, too, that display of challenge cups in an office suggested a good deal of vanity and self-love – the kind of character that can't put up with being outdistanced, or with open failure in any way. It struck me it might be useful to find out what there was about a sports cup Maddox didn't want seen, so I made an excuse to have a look in his room at his firm's offices, and found one cup had disappeared – if Owen's reckoning was correct. That seemed still more curious, and I sent off a cable. To-day the reply came that an Englishman named Claude Maddox had won a cup offered in a knife-throwing contest at a town up-country in the Argentine.'

'He threw the knife,' Penfold exclaimed. 'It was there, and he knew just how, and he threw it – that explains why we could never find any bloodstains.'

'That's the theory I should put up,' Mitchell agreed. 'I expect Maddox's nerve was beginning to wear thin – he had tried it a bit too highly, perhaps when he ran that bluff of coming back to where he had done the murder. Anyhow when he saw Owen looking at the challenge cups he couldn't help showing uneasiness, and afterwards thought he had better get rid of that one. That meant he had something to hide – a clear invitation to us to find out what.'

'She must have got them both pretty well worked up,' Ferris said musingly, 'to make one of them ready to commit forgery for her, and the other to sling a knife at her throat.'

'Beauty of woman,' Mitchell said slowly, 'it can make even a wise man mad, and neither of these, I think, were wise.'

'She wouldn't think much of the ring he bought,' Ferris observed. 'Not when she had two hundred pounds in her bag. He may not have meant murder at all, but only to show her the ring to prove he meant business, and then she could come and choose another, as he hinted in the shop. But if she turned up her nose at it when it came out, or laughed at him for being mean, that might have started a quarrel between them, ending in the knife-throw.'

'I don't suppose anyone will ever know which way it was,' Mitchell remarked, 'unless he chooses to tell himself.' He looked at his watch. 'Late,' he said, 'or early, according to which way you take it, but all the more likely to catch our man in bed. We'll push along, I think.'

This time Penfold did not accompany them. Instead Mitchell took with him Ferris and Bobby, and two uniformed men as well, in addition to the chauffeur. It made a full car-load, and, some hundred yards or so from the Maddox residence, Mitchell ordered a halt.

'It's our ringing him up with that inquiry about his automatic that's worrying me,' he explained. 'It may have made him suspicious, and if he hears a car at this time of night he may take the alarm.'

They completed their journey, therefore, on foot, and, when they reached the house, Mitchell sent one uniformed man to the rear, and put Bobby and the second uniformed man to watch the side windows.

'Don't want to take any risk,' Mitchell observed. 'He may try to make a bolt for it.'

These dispositions complete, he and Ferris went to the front door, and knocked and rang, though not loudly, for Mitchell had no wish to attract the attention of neighbours, though in fact one or two windows did go up, and the policeman on duty on that beat, hearing the knocking, thought it his duty to come along and see what was happening. Pausing under the nearest street-lamp, he stood there, opposite the house, waiting for possible developments.

Almost immediately a light showed in one of the windows to prove they had been heard. Then another light appeared, and Mitchell knocked and rang once more, though again quietly, for he still hoped to avoid attention, and then all at once from behind the house there broke a sudden clamour, a sound of scuffle and loud shouting.

'He's off,' Mitchell cried, and he and Ferris raced round to the rear, Bobby and the second uniformed man preceding them at full speed, and the policeman on the beat running from his post under the lamp to follow behind.

They found the back door wide open, and before it the first uniformed man, sprawling at full length, his helmet yards away, his truncheon half drawn, his head bleeding from a badly contused wound, he himself dazed and half unconscious. But he managed to gasp out something about 'a barefooted man in pyjamas,' and 'landed me one before I knew it,' and, when he heard that, Mitchell lost no time, but dashed into the house, where the inmates were now running about in a state of considerable agitation and alarm.

'I'm a police officer. Where's the phone?' he demanded, and, finding it, issued at once quick far-reaching orders so that almost simultaneously, so ready was the organization, so smoothly did it work, the majority of the London police were keenly on the look-out for 'a bare-footed man in pyjamas.'

'Won't be long before we have him,' Mitchell thought, with satisfaction. 'That is, unless he means to do himself in, and he'll hardly have time even for that.'

Satisfied that the net had been spread so widely and so swiftly that a quarry so well-marked as 'a barefooted man in pyjamas' could not escape it for long, Mitchell went back to where the injured constable was receiving first aid from both his colleagues – the man on the beat, that is, and the other uniformed man, both of them anxious to secure a little practice in first aid, and both of them getting very much in each other's way.

'Came at me like hell and laid me out and gone before I knew nothing hadn't happened,' confessed the slowly recovering constable, an elderly man of the old school. 'I saw a window go up, and I watched out, ready for him if he jumped, and then bang went the door and out he comes all in one jump, so he was on me before I knew it. In pyjamas he was, and something the light shone on like a pistol, or a knife, in one hand and a spanner in the other – a whopping big one – and bare feet. Just one jump he made, and on me like – like hell,' said the constable, whose stock of metaphors seemed limited, 'and laid me out before I knew it, and I don't believe Jack Petersen himself or no one wouldn't have caught it just the same, that quick he was, and one over the head before you knew it, and down away through the garden there like – like' – he searched his mind for a moment, and finding the *mot juste* at last – 'like hell,' he declared.

'Well,' commented Ferris, 'he won't get far, that's one thing – not like that; not in bare feet and pyjamas. Even if no alarm had gone out, the first man who saw him would want to know what was up.'

On that, indeed, they were all agreed, as on the obvious, for what chance had, in fact, a man at that time of night, dressed only in pyjamas, without shoes even, of avoiding arrest or notice for long?

Mitchell went back into the house, where there now had to be carried through the always painful and distressing task of explaining to incredulous, bewildered women that one of their menfolk was suspected of crime. Though Mrs Garvie, Claude's sister, did not show much surprise.

'It's that girl – that Carrie Mears,' she said at once. 'It's been all her doing from the very start.'

'Do you know anything about that?' Mitchell asked her. 'You understand, we are police officers, inquiring into her murder.'

'All I know is she drove him mad, playing with him and leading him on and not meaning it,' Mrs Garvie retorted. 'It's all been through her from the very start.'

It was quite evident she thought she was defending her brother, and did not in the least realize that she was implicating him more deeply by showing adequate motive. Mitchell said:

'Any statement you can make, any information you can give us, we shall be very glad to have. If the case proceeds to trial, you will probably be asked to give evidence. May I see Mr Maddox's room now?'

This suggestion of taking a statement from her, and of her having to give evidence at a possible trial, silenced Mrs Garvie very effectually, as, indeed, Mitchell had expected it would. In silence she led the way upstairs to the room her brother had occupied. The disarranged bed, the clothing lying about the floor, the general disarray – all showed in what haste and panic he had fled. In one corner of the room stood a writing-table, whereof the drawers were locked. One drawer looked as if an attempt had been made to force it open, and when Mitchell asked for the keys to the drawers none could be found. A maid, who now had appeared, wide-eyed and excited, obviously quite enjoying this dramatic interlude in the dailiness of daily life, volunteered the information that, hearing a noise at the door and concluding immediately that the house must be on fire, she had rushed down from her own room on the floor above, and had opened 'Mr Claude's' door to give him the alarm. But he was already awake and up, she said, and banging at his desk, trying to get it open. When she called to him, he turned round and rushed past her.

'Did you say anything to him?' Mitchell asked.

'I told him it was the police,' she answered, 'and the house must be on fire. When I was woke with the noise, I looked out of the window, and I saw a policeman, quite plain, under the lamp.'

'Did he say anything?' Mitchell asked, resignedly accepting the bad luck that had brought the man on the beat on the scene at the very moment best calculated to spoil the plan of operation.

'No,' she answered. 'He just rushed past and downstairs like mad – nearly knocked me over, he did.'

'What was he using to try to open the drawer?'

'He was banging away at it,' she answered, 'frantic-like, if you know what I mean, I think it was the ruler he had, and he threw it down and made a sort of run at me when he saw me, and then he seemed to see his keys on the table behind a book. He stopped, grabbed them quick-like, and I said the police was here and was it fire, and he never answered, but he looked awful, like a dead man come alive, but the grave still with him, and he rushed away, nearly knocking me down, so you would have thought he didn't dare stop another minute.'

'I don't suppose he did,' Mitchell observed grimly. 'Not after you told him police were here.'

At a sign from him Bobby picked up the indicated ruler from the floor. It showed plain signs of having just been put to violent use, and it fitted well enough the marks made on the still-locked drawer, though evidently it was far too light a thing to have been of much help in the attempt to break the drawer open.

'Seems,' remarked Mitchell, 'he couldn't put his hand at once on his keys, in his panic and excitement, so he grabbed the first thing he could to try to get the drawer open, and couldn't manage it. Then, as he was rushing off, he saw the keys, where they had been all the time lying on the table.

I suppose he didn't look there because it was the natural
place for them. Evidently the keys were what he had in his
hand that our man saw the light shining on and took for a
pistol or a knife – lucky for him it was keys. And then, somewhere in the house, he picked up the spanner he used in
escaping.'

Indeed further evidence showed that a spanner had been
left lying in the hall the night before, and later on it was
discovered in the garden, where Maddox had evidently
thrown it away after using it to knock out the unlucky uniformed man.

But that was later, and now Mitchell was chiefly occupied
in getting open the locked drawer. When he succeeded,
there was found within a passport and a considerable sum
of money in French, English, and Italian notes.

'All ready for a getaway,' Mitchell commented, 'only we
came a bit too suddenly. He lost his head when he heard
police were at the door – couldn't find his keys – couldn't
get the drawer open – had to leave it.'

'His wallet is here, in his coat pocket,' Bobby said. 'About
ten or twelve pounds in it.'

Mitchell thought a moment:

'He has left his money and his clothes behind him, he is
in pyjamas, without even shoes, barefooted, and the alarm
was given within two minutes of his escape,' he said slowly.
'Well, I think we can be sure he hasn't one chance in a
million – one chance in a billion, for that matter – of escaping. We shall have him before twelve hours are over – before
it's even morning, most likely.'

And Ferris, and Bobby, and, in fact, all the police force
of London, were all of the same clear and confident opinion.

CHAPTER XXV

DISAPPEARANCE

BUT this assumption proved unfounded. Yet it had seemed reasonable enough – even certain. The fugitive had had scarcely five minutes' start. He was without clothes or money – barefooted even. It seemed impossible he could evade arrest for more than an hour or two. Yet it was as though he had stepped off the planet altogether. No one had seen him; no one had heard of him; not even so much as the hint of a rumour came through of any glimpse of a barefooted man in pyjamas having been had anywhere by anyone that night.

The newspapers, seeing the chance of a popular sensation, took it up, and demanded, in huge headlines: 'Where is the barefooted man in pyjamas?' For a few days it raged as a popular catchword – the standard joke of the season. The fact that a human life was in question, became forgotten or ignored. The music-halls jested about it; three popular songs, with the refrain, 'Have you seen a barefooted man in pyjamas?' scored an enormous success, and one found its way into Mr C. B. Cochran's latest – and best – revue; gay young sparks began to lean out of sports cars to beckon traffic police and demand of them the same question, speeding away before outraged law could assert itself; one of the Sunday papers published an article by the most popular writer of the day, torn reluctantly from his garden, on 'Celebrated Pyjamas of History'; a daily paper offered a reward of £1,000 for the solution of the mystery, and one of its rivals at once offered a counter-reward of £3 a week for life, a new seven-roomed house, furnished by Mage, and a free ticket for a month's cruise in the summer; a third filled its front page with an enormous photograph (exclusive) of Maddox, and most of the rest of that issue with specimens of his handwriting and of his (alleged) finger-prints; the correspondence columns of all the papers alike swarmed with letters offering every kind of solution, possible and impossible; a lecture on 'Dematerialization,' at the Albert Hall, by a well-known student of the occult, 'with special reference to Ancient Wisdom in Modern Crime,' achieved a resounding success – a hint that tidings might presently be received of the sudden appearance of a barefooted man in pyjamas in a monastery on a peak in Tibet causing unparalleled excitement. In fact it was the biggest sensation known for years – it even spread abroad; several prominent Nazis expressed their firm belief that the Jews were at the bottom of the whole thing; several French newspapers sent over special correspondents – all eminent men of letters – to report on this strange manifestation of '*l'hystérie Anglaise*'; the Italian Press congratulated itself warmly on the fact that in the Corporate State such things did not happen, the Duce never having given permission; and even America admitted that Europe, like nature, was creeping up, though still with a long way to go before attaining real gangster levels.

As for Superintendent Mitchell, he openly confessed himself puzzled, baffled, and bewildered as he never remembered having been before in all his long experience.

'The thing's not in nature,' he declared. 'It was three in the morning, and within ten minutes every man of ours on duty was on the look-out for him. Nothing could be much more conspicuous than a man in pyjamas with bare feet. The merest glimpse of him would be remembered. But not a soul seems to have seen him. He had no cash, apparently, no means of getting clothing, and yet he's vanished, like your money when you back the favourite and nothing left even to show it was ever there.'

After a long pause, he added:

'It's against all reason, sense, and possibility, and yet there must be an explanation if only we could think of it.'

The joke began to pall, though the mystery deepened. Mr C. B. Cochran tried out on Manchester another revue –

his newest and his best – without a single reference to the barefooted man in pyjamas; the stream of royalties to the authors of the three popular songs with that refrain dried up, as it were, in an hour; the newspapers discovered other and newer sensations; the French papers recalled the eminent men of letters who had been acting as their correspondents; and prominent Nazis hinted darkly at an Israelite conspiracy to hush up the truth, which was probably, they declared, connected with a case of ritual murder.

The general opinion turned to a certainty that Maddox had committed suicide, though, in that case, what had become of his body still remained for explanation. Besides, how, in that brief ten minutes before the hunt became general, suicide could have been carried out in such a manner as to evade observation at the time, or discovery of the body afterwards, seemed utterly inexplicable. Nevertheless, every empty or unoccupied house for miles around was searched without result, except that here or there unlucky vagabonds, who had found a cheap resting-place, were duly routed out. As for the Thames, inconceivable that a man in that state of undress could have traversed the four miles from Brush Hill to the river without being seen.

'Suicide won't do for an explanation,' declared Mitchell. 'Somehow or another he must have got away – found food, shelter, money – and that within ten minutes, and all within a radius of about a mile or so. Beats me.'

'Could he have met a pal in a car, and been whisked off right into the country?' suggested Ferris.

Such a coincidence, had it happened, would have bordered on the miraculous. It would have required not only an accidental meeting at three in the morning with a friend able to help, but also required that that friend should be prepared to risk the severe penalties incurred by those assisting fugitives from justice.

Nevertheless the possibility was thoroughly considered. Every friend and acquaintance of Maddox who could be traced was asked to account for his movements on that night.

All could do so satisfactorily, but, all the same, all were kept under observation – without any result. Nor does the passage of a motor-car through a quiet suburban district at three in the morning easily escape observation, yet nobody, certainly none of the police on night duty, seemed to have noticed one. Nor was there a boarding-house, hotel, or lodging-house within reasonable distance that escaped questioning.

Every effort failed completely. The mystery deepened. Yet it was a search not for a needle in a haystack, but for a haystack itself, or, at least, for an object that should have been as conspicuous. But in spite of failure, so complete and so bewildering, the search still raged – there is no other word for it; Mitchell's perseverance was of that kind. The more hopeless it seemed, the more bewildering the utter lack of result appeared to be, the more determinedly he drove on his assistants to fresh effort.

'Because,' he explained, 'there must be some explanation how a man without clothes or money, without even shoes on his feet, could vanish in ten minutes, and, if there is an explanation, it must be possible to find it, and we've to go on trying till we do.'

But still the days passed and nothing was discovered. The adjourned inquest on Carrie Mears was held, and resulted in a verdict of 'Wilful Murder' against Claude Maddox, with a rider to the effect that the police should be urged to effect his arrest without delay.

It was a rider little appreciated at Scotland Yard, where everyone was doing double work, and the word 'leave' had become a mockery and a byword, so that men hearing it spoken would go to the dictionary to look it up and find out what it meant. A poor revenge, indeed, was attempted by the circulation of a story that the jury, used to investigating motor-car fatalities, had added a further rider, from force of habit, exonerating the murderer from all blame, but this was only a passing consolation.

The next day another inquest was held – that on Leslie

Irwin – and attracted more interest, for many rumours had been in circulation. However the police made it plain that their investigations inclined them to accept Paul Irwin's story, and he himself told it simply and frankly in the witness-box, with little visible trace of emotion, and with a complete recovery from his first collapse to his normal complete self-control. In effect his statement was that his son had been very depressed over recent events, and was moreover probably aware that the forgery of which he had been guilty was known to his father.

'On that night,' Mr Irwin said, 'he made what I took to be a reference to the forged cheque. He did not wait for me to answer him. He went immediately to his room. I was following, when I heard the shot. I went into the room, and found him dead. I picked up the pistol, and went out to get a doctor, I think. There was no one else in the house. Our housekeeper, Mrs Knowles, was spending most of her nights, just then, with a sick relative. I think some minutes passed before I did anything at all after I found out what had happened, but I don't remember very clearly. I do remember seeing a motor-car passing and recognizing police in it, and I suppose I thought help had come, and I went back to the house to tell them. I am afraid I don't remember details very clearly.'

The evident truth and simplicity of the statement won credence, and it was supported both by the doctor's evidence and by Bobby's that accounted for the possession by the dead boy of Claude Maddox's pistol. Without hesitation the jury returned a verdict of 'Suicide During Temporary Insanity,' and added a rider expressing sympathy with the bereaved father.

All this time the search for Maddox still continued, without the least success, till a day or two after the inquest on Leslie a coffee-stall keeper on the Embankment came forward to say he believed he had recognized Claude Maddox in a customer who had purchased coffee and sandwiches at his stall one night.

'Noticed him first,' explained the coffee-stall keeper, to Bobby, who had been sent post-haste to investigate, 'along of his doing himself well – mightn't have had anything to eat for a week of Sundays. Of course, in a manner of speaking, I get all sorts – toffs what thinks it's seeing life to have a cup of coffee, and coves what's had nothing since the day before, and now only enough for a coffee and bun. But this fellow was eating solid, and all the best, and he give me a pound note to change, so he wasn't hard up, and I wondered why he didn't go to the Corner House with the slap-up swells. Then I noticed the suit he had on – grey tweed lounge it was – seemed too small for him. Tight it looked, and his arm sticking out so you saw it half-way up to his elbow, and then the pound note he gave me was that clean it looked as if it had come out of the bank that day almost. So with one thing and another, and me watching him with there not being no other customer just then, it came to my mind he was like the picture was on the *Daily Intelligence* front page last week – wonderful how they get them things, isn't it? Well, it came to me sudden-like, and, yielding to the impulse-like, I says to him : "Aren't that Claude Maddox bloke, are you?" expecting him to take it as a joke and have a laugh. Well, he didn't – off like nothing, he was, and on his bicycle and away. And what's more – and that's what made me think you fellows had better know – he didn't wait for his change, which was seventeen and 'ten.'

'Was it an ordinary bicycle, or a motor one?' Bobby asked.

'Push bike, and off on it like nothing, so as I hadn't even time to yell – there, in a manner of speaking, he was,' said the coffee-stall keeper impressively; 'and there, in a manner of speaking, he wasn't.'

Bobby secured the note with which the unknown had paid for his refreshment, and went back to the Yard with it. It was, as the coffee-stall keeper had remarked, quite new and fresh, so that it could not have been much in circulation, and Mitchell, when it was shown to him, examined it with great interest.

'If it was Maddox,' he said, 'it means someone must have provided him with shelter, money, and clothing, and yet he has to run the risk of getting his food outside. Also he has to put up with a suit obviously too small for him. Looks almost as if he had broken into some unoccupied house and had found money and clothing there, but no food. Only, how on earth did he manage that in such a short time? Besides, there's hardly a house anywhere near that hasn't been investigated – bicycle, too, apparently. Possibly this note may help us.'

To trace one-pound notes is generally impossible, few people taking the trouble to keep record of their numbers, but inquiry showed that, as Mitchell had hoped, this note belonged to a series only just issued. It had gone, with others of the same series, to the London and Suburban Bank, and Mitchell was not altogether surprised to find that it was to the Brush Hill branch of that bank that it had been sent. Thither, therefore, Bobby was forthwith dispatched to make inquiry. Before long he was back.

'Well, what luck?' Mitchell asked, when he appeared to report.

'They say,' Bobby answered, 'it was one of a number paid out to meet a cheque for five hundred pounds, drawn by Mr Paul Irwin on his private account, and cashed by him personally two days ago.'

Mitchell was not often taken aback, but this time he fairly gasped.

'What on earth is the meaning of that?' he demanded at last. 'How could a note paid out to Paul Irwin get into the possession of Claude Maddox?'

'I don't know, sir,' answered Bobby simply.

CHAPTER XXVI

CHANGED OUTLOOK.

MITCHELL decided now that it would be as well for Bobby to go at once to Brush Hill to interview there Mr Irwin again, and see if he could throw any light upon what appeared so inexplicable a circumstance.

'Mr Irwin's quite got over his illness: he has been back at his office some days,' Mitchell said. 'You can see him either there or at his home. Of course, it may not have been Maddox at all our coffee-stall friend saw; in a case like this there are always plenty ready to swear they've seen anyone missing. Or there may be some quite simple explanation – the more impossible a thing seems, the simpler the explanation, as a rule. Or the bank may have made a bloomer. You had better check up there, first, I think, Owen.'

'Very good, sir,' Bobby answered.

'Well, there's one thing,' observed Ferris, who had been called into consultation. 'We can depend on old Mr Irwin to give us all the help he can now. There won't be any more of that "I have nothing to say" business, that's like a stone wall in front of you, now he knows Maddox did it, and but for Maddox his Leslie would be alive still, most likely. A tough old boy,' he added musingly. 'Something rather terrifying about him – no softness or sympathy; hard on himself, and hard on others. The sword of the Lord and of Gideon style.'

'If he had been a little less hard,' observed Mitchell, 'a little less sure of being right, most likely all this would never have happened. It's that was the root of it all.'

'Anyhow,' repeated Ferris, 'he'll be willing to do all he can to help. He was so wrapped up in that boy of his, he won't want Maddox to get off scotfree.'

Bobby was of the same opinion. Anything that stern, relentless old man could do to help, would certainly be done. Of that much, Bobby felt sure, and yet had to confess himself both worried and puzzled by the coffee-stall keeper's story. It seemed against all reason, common sense, and credibility, but then so was, in the conditions, the disappearance of Maddox. He was inclined to suspect that there must be some mistake at the bank, but this suggestion, when he put it forward somewhat light-heartedly to the branch manager, was received with cold contempt. Banks, it appeared, above all the Brush Hill branch of the City and Suburban Bank, did not make mistakes. Customers might – customers, indeed, made little else; science and religion could err, and art follow false paths; proneness to error might be integral in human nature, but banks – well, one did not so much define banks in terms of the infallible, as the infallible in terms of banking. More especially, the manager implied, did all this apply to the Brush Hill branch of the City and Suburban.

Bobby, suitably crushed, but rallying bravely, inquired if it were equally certain that Mr Irwin, in person, had received the money.

Of that, too, there was no doubt. Mr Irwin was well known – as well mistake Trafalgar Square for a cocktail before dinner as Mr Paul Irwin for anyone else.

'It's all told on him,' the manager observed. 'He looks his age now, especially with his hair turned white, but he keeps up wonderfully. He's begun to use a bicycle, too, instead of walking so much, but that's about all – wouldn't hear of a car, I'm told. It must have been a terrible blow to him; he was wrapped up in his boy.'

'I always felt that,' Bobby said. 'It makes us feel we can rely on him now for all the help he can give.'

'You know,' the manager went on, 'young Leslie thought a lot of his father, too. Only he was afraid of him as well. Fear. Love drives out fear, perhaps, but fear masks love. Don't wonder, though, at anyone being afraid of Mr Irwin.

Everyone respects him, but they all know he makes no allowances – no discount given in his accounts.'

'He is like that, isn't he? He makes me feel all weighed up and found out and judged,' agreed Bobby. 'Yet thaw follows frost,' he added, and then felt surprised at his own expression of this thought that had come abruptly and unexpectedly into his mind.

From the bank Bobby proceeded, after some hesitation, to Mr Irwin's private residence rather than to his office. It was beginning to grow near the close of business hours, for one thing, and for another he thought that there would both be fewer interruptions at the house, and that there Mr Irwin would be more likely to talk freely.

The old housekeeper, Mrs Knowles, told him that Mr Irwin was not back yet, but that she expected him in soon for his tea. Afterwards he would probably return to the office, and be there till late – so late that now she did not wait up for him, but put his supper ready on a tray in the study and then retired, for, now that her sick relative was convalescent, she was again sleeping at home.

'It's because of another society joining up with them,' she explained. 'He works till all hours – making things right.'

'How does Mr Irwin seem?' Bobby asked.

'Well enough,' she answered, with a certain air of disapproval, 'as you may say, but he's a changed man, for all that. It'll be different, very like, when you've done your duty and got that Maddox safe under lock and key – where he ought to be, and a shame and a scandal such as him should be running free.'

'We are doing our best,' Bobby explained meekly, and a snort from Mrs Knowles showed very clearly what she thought of that 'best.' Bobby added: 'You were saying Mr Irwin had changed?'

'There's something gone out of him. He's not the same man,' she answered. 'Broken, you might say, though he has his faith that ought to keep him up.'

'Do you mean he seems feeble – ill?' Bobby asked.

'Not in body,' she answered. 'It's something in him that's clean gone – why, he preached and prayed last Sunday same as usual and never once did he so much as mention hell or God's punishment on sinners, but all about understanding each other, as if sin was to be understood and not just stamped on. What I say is, it's this Maddox getting away scotfree that's telling on him.'

'Maddox hasn't gone scotfree yet,' Bobby reminded her. 'In fact, we have some idea he may be hiding somewhere in this part – in Brush Hill itself, perhaps.'

'Well, then, why don't you find him, if you know where he is?' she demanded fiercely. 'I would, if I had to tear down every house with my own hands, rather than let him go free that's been the cause of Mr Leslie's killing himself.' She spoke with great bitterness and vehemence, and then added, more quietly: 'The papers say he murdered Carrie Mears, and very like no more than she deserved, and no better, I daresay, than she should have been. But it was all on account of that Mr Leslie shot himself, and worse for Mr Irwin, for he thought all the world of that boy. Worse than murder, I call it: and when Maddox hangs I shall go down on my knees to thank God right's been done at last on him, that Mr Leslie would be alive and well to-day but for what he did.'

'I daresay Mr Irwin feels like that, too,' Bobby remarked.

'If you had seen his hair go white, day after day,' she answered sombrely, 'you wouldn't need ask that, young man – and enough to turn the mind of anyone, and him so strong and young before. If I wake in the night, I can hear him praying, and I know what for, for he told me himself it's for God's punishment to fall on Claude Maddox.'

A grim old man, Bobby reflected, repelled, even appalled by this picture presented to him of one who had striven so long, and with such prodigies of self-control and self-denial, to serve Him, now battering His Throne with cries for the revenge of a private wrong. But it was perhaps this very intensity of his desire for vengeance that kept up the old man's strength, and when Bobby expressed, though vaguely, some such idea, Mrs Knowles seemed to understand.

'He's keeping well enough,' she admitted. 'He doesn't sleep much, for often and often I hear noises in the night that's him moving about; and he's at his prayers early and late, but he eats well – better than he used. Now that he's late at the office almost every night, I put the tray ready for him in the study, and there's little left when I clear away next morning. He was a bit queer after Mr Leslie shot himself, poor lad, with that fit he had while you were here, but that didn't last.'

'In what way do you mean he was queer?' Bobby asked.

'In his ways, like. One night he took back all the housekeeping money he had given me for the bills. Said he wanted it, when it was the middle of the night then – so how could he? But he took it, and got more next day for me. And he wanted me to go on sleeping at my sister's – pretended he would rather be alone at night. I told him flat I wouldn't have it. He wasn't fit to be left alone that way. Excited and funny-like, too. He went over Mr Leslie's things, when I wanted to do something about them, seeing the poor lad will never want them more. Told me I wasn't so much as to touch a thing in his room, not even to open a drawer or a cupboard, nor even his old tools in the attic he's never been near for years.'

They heard a key in the door, and Mr Irwin came in – old and bowed now; his thin form bent; his features pinched and thin beneath the mass of snow-white hair. He looked a little startled, Bobby thought, at seeing him, but said a word or two of greeting, and then led the way into his study.

'You can bring us some tea here,' he said to Mrs Knowles, and then indicating a chair, he said to Bobby: 'Sit down, won't you? You've come to see me, I suppose?'

Bobby seated himself, feeling curiously at a loss. It was not only physically that Mr Irwin had changed, there were other and more subtle alterations more difficult to define. His snowy hair certainly now served to accentuate that air

of the prophet there had always been about him, and his
eyes had still that clear bright stillness that shows in those
used to gaze upon a light others do not see. The word that
Mrs Knowles had used had been 'broken'; the word that
came into Bobby's mind was 'benign,' though why he hardly
knew, and it astonished him.

'You wanted to speak to me?' Mr Irwin repeated. He
smiled slightly – very slightly – yet with a smile that seemed
to caress and to understand. 'You are very young,' he said.
'As young as Leslie, I suppose?'

'I think I must be a little older, sir,' Bobby answered,
wondering to notice how simply and how naturally the reference to the dead boy had been made.

'Yes, yes. Perhaps you are,' Mr Irwin agreed. 'I suppose
it is about Claude Maddox you are come? You have no idea
yet where he is?'

It was an assertion more than a question, and yet it had
in it a faint touch of uneasiness. Bobby repeated briefly the
coffee-stall keeper's story.

'It seemed so incomprehensible,' Bobby concluded, 'that
a pound note apparently paid out to you should turn up
in that way that we felt we would like to know what you
thought about it.'

Mr Irwin listened gravely. When Bobby paused, he was
silent for a time, and then he answered, as he had answered
before:

'I have nothing to say.'

But this time he uttered the words with a tone and accent
singularly changed. Before his voice had had the hardness,
the clarity, the finality of ice; now there sounded in it a certain tenderness, a touch almost of humour, that Bobby recognized, and that again a good deal puzzled him. He said,
half-defensively, half-questioningly:

''Maddox is a murderer. He killed Miss Mears. And he
would have let your son hang for it, too – or at least never
said a word when he knew Leslie was suspected and likely to
be arrested. But for him, and what he did, Leslie would be

alive to-day. Surely we can depend on you to do all you can to help us find him?'

The old man did not answer. He was looking, as it were, far away – to distances beyond the sight of every day. Embarrassed, though why he hardly knew, Bobby muttered:

'Mrs Knowles said ... told me ...'

'What?' Paul Irwin asked, as Bobby's voice trailed into silence; and now there came again into the old man's tones something of their former tremendous force, of their old fierce vigour. He said: 'I know. She woke in the night. She thought I was ill and came downstairs and heard. She told you I was praying for punishment to fall on Claude Maddox. Well, she is right – but there are many kinds of punishment.'

CHAPTER XXVII

MURDER ONCE MORE

But as if he felt that he now had said too much, betrayed too clearly the intimacy of his private feelings, Paul Irwin, after this, grew silent, and would answer no more questions. His refusal was very gentle and very quiet, but none the less determined. At times he would make a brief and smiling comment on Bobby's questions; once or twice, even, he replied with a quiet pleasantry that in him, or rather in contrast to him, as he had been before, astonished Bobby considerably. But never came a single word that offered any enlightenment on the points Bobby was attempting to clear up. When Bobby remarked that the cheque, on which the one-pound note traced to the supposed Maddox had been paid out, had been drawn for an unusually large sum – especially for clearance in cash over the counter – and that an explanation would be welcome, he was answered by a non-committal 'personal reasons,' beyond which Mr Irwin was plainly determined not to go.

Utterly baffled, completely at a loss, Bobby retired to headquarters, where first he told his tale to Ferris, who received it with gloomy head-shakes.

'I don't trust that old chap,' he declared. 'Got something up his sleeve, as like as not.'

'I had a little bit that idea myself,' agreed Bobby, 'only I can't imagine what – or why?'

'It's hard enough to worry out the truth in these murder cases,' Ferris observed, still gloomy, 'but when you get religion, too – well, it's the devil.'

'Religion so often is,' murmured Bobby, and now Ferris looked shocked.

'That's not at all what I meant, young man,' he said sharply. 'We had better see what Mr Mitchell thinks.'

But Mitchell was as much at a loss as anyone. He cross-examined Bobby closely on every detail of the interview with Mr Irwin, and evidently regretted he had not had time to go himself, as he would have done had not some important returns to the Home Office, on the sale of chocolates after prohibited hours, required completion.

'One can understand,' Mitchell remarked, 'his refusing to help us before, when it looked as if his son might be implicated, but what is he lying low for now?'

'Put it this way,' Ferris suggested abruptly. 'He means to do the job his own way instead of leaving it to us.'

'How do you mean?' Mitchell asked, startled, and yet aware that this suggestion responded to a thought in his own mind.

'He doesn't want human justice, he wants divine justice, and he means to be the instrument himself,' Ferris answered slowly. 'There's something about the old man that always frightened me. The sword of the Lord and of Gideon,' he repeated.

Bobby fidgeted. He would have liked to say something, but neither of his two seniors was paying him any attention and discipline bade him hold his tongue.

'I've felt like that with him myself,' Mitchell admitted. 'Only, what have you got in your mind, Ferris?'

'Put it this way,' Ferris said. 'It looks like money paid out to Paul Irwin goes at once to Claude Maddox. That means connection of some sort. Perhaps not direct, but there all the same. Put it this way. Mr Irwin means to land Maddox himself. Some way he's got a hint where Maddox is, and he thinks Maddox responsible for his son's death – thinks of him as his murderer. Well, the one-pound note was ground-bait, the five hundred is bait for the hook to catch him, and Mr Irwin's not saying a word beforehand because he means to bring it off himself – and there won't be much left for us to do afterwards, either. The sword of the Lord and of Gideon.'

'There's a tremendous change in him,' Bobby could not prevent himself from interposing.

'Yes, you put that in your report. I don't like that, either,'
Ferris answered. 'Penfold said something of the same sort
yesterday, when he rang up. Everyone noticed it, he said.
Penfold said no one could understand what had changed
him so, and I put it to Penfold at once, I didn't half like it.'

'Why? Do you think he is fey?' Mitchell asked.

'Oh, I don't think it's drink or anything like that, sir,'
answered Ferris, rather badly misunderstanding the meaning of the Scots word that presumes a sudden alteration in
character to indicate the near approach of death, as if in
that great coming light all things must needs grow different
and change. 'I just don't like it. Looks like he was planning
something – trying to put people off. If we don't mind, we
shall have another murder case on hand, with Claude Maddox not in the dock, but chief exhibit. That's why Irwin's
gone so quiet and soft spoken, so as to hide what's in his
mind.'

Mitchell looked uneasy. So did Bobby, to whom this was
a completely new view. But both of them felt it was possible,
even that it had about it a certain air of plausibility. Bobby,
in especial, found he could not dismiss the suggestion as entirely fantastic. That new softness and gentleness he had seen
in Paul Irwin might indeed have been assumed to hide a
deadly resolve, and the cheque for five hundred pounds have
been drawn to provide the necessary means for carrying it
out – for bribes, rewards, and so on. Mitchell was beginning
to drum with his finger-tips on his desk – a sure sign that
he was seriously disturbed. He said heavily:

'We'll have to watch out. Then, too – even supposing Mr
Irwin has any such mad idea in his mind – it doesn't follow
that's the way it'll work. Suppose he does find Maddox –
even suppose he comes upon him unexpectedly? Well, he
would have that much advantage, but Maddox is a good
deal younger – desperate, too.'

'I would back Mr Irwin,' Ferris declared, 'to come out
on top all right – he's that sort.'

'Because he's always so dead sure that God is with him,'

Mitchell said. 'I know. Many a man has gone all the way to hell quite convinced of that. It's a belief that helps you to get to your destination, though I don't think it alters it much. All the same, Owen, I think it would be as well to keep him under observation. The house, too. It is just possible that five hundred is meant for a bait to draw Maddox. You remember Leslie Irwin said Maddox had a key at one time, so he could let himself in when he wanted to use their workshop in the attic. He may have it still, and Mr Irwin may know or suspect as much. Somehow he got that pound note to Maddox's hands. Suppose he also gets to him the information that there is five hundred in the house in cash – the house being left all day in the charge of one old woman, who must go out sometimes to do her shopping. You know, it does begin to look a bit like a trap. What do you think, Owen?'

'Yes, sir, perhaps,' Bobby agreed, though reluctantly. 'Only, I don't quite see how the trap's to be sprung if the house is left all day in the charge of one old woman, and she's out sometimes.'

'No, I don't see how it's to be sprung, or who is most likely to be caught in it, either,' answered Mitchell grimly. 'Possibly Irwin leaves someone on watch. Or he may have some other scheme. Better get along to Brush Hill, Owen, and see what you can do there. Find out if the house seems under observation, if you can, and if Irwin sometimes leaves his office without explanation. Are you on terms with Mrs Knowles?'

'I think so, sir. She doesn't think much of us, but she's keen to help. I expect she thought a lot of Leslie Irwin, and there's nothing she wouldn't do to get Maddox arrested. She thinks he is the cause of it all, and resents any chance of his getting off scotfree, as she calls it.'

'So much the better,' Mitchell said. 'Try to get her to let you go over the house. If it's necessary, hint you are afraid burglary may be attempted, but don't alarm her more than you can help, and give her a hint not to say anything to

Mr Irwin – put it, for fear of alarming him unnecessarily. And keep your eyes open for anything unusual – clubs behind doors; poisoned bottles of whisky; any old thing you can imagine, in fact – for in this business I'm beginning to believe anything and everything is possible. And I'll get on the phone and ask Penfold to place two men on watch at the house – one in front and one at the rear.'

To Brush Hill, accordingly, Bobby returned, and there made little progress. It was certain that Mr Irwin was present at his office early and late, hard at work on the details of the proposed amalgamation, and not allowing in any way the recent tragic happenings of his private life to interfere with the routine of his business engagement. A true descendant of the 'Ironsides' he was showing himself, steadfast in every circumstance of life, though it appeared that in the office, too, a new gentleness and benignity of manner had been noted. At the house, Mrs Knowles, by no means above a weakness for gossip, showed no displeasure at Bobby's reappearance and made no difficulty about allowing him to go through every room. Burglars, she admitted, she had a dread of, and after what had happened and all the talk in the papers, and the pictures they had published with an 'x' in the corner to indicate this or that, no one could be surprised at anything that happened next, and if this polite police young man could suggest any further precaution to take, it would certainly be adopted.

But she made a point of accompanying Bobby on his tour of inspection, and used the opportunity to comment, frequently and unfavourably, on the total failure there had been to find Maddox.

'And him in pyjamas and his feet bare,' she reminded Bobby, who had not forgotten those facts, 'so it stands to reason he can't have got far, and no money, either.'

Bobby admitted he and his colleagues were completely baffled. It didn't seem possible for a man in such circumstances to have evaded notice and pursuit, and yet that Maddox had completely succeeded in doing. Mrs Knowles indicated, not obscurely, that the probable explanation was complete incompetence on the part of the police, and Bobby found no adequate defence to put up, since the only defence acceptable for even a moment would have been the discovery of the vanished Maddox.

With such converse they passed the time as they went over the house together. It was not a large one. On the top floor were the attics, and above them a space in the roof occupied only by the storage cistern. Access was obtained by a ladder, and Bobby got Mrs Knowles's consent to put it in position and ascend, when only a glance was needed to tell him no one had been there since the last time a plumber had dozed over the job of putting right a defective ball. The attics consisted of two small ones at the back, and one larger one in front. Of the two small attics, one was a lumber room, full of odds and ends, the other was Mrs Knowles's bedroom. The front and larger attic was the one Claude Maddox and Leslie had used in past years as a workshop when they were boys together. Bobby paid it particular attention. It still contained the bench at which the youngsters had worked, a supply of wood of various kinds, a tool-box, and so on. Everything was clean and in good order, and Mrs Knowles explained that it was part of the household routine to sweep and tidy the place at regular intervals.

'I did it myself yesterday,' she remarked. 'Mrs Harris does it generally, but I saw to it yesterday.'

Mrs Harris was, it appeared, a woman who came in to help with the house-work every week-day.

'It needs papering,' Mrs Knowles remarked, 'but Mr Irwin says no one uses it now, so it doesn't matter.'

Bobby had been looking at the wallpaper, which was in fact a good deal faded, and stained here and there with damp, though it was not those facts that had caught his attention, but the variegated and complicated, and even startling pattern, which he supposed must have represented some very early cubist design. At any rate it seemed a quite mad confusion of lines and angles, without so much as a single curve

among them. However, an eccentric wallpaper pattern was
evidently of no interest or importance to his quest, and
Bobby turned his attention to the windows. A glance showed
that they, like those in the other attics, had not been opened
for a very long time, for Mrs Knowles held fresh air in some
suspicion, associating it with draughts, and draughts with
sudden death.

'Open windows lets in the dirt,' pronounced Mrs
Knowles, though it was draughts and death she meant, for
experience had taught her the first excuse was more likely
to be sympathetically received. 'The window-man does the
outside,' she explained, 'and we rub them up inside, and
no need to bother opening them.'

On the first floor were two larger bedrooms in addition to
the bathroom, and the smaller room over the front door that
Leslie had used for his own, and where so unhappily he
had ended his life. On the ground floor were dining- and
drawing-rooms, and the smaller room Mr Irwin used as a
study. The kitchen and other offices were built out behind,
and were reached by a narrow passage continuing from the
entrance hall round the foot of the stairs – an arrangement
calculated to ensure that food should always be cold before
it reached the dining-room. Noticing the attention Bobby
was paying to the fastenings of the windows, Mrs Knowles
told him she always made sure herself before retiring to bed
that all bolts and fastenings were in good order.

'I make sure they're working proper,' she told him; 'well-
oiled and all. I put my trust in the Lord, but that's no reason
for leaving windows so any man could open them with a
knife. Ours have all got proper screws.'

Bobby agreed that all fastenings were secure, and that if
all windows and doors were as well secured burglary would
soon become yet another of Britain's lost trades. Then he
departed, well assured that if Mr Irwin were really planning, as Ferris suggested, to use his £500 as a bait to draw
Maddox from his place of concealment, then he must also
be planning to provide some special mode of entry.

It might be, of course, that the plan involved a door or window deliberately left open, and a picture framed itself in Bobby's mind of an open window, of Maddox climbing through to secure the money that would give him his chance of escape, of the old man grimly waiting the coming of his victim.

But there was, too, Mitchell's remark to reflect on – that even so the issue might be doubtful.

'Youth on one side, surprise on the other,' Bobby thought, remembering what Mitchell had said. 'And which'll win?'

Probably, however, in spite of the Firearms ·Act, Mr Irwin had provided himself with a revolver or automatic pistol, and Bobby remembered, too, that to shoot a burglar entering your house might easily pass ·for an act of self-defence.

It might well be, Bobby thought, that was what was in contemplation, and he could not help shivering slightly at the possibility, for, though he would scarcely have believed credible a scheme of that nature in the case of the ordinary citizen, he felt in Paul Irwin a strength, motives, standards, beliefs that were the old man's own.

'He is his own judge,' Bobby reflected. 'Or rather, he has made up his mind that only God shall be his judge.'

From all this, therefore, it followed that he took especial care to see the observation kept upon the house was as careful as complete. One man was to watch the front, one was stationed behind; they were warned that no relaxation of vigilance was to be permitted for even a moment for any reason whatever. Even a blowing of police whistles near by was not to draw them from their post. Any person answering in any way to the description of Maddox was to be challenged instantly, and the most careful notice was to be taken of any unusual noise or occurrence.

With such precautions taken, and approved by his superiors, Bobby went off duty with a mind at ease, and from his first slumbers he was wakened by the loud ringing of the phone bell at his bedside. He answered it mechanically be-

H

fore he was well awake, but his senses were shaken into full consciousness when he heard the far-off tiny voice directing him to repair at once to Brush Hill.

'There's been fresh murder done,' the voice said dispassionately, 'and the Super. wants you to report to him there at once.'

CHAPTER XXVIII

DISCOVERY

ALREADY when Bobby reached Brush Hill the full routine of investigation was in progress.

The news, too, had spread in the neighbourhood, in spite of the lateness of the hour, so that a little crowd of curious onlookers had gathered to watch the coming and the going of the detectives, and to be thrilled by the occasional arrival of motors. And, at the windows of the houses adjacent, lights were showing and heads appearing as people roused themselves from their beds to stare at these new happenings.

Two burly constables in uniform guarded the entrance to the front garden of the house, permitting only those to pass who were engaged in the investigations, or who were connected with the Press, for this sensational sequel to recent events had already reached the newspaper offices, and every crime specialist of Fleet Street was either on the spot by now or hurrying to it at his best speed.

To one of these guardians of the door, with whom he chanced to have been on duty during his days in uniform, Bobby said, in passing:

'What's happened? Do you know?'

But the constable, to whom all this was the mere dull daily grind of duty, signifying only extra work and no more pay, shook his head:

'Someone done someone in,' he answered vaguely. 'Stand back, sir, if you please,' he added, to an enterprising youth who had tried to slip by. 'Can't help it if you are a friend of the family – and if you're Press, show your card.'

Bobby went on up the path to the house, where now, in the dark night, lights flared at every window. No blinds had been drawn, and behind the windows could be plainly seen the figures of men moving to and fro, intent on their grim business of discovery and pursuit. Another constable was stationed at the door of the house itself, yawning ferociously, for he had been called from bed after a long day's duty. But he no more than his colleague at the garden gate could tell Bobby exactly what had happened.

'It's murder,' he said morosely. 'A fellow gets no time off -- nothing but work, work, work, duty, duty, duty -- when there's murder done.'

It was a point of view, Bobby thought, as he entered that sad house of tragedy, and in the hall saw Inspector Penfold, who nodded a greeting.

'Mitchell was asking for you,' he said.

'I came along as quickly as I could,' Bobby answered. 'What's happened?'

'Old Mr Irwin done in,' Penfold answered. 'House-keeper did it.'

'Mrs Knowles?' Bobby repeated incredulously, utterly bewildered. 'But surely that's ... impossible.'

'Well, there it is,' retorted Penfold. 'House was under observation, back and front, by two of my best men, and both of them swear no one has been in or out since Mr Irwin got back from his office. He can't very well have smashed himself up the way he is, and there's no one else, not a living soul in the whole place, except Mrs Knowles, with the poker in her hand and blood all over her -- and every door and window fastened on the inside so tight the first men here had to break in. So there you are. It was either her, or it wasn't anyone.'

'But an old woman like that?' Bobby protested.

'When a woman gets going, even an old woman,' Penfold said, 'it's an all-in job. I remember, when I was a sergeant, having to tackle an old girl of seventy who had just laid hubby out with a flat-iron. Took four of our men to get her to the station, and two of them went on the sick list next day.'

'How was information received?' Bobby asked.

'She rang up herself. Went off her head after doing it – or before doing it, very like. Yelled something about murder, and help, and come quick, and when we got here – we had to smash in the back door – Mr Irwin was in the study, all knocked about, and so near dead as doesn't matter, and she was in a faint near the phone. Called us up, and then collapsed. Had the poker she did it with in her hand, and not another living creature in the house, so it was a clear case, every door and window fastened, and my two men on watch outside. So there you are. Sounds impossible, but no getting away from it.'

'But – –' began Bobby, and paused.

'Can't get away from facts,' Penfold repeated. 'If there's no one else it could be, seeing there's no one else in the house, then her it must be. Sort out all the impossibles, and what's left must be the truth. Not that there's much sorting out required this time. The old boy didn't do it himself – impossible he could have. There was no one else to do it, except her. Well, it can't have been no one, so it must have been her, and good enough to hang anybody. And there's something else.'

'What?' asked Bobby.

'Just this. It's her who did the other cases, too.'

Bobby didn't answer. He only stared. With a touch of complacency in his voice, Penfold continued :

'A bit of a staggerer, eh? It was to me, when I tumbled to it. Just think, though. She wasn't going to have her precious Leslie marrying a Carrie Mears, so she outed the girl to save the boy. I've been doing a bit of investigating in my own time, and I've got a letter Mrs Knowles wrote to her sister about Mr Leslie mustn't be let marry the girl, and it would be the ruin of him, and she would stop it herself to save him in both worlds, this and the next one. And then Leslie began to suspect what she had done, and tackled her about it, and let her see what he thought, and she got scared of the hanging she saw getting near and put a bullet in him, knowing no one would ever think of her.'

'But – –' repeated Bobby; and then : 'Claude Maddox ran for it?'

'Panic,' explained Penfold. 'They do at times ... silly, and gives us a lot of trouble, same as this time, but it's just panic. Panic, and their one idea is to bolt for it, anywhere to be safe; and I don't wonder so much in his case, for it looked bad against him till this came up.'

'But Mrs Knowles wasn't in the house when Leslie Irwin was shot,' Bobby objected.

'I know,' answered Penfold. 'Alibi, she had all right. Who checked up on it? No one. No one ever even thought of suspecting her, and so they never troubled. House wasn't properly searched, either. No one thought of looking under beds or in cupboards. Told you I had done a bit of investigating on my own. Supposed to be spending the night with a sick sister, wasn't she? Well, that night she was out late. Said she got in the wrong train on the tube. That's as may be, and she may have been lost on the tube, or she may have been hidden here. No one thought of searching here – not what you would call searching.'

'Has a search been made to-night?' Bobby asked.

'It has,' Penfold answered. 'I saw to that. Every room. Under the beds and all – even the cistern in the roof, and every cupboard. Not a mouse could have escaped us. Not a sign of a trace of any living creature anywhere about, and two of my best men to swear it's impossible for anyone either to have entered or left since it happened. So there you are. When there's only two people in it, and one's murdered, then the other did it.'

'Yes, but ... but ...' muttered Bobby, a little dazed. He put one hand to his head. 'That old woman ...' he muttered.

'Ah,' answered Penfold. 'Never thought of her, eh? The most unlikely person, you know. Good rule – only we forgot it. The most unlikely person; got to remember that another time,' he said, with a touch of complacence in his voice.

'Where is she?' Bobby asked.

'Hospital. Ambulance took her off. She was having hysterics when she wasn't fainting, and fainting when she wasn't in hysterics. I don't wonder, either – three murders one on top of another; bit of a nervous strain for an old party like Mrs Knowles.'

Bobby was still gaping, unable to find words. Penfold gave him a little satisfied nod. The C.I.D. might think a lot of themselves, but sometimes the uniformed branch could show them a thing or two. From one of the adjoining rooms, where till then he had been busy, Mitchell came quickly into the hall. He had with him a finger-print expert, who was looking very gloomy.

'Nothing to help us so far, sir,' he was saying. 'And I don't think the poker will be any help – it's smothered in blood. No prints on it we can find to recognize, except those of the woman herself – where she was holding it.'

'Now, I ask you,' Penfold muttered, 'how could there be, when there wasn't another living creature in the house?'

'Ah, there you are,' Mitchell said, noticing Bobby. 'Stand by till I want you.'

Bobby waited accordingly, taking while he did so an opportunity to glance within the study. It was not a pleasant sight, for the attack had been delivered with an almost maniacal fury, and, feeling a little sick, Bobby went back to the hall to wait. It was not long before Mitchell returned.

'Bad business, Owen,' he said, signing to the young man to join him. 'What do you think of it? Penfold been telling you?'

'Yes, sir,' Bobby answered. 'Only ...'

'Well, there it is,' Penfold interposed. 'Cut out the impossible, and what remains must be. The house has been gone through from top to bottom, from cellar to attics. Not a sign of another living soul, and Mrs Knowles said herself there was no one here but her and the old man, and couldn't be. So there you are,' he repeated.

'We'll have another look round,' Mitchell said.

Penfold shrugged his shoulders, though not till Mitchell had turned away, and put on his most patient smile. Still, the whims of superiors have to be tolerated. They began with the cellars, and soon assured themselves afresh there was no possibility of anyone being hidden there. Then on the ground floor and on the first floor the same careful search was continued, with the same result. Modern drawing-rooms, dining-rooms, bedrooms, offer small chances of concealment, and even modern chimneys offer small facilities for escape or hiding. Examinations proved, too, that, even without the evidence of the police on watch without, any escape by door or window was impossible, since all were securely fastened on the inside.   .

They went on to the attics.

'Is there any space under the roof?' Mitchell asked.

'I've been up there; had a good look round,' Penfold answered. 'There's dust and dirt enough to show no one's been there before us for donkey's years.'

They went into the attic at the back – the one Mrs. Knowles had used for her bedroom – and Penfold said musingly :

'Funny to think of that old creature planning it all here and then creeping out about the job.'

Mitchell made no comment. There was obviously no possible place of concealment in the room, and once again Mitchell assured himself of the security of the window fastening. Thence they went into the front attic, a large, bare, gaunt apartment, furnished with a few chairs, a table, a work-bench, and two chests of tools.

'Where Claude Maddox and Irwin used to play about, when they were youngsters, I suppose,' Mitchell remarked. 'Someone told me they did real good work; young Claude Maddox in especial had a real knack.' Then he turned his attention to the wallpaper, that somewhat remarkable effort in early cubism which already Bobby had noticed and wondered at. 'Where on earth did they find it?' he remarked. 'Enough to make you dizzy.'

'Picked it up cheap, I expect, sir,' Penfold suggested, 'and thought it wouldn't matter up here.'

'Might be that; might be that; mightn't be that,' muttered Mitchell, staring at it with an attention so concentrated and so prolonged that even Bobby wondered why his chief should spend so much time upon what was after all merely an eccentric development of an eccentric and now half-forgotten art theory. Penfold could not prevent himself giving a discreet cough, an even more discreet shuffle of his feet. There was far too much to be done, in his opinion, for time to be wasted in staring at wallpapers. But Mitchell still remained lost in contemplation, as if wallpaper patterns were the one thing in all the world that interested him, as if in comparison with them murders were but trifles; and Penfold said, in a loud whisper, to Bobby:

'Notice how clean and tidy it all is – not a speck of dust anywhere.'

'Mrs Knowles told me it was part of the housework to tidy up here every so often,' Bobby remarked.

'Well, anyhow,' observed Penfold, 'no hole or corner here where even a mouse could hide.'

Mitchell seemed to come out of his trance of contemplation.

'Bit nightmarish,' he remarked. 'Wonder who chose it – and why!'

'Why?' repeated Bobby, puzzled by something he seemed to detect in his chief's voice.

Penfold wandered, a little ostentatiously, towards the door. Discussions on wallpaper patterns did not interest him, and all creation knew there was enough hard work waiting, and no chance of rest or sleep till it had been attended to.

'You know,' he remarked, over his shoulder, 'what I say, sir, is they'll bring it in homicidal mania.'

'Not so sure of that,' Mitchell answered.

'Oh, well, sir, an old lady like her,' protested Penfold, 'three murders one after the other ... it's not natural.'

'No more than a wallpaper like this in an attic,' observed Mitchell. 'And what is not natural should always be explained.'

Penfold looked as if he thought the superintendent was suffering from some sort of mania himself. Bobby was inclined to make a little joke about such a pattern being above all explanation, but then told himself that neither the time nor the circumstances nor yet Mitchell's manner invited pleasantry.

'There's a recess on one side of the fireplace,' Mitchell was saying, 'but not on the other.'

Penfold cast one uninterested glance towards fireplace and recess, and another, much more alert, towards the door. Bobby gave a little gasp. Dimly he groped for what was coming, and dimly guessed. Mitchell went on:

'Both boys had the knack of handling tools – first class professional work they turned out. Boys often have a fancy for secret hiding-places, hidden dens – all that kind of thing. Old Mr Irwin kept them under strict discipline, and perhaps it was handy, too, to have a safe place to keep things – or themselves – away from him. I can imagine, for instance, Maddox hiding up here ready to join Leslie in secret excursions at night, or perhaps when returning from them.'

'Yes ... but ... hide ... where?' Penfold stammered.

Mitchell put out a hand, and knocked heavily on the wall by the fireplace where no recess showed.

'Sounds hollow,' he said. 'And all that muddle of line and angle and whatnot on the wallpaper would go a long way towards hiding any crack that could betray a concealed door.' He struck again upon the pseudo wall – a heavy and resounding blow. 'Like to come out, Mr Maddox?' he called.

There was a pause, a hesitation, and then a door opened in what was in reality a partition of stout wood put up to enclose a recess corresponding to that on the other side of the fireplace. Very slowly Maddox stepped out.

'I'm almost glad you've found me,' he said.

CHAPTER XXIX

CONCLUSION

IN the hospital the nurse, watching by Paul Irwin's bed, reported signs of returning consciousness. But the doctors gave no hope.

'The injuries are too serious,' they said. 'Even a much younger man would hardly have a chance.'

Indeed already there were symptoms of pneumonia, and the doctors advised that the sick man's relatives should be warned. The few that he possessed, however, were resident in the north country, and there would have been little chance of their arriving in time. But, when he was able to speak, it was not for them the dying man asked, but for Bobby.

'That young policeman,' he managed to murmur. 'A boy called Owen ... can he come?'

A message was accordingly sent to Scotland Yard without delay, and Bobby was at once dispatched.

'It'll be a case of taking his depositions, from what the hospital says,' Inspector Ferris told him. 'You had better see Penfold first. He knows what to do – he was warned to be ready.'

But though it was therefore in the company of various important official personages that Bobby arrived at the hospital, it was only Bobby himself who was allowed access to the dying man.

'He's in no condition to be argued with,' one of the doctors said. 'Any excitement, even the least, might be fatal on the spot -- probably would. It's a Bobby Owen he is asking for, and no one else. Afterwards he may be strong enough to see some of you others, if he wants to. I won't take the responsibility of allowing anyone else; even the effort of explaining who you are and what you want might easily be too much for him.'

So Bobby went alone to the small private ward where Paul Irwin lay, and there was greeted with a faint smile of recognition. For, though death was plainly not far distant, the injured man's strength seemed greater than the doctors had appeared to think. Though that it might be only a last effort, was plainly evident.

'You're so young – like Leslie – that's why I wanted you,' he murmured, in a voice that was certainly feeble enough and yet was fully audible. 'When you're old, youth seems a lovely thing.'

'Yes, sir,' said Bobby, who did not understand this, for though he knew he was young and couldn't help it, 'lovely' was about the last epithet he would have thought of applying to himself. 'You were wanting to say something?' he hinted, afraid the other's strength might not last.

'Like Leslie,' Paul murmured again; and then more clearly: 'You thought he was innocent – you knew it before I did; better than I did. I saw him coming out of the room, I thought, but that was wrong. He had only been about to go in when he saw me, and then he went away, and he never knew at the time what was there. But, when I went in and found her, that was my first thought – that he had done it. I knew already about the cheque – that's what I wanted to say to her. I thought he had forged the cheque for her and then she had turned on him. And then he thought the same of me when he knew you had found my hat there.'

'You left it here on purpose, didn't you?' Bobby asked.

'To make you think it was me, not him,' Paul answered. 'I don't know if it deceived you, it did him, though I never thought of that. Funny, to make Leslie think it, but not you. And we never spoke or asked each other anything – not once. We daren't. I daren't because I was afraid what he might say; and he was afraid, too, because of the cheque he forged. That made him afraid ... bad, bad, when a son's afraid of his father.'

'That's all over now, sir,' Bobby said gently.

'Yes, all over now. It was Maddox I wanted to ask you about – Claude Maddox.'

'We got him all right,' Bobby answered, with satisfaction. 'Found where he was hiding before he had a chance to get away.'

He said it with full confidence that the news would ease the dying man's last hours, even that it might serve as a tonic to rally his strength still further. But to Bobby's astonishment he almost visibly drooped and shrank as he lay there in his bed, propped up on pillows. What faint show of colour had come into his cheeks ebbed away again, his breath fluttered. Bobby had the sensation of having dealt him a cruel, a violent, an unexpected blow.

'I thought ... I hoped ... I believed ... he might have escaped,' Paul whispered. 'I prayed ... you wouldn't ... find ... never'

'You didn't want him to get off, did you, sir?' Bobby asked, utterly amazed.

'I hoped ... I tried ... I hoped ... I couldn't do more ...' Paul answered in his stammering, uncertain voice. 'He was afraid ... fear ... like Leslie, too ... fear spoils all ... fear not, we are told and we do ... I taught it ... fear I mean ... Claude, too.'

'Do you mean you knew he was hiding up there?' Bobby asked.

'From the first night,' came the faint response. 'Years ago ... he and Leslie ... they made that place to hide in ... they thought we didn't know ... Miss Temple and me ... she was housekeeper then ... we never said anything, but we knew ... there was nearly a week once when Claude hid there and Leslie fed him ... they thought no one knew ... it's so easy to think no one knows ... that night you went to arrest him and he got away ... Claude, I mean ... barefooted, in pyjamas, no money ... alone, no friends ... and you hunting for him everywhere ... then I suppose in his despair he thought of that secret cupboard he and Leslie made to hide in when

they were boys ... he had the key to the house he had kept
all those years ... he went straight there ... he let himself in
that night within ten minutes of his escaping you .. less, five
minutes, if he ran, and I expect he did ... of course I knew
at once ... the only possible refuge ... in the only house in all
the world no one could have thought of ... that first night I
took back the money I had given Mrs Knowles and left it
for him ... and food ... I used to leave my supper out on the
tray for him every night ... he used to slip out sometimes,
when he thought we were in bed and it all seemed quiet ...
and then crept back before it was light ... he daren't show
himself in the daytime ... I left the evening papers where he
could see them ... he took a suit of Leslie's to wear ... I told
Mrs Knowles she wasn't to touch Leslie's things, so as to
stop her noticing any were missing ... but I knew it couldn't
last ... I cashed a cheque to get money to help him get away
... abroad somewhere ... I waited till I heard him slipping
down the stairs ... for food ... or to go out ... I opened the
door ... silly ... I only wanted to give him the money and
explain, but he thought he was discovered ... he thought I
would tell ... he was afraid ... fear ... fear ruins all,... he was
carrying something, and before I could make him understand
he was hitting out with it ... over and over again ... frenzied,
mad, panic, that's all ... Mrs Knowles heard ... she came
running and crying out ... it was dark in the hall, and I
suppose when Maddox heard her screaming he hid behind
the banisters or in a corner somewhere and then ran back
upstairs ... I thought if you hadn't found him he might still
have a chance to get away ... I meant to lie and say it was a
burglar ... I thought the first lie of your life when you're
dying and have never lied before ... I thought perhaps it
wouldn't matter so much ... but if you've found him, that's
no good ... lies never are ... but it was only panic ... not
murder.'

Bobby was writing all this down as quickly as he could.
He said, still very much puzzled:

'You wanted him to escape ... you meant to help ...'

'With five hundred pounds he might have managed it,' Paul murmured. 'And there's no worse use you can put a man to than hanging him.'

Bobby wrote that down too. He said:

'Will you sign this, sir?'

But Paul did not answer, and the nurse in attendance leaned across the bed, and said:

'He's gone ... it's not often they go so quietly as that, so quietly you couldn't tell.'

THE END